BREAD *from* HOME

A Collection of Short Stories about Life in an American Orthodox Parish

STEPHEN SINIARI

ANCIENT FAITH PUBLISHING CHESTERTON, INDIANA

Front Cover Photo: SuvorovaElena—Shutterstock
Back Cover Photo: Alejandro Piorun—Shutterstock
Author Photo provided by the author

Published by:
Ancient Faith Publishing
A Division of Ancient Faith Ministries
1050 Broadway, Suite 14
Chesterton, IN 46304

ISBN: 978-1-955890-45-8

Library of Congress Control Number: 2023935638

Printed in the United States of America

ALMER BURIAL GROUND
GATE HOUSE
ST VERONICA'S CATHOLIC CHURCH
PARKING ST VERONICA'S
PUTTY FACTORY PARKING
LADIES' ENTRANCE
SHOOKY'S TAPROOM
THE PUTTY FACTORY
LOADING DOCK
SHMIDT'S BAKERY
TROLLEY BARN
RTE 15
RTC
OFFICE
TURN AROUND
PENN TREATY PARK
LITTLE HARRY & GETZY'S SALVAGE
1682
WILLIAM PENN
THE DELAWARE RIVER

To my Margot

My grandparents,

Llamba and Stefan Sinjari

Florence and James Gill

My parents,

Claire and Nicholas Siniari

Und Meine Liebe Muttie Margot Fōrst-Craig

On Father Stephen

IT WAS A SATURDAY NIGHT. Father Stephen's wife, Margot, and I were by his bedside in a Camden, New Jersey, hospital. He was unconscious and literally on ice. Earlier that night he had collapsed suddenly in his car by her side with what turned out to be a heart attack, and it was hoped that cooling his whole body down might stabilize his condition.

The doctor came in and told us that they would begin "warming" him up the next day, on Sunday—but they were not sure if and how his body would react and in what condition he might return.

So we waited.

On Sunday morning before the Liturgy I received a call from Margot that he had come back and there were positive signs for recovery. And in remarkable and mysterious ways, he did indeed return and has never been quite the same.

Yet I have known Fr. Stephen for nearly forty years, and this near encounter with death or ultimate reality only confirmed my observations that he has always been on the threshold of here and beyond, of conviction and the challenge of uncertainty. At the end of our frequent conversations when he lived in the

Philadelphia area, he would always conclude by saying, "I'm out here if you need me."

In addition to his pastoral responsibilities, he often did overnight street ministry with homeless teenagers while working for Covenant House in various inner cities. So, in one sense, he was out there and prepared for whatever would happen. But his various life and pastoral experiences combined with his creative talents have generated a unique and expressive approach to how the dynamics of life can be explored and interpreted.

For twenty-eight years I edited *Jacob's Well*, the publication of the Orthodox Church in America's Diocese of New York and New Jersey. Father Stephen and I were the only ones who wrote articles for each issue (these articles were the forerunners of his current published works, and many are still available online). It became obvious to our readers that there was a "Siniari" literary style unlike anyone else's (just as he had his own approach to punctuation!).

But like the best writers, he has led us as readers in one direction, only to disclose gradually that his intent was to take us somewhere else so as to share the experience of something more revealing.

I've been grateful for his friendship and his startling modes of expression. I'm so glad that he came back that night and continues to explore what it's like to live between two worlds.

—Fr. John Shimchick

Contents

Bread from Home

WE REMEMBERED THE FIRST TIME he led her into church. His Olivia.

He did everything backwards, Pandi Thomo, and he wasn't old when his wife, Olivia, died.

For some reason her folks'd had a big insurance policy on her, and they'd made Pandi the beneficiary. Made him sadder than he had to be.

Came to Naum, Pandi, said, "Father, I'm walking backwards to the monastery." He didn't say which one.

People said Pandi was hard to talk to. They meant by that, he didn't get the things they said the way they wanted him to get them. Pandi had his own way.

Naum knew he wasn't being abstruse on purpose. That's just the way his thoughts came naturally to his tongue.

"I can't help it if sometimes I talk like a sun shower. Maybe there's gypsies singing sad songs causa the devil's daughter's getting married."

Only thing Naum knew for sure, Panteleimon Koukouzelis Thomo loved to sing and had a voice that made people stop and listen, a way of telling a story that sounded like he was singing a sad, sad song that at the same time gave you hope.

And "Such a handsome boy," they said, the thirty-something happy guy with the long auburn beard. Slicked-back hair and eyelashes to match.

Eyes the color of root-beer barrel candy stared at Naum for two minutes without a word before Pandi told him, "Father, having all this money from my Olivia makes me feel like I'm walking with my shoes backwards unlaced on the wrong feet."

How do you cash a check for such a big amount? Naum had no idea. And when Pandi told Naum, "I'm tithing ten percent to me and giving the church the rest," Naum had to call Doreen, who was parish treasurer that year, and make sure she handled whatever paperwork was necessary to explain a six hundred thousand-dollar donation when tax time came.

"Pandi," Naum said, "you sure?"

"Who can be sure?"

Naum looked at him.

Pandi said, "Ain't it was you told me that?"

"Pandi." Naum saw Pandi'd made up his mind. "What can we do for you?"

Pandi wanted two things.

First. "Please pray me Many Years and memorial my Olivia."

The choir intoned the Many Years for Pandi. Everybody cried. And cried again when the Deacon started us in Memory Eternal for Olivia.

Second. "I'm gonna send you a postcard on Tuesdays where I'm gonna end up every Sunday, and if it ain't no trouble, 'cause I can't carry that much in postage—I only got twelve pockets—you can send me bread from home. I like bread, but only the church bread we got around here."

Naum was standing on the veranda early Monday morning at his office-cleaning janitor job, saying morning prayers and watching the sun come up, when he heard Pandi singing the trisagion prayers, walking east out of Fishtown, backwards.

Naum came off the veranda and said, "Pandi, I give you a blessing to not walk backwards."

"Okay," Pandi said. "If I have your blessing to walk not backwards, I won't."

THE NEXT FRIDAY, Tuesday's postcard arrived in Fishtown:

> *Father Naum and neighborhood friends . . . Sunday Pandi's gonna sleep in the woods at the monastery by the lake in the Poconos . . . Send bread from home.*

There was something in the living water of the monastery well that made the bread come alive. Pandi got up from his sleeping bag beside the little church that housed the well. He took the tin cup on the tin-twisted chain and lowered it into the watery darkness.

Pandi was careful not to spill. One link at a time, he drew the water up into the alabaster daylight of the tiny cross-topped shingle-sided cedar-shake cupola-capped church.

Pandi looked up and saw her.

She was there at the monastery well, looking for her husband.

Pandi extended the cup.

She said, “If you see my husband, tell him to come home.”

After she left, Pandi walked through the woods by the well. He saw a flat boulder in front of a large mosaic icon of Saint Seraphim of Sarov.

Pandi sat by the rock. He made the cross. He unfolded the napkin. He removed two of the crusts of bread.

Pandi drank another cup from the well and consumed the bread from home. He said, “This bread brings me home. This bread brings home to me.”

The next day he started on his way. Route 80. Not intending to end up somewhere between Youngstown and Pittsburgh but landing there anyway . . .

Vitaly, the independent cross-country trucker from Ukraine, saw the man with the beard walking on the side of the road. The man reminded Vitaly of Nazarios, a childhood friend from his home village of Kariv. Nazarios who became a priest.

“It’s too cold to be walking,” Vitaly said to the man with the beard. They were sitting along the counter inside the truck stop café.

The man with the beard said, “Yes. I should be riding with you. I’m glad you picked me up.”

Vitaly saw him make the cross, our way, before unfolding a napkin and removing two crusts of bread. Taking Vitaly’s hand, Pandi said, “This one is for you.” Pandi placed the dried bread in Vitaly’s palm.

Vitaly made the cross. The bread was hard. The bread had a crunch. Bread with a fermented yeasty goodness.

Pandi began to sing. Vitaly knew the melody, but had never

heard "Bless the Lord, O my soul" in English. Vitaly sang it in Ukrainian.

Pandi sat back. He had never been so high off the road.

Blonde Vitaly piloted the eighteen-wheeler effortlessly along the highway. Happy blue eyes, telling Pandi, "No truck across this great country. Luke Skywalker. Me. *Star Wars*. No truck. This is my Landspeeder X-34."

Pandi was sure they were floating.

Vitaly said, "My daughter, she's sixteen, Larisa. She runs away with a motorcycle guy. Smokes the dope. Posts lewd pictures on social media. Her mother's and my heart, our hearts are broken. The motorcycle man got her pregnant and beat her till she loses baby."

For many miles out the window it was just two men, high off the road, wordless in a hovering X-34 while the great country of America went land-speeding by.

Pandi knew sometimes silence is the best thing to say.

After a long, long stretch of bumps and highway sound, Pandi said, "My wife died. She was very young."

He was looking straight ahead. Vitaly was certain Pandi was seeing something other than the careless, weaving drivers and the highway-gray of the never-ending concrete road.

Vitaly had been reaching for the lid of the center console. He stopped. Sat back, looked across the cab at Pandi and said, "I'm sorry."

"We all want bread from home," Pandi said.

Vitaly could still taste Pandi's bread. It made his sadness unpronounceable on his tongue. There were no words.

Then after a while he said in Ukrainian, "When shall I behold the face of God?"

Pandi said, "Brother, my tears have been my food both day and night."

Vitaly said, "You speak Ukrainian?"

Pandi said, "No."

The truck made a sound on the highway like the sort of ringing Pandi heard in his ears ever since the summer he slept under the unoiled rusty ceiling fan on its last thread, tilting overhead in the sodden airless room of his uncle's Fishtown third-floor walk-up, with the El train running by into the night.

At the intersection, as Pandi climbed down, Vitaly made the cross and said, "I was reaching in the console for my Makarov nine-millimeter to shoot us both. Something was telling me to pull to the side of the road and do it. All I wanted was that trigger. But you didn't say a word when I told you about our daughter. I could not have taken any more scripture or pious quotes."

Pandi said, "Either I."

Vitaly said, "Your bread from home was enough."

Vitaly stretched over and left Pandi standing in the sound of the big-rig latch as the passenger door clicked tight.

FRIDAY IN FISHTOWN, Tuesday's postcard arrived, saying:

Father Naum and friends . . . Sunday Pandi's gonna sleep in the cemetery at the women's monastery by the grave of the princess . . . Send bread from home.

She was tall, the nun standing over Pandi, and shapeless as a square-peg clothespin turned black from being left too long on the line.

Pandi was content to remain on his back by the grave. He opened his eyes and smiled up like he recognized her.

She said, "Pandi, I don't know if you remember me. I'm Emma, the girl who came to Pascha in Philly with Professor Candace. She brought me and became my godmother in the Orthodox Way."

Pandi lifted to his elbow and then squatted to his feet, and as she brushed the leaves and debris from him, she couldn't help laughing at the damp wetness from his shoulders to his shoes, perfectly distributed down the back side of his lanky figure. The front of his clothes stiff and dry as a towel in the sun.

"I remember you, Em," he said. "You're Mother Macrina."

And Pandi calling her "Mother," she started to cry.

Nearby was a wet bench under a tree that had no leaves. Pandi wiped it down with his jacket and made a place to sit.

She said, "I wanted to reach out to you for a while. It's actually been weighing on my heart for such a long time, and apparently so much so that instead of sleeping, I googled your email address to write to you and ended up calling Father Naum, and he said you were off on a pilgrimage, and I am so sorry, Pandi, to hear about your Olivia."

Pandi picked a leaf by the stem and watched it twirling between his finger and thumb.

Mother Macrina said, "I don't know if I ever told you, thank you for everything. The first time I met you and Olivia, it was such a dark time in my life, and with your help, you and Olivia, and finding a church home like Saint Alexander the Whirling Dervish—a group of people worshiping together, and old Father Naum . . . It made such deep down sense in some part of me that was withering. I found my way out of the maze."

Pandi said, "I didn't know."

The woman, who had been a dedicated physician and the head of adolescent medicine at our premier children's hospital, told Pandi, "Since then a lot of changes have happened in my life. Like being here. New calling. New relationships.

"But negative things have also happened," Mother said. "My former colleagues, my family, some don't get it, and we aren't as close anymore. And sometimes the things I see people here at the monastery doing and the things I've discovered about my own inner motives, my doubts, sometimes really have me questioning my faith.

"The last time I attended church and was able to just *be* . . . that was a few years ago, and part of me feels like running away and finding a new way to live, because a big part of me feels like a fraud. How can I continue to stay with all this?" She gestured to the graveyard and the grounds, her headdress and long black habit. "My lack of inner attendance at liturgy. My doubts. My questioning?"

She said, "How do you find your way in a mess like that? I miss the feelings of hope, the joy after that first Pascha. The feelings of peace after spending time with the faithful in Philly, and the sense of community and connectedness from services there on Sunday.

"I guess what I'm looking for," Mother said, "is guidance or reassurance or . . . I don't know . . . I just feel lost. I'm sorry for the rambling, Pandi. It's been a lot weighing in my heart and my mind. I appreciate you taking the time to listen, even though it's all one big verbal mess."

Pandi was surprised by the sound of the voice that came out of his mouth. He tried putting his hand over his lips but that just made him mumble. So he sat there spinning the leaf and let the words tumble out till his tongue went empty.

Pandi Thomo did everything backwards. We all knew he couldn't help it.

He said, "It's good to be a fraud. It's natural for con artists like us. What, should we be honest and lie to the devil? Stay the way you are, Em. Never change, Em. Be happy. Be questioning. Be a question. If we're questioning, Naum said, it means our soul is alive and still on active duty. Did he or didn't he call us pilgrims? Pilgrims pilgrim, right? That's what pilgrims do."

Pandi said, "I can't remember, did he tell me never stop questioning, or did he say God can't take it and the church doesn't need it to be honest?"

Mother was watching Pandi open his bag. She saw him make the cross before unfolding a napkin and removing two crusts of bread.

Taking Mother's hand, Pandi said, "Mother, this one is for you." He placed the dried cube of *nafora*, what others call *antidoron*, in her palm.

She made the cross. The bread was hard. The bread had a nut-like crunch. The bread with a fermented yeasty goodness.

Pandi began to sing. Mother knew the melody but didn't remember "Bless the Lord, O my soul" in Albanian. She sang it in English.

After, Pandi said, "How does a throwback to the Garden of Eden who remembers the future find her way in a mess like this world?"

Mother was used to his Pandi backward syntax cadence. She said, "How?"

Pandi said, "By not loving God. Forgetting to love others and striving not to see the good? That might be a way. But maybe the doctor in the throwback overthinks things and constantly second guesses herself?" Pandi paused and said, "Nah, not possible."

She raised her eyebrows, same as when she was a doctor and wasn't quite ready to commit to a diagnosis.

Then he said, "We know a monastic should *not* stay put. You're a born wanderer, a spiritual wayfarer, like me. A pilgrim of the Absolute called to be in more than one place at a time. Your perfect church is not here or anywhere. We're not already in front of the Throne, are we?"

Mother wanted to ask how he ended up sleeping in the graveyard. She knew Pandi somehow always ended up being where he needed to be. Or if not quite there, he was at least always on the way.

"Me?" Pandi said. "If I find the perfect church, I'll write you right away. But I know as soon as I get to the perfect parish it'll no longer be perfect. 'Cause I'll be there."

The bread was all gone.

It was as if Olivia were tapping him on the shoulder and whispering in his ear.

"Mother, I know the Holy Spirit is in you, no doubt. You're a blessing to me and will be a blessing to many if you stay put."

Mother Macrina could still taste the bread. Bread from home. It made her doubt unpronounceable.

Pandi said, "Mother, bless me."

She said, "Pandi, I don't love you. I never think about you. I don't miss you. I hardly ever pray for you and Olivia. I'm not happy to see you, and . . . I think you're ugly."

What better blessing?

An older nun came. She saw Pandi and kissed his forehead. Macrina said, "Mother Nikki, this is Pandi."

Mother Nikki said, "I know."

Halfway down the road, Pandi stopped and turned to pray when he heard the wood.

The syncopated, resonating rhythm of the monastery semantron . . . The large, heavy, fixed block of timber suspended on chains, being struck alternating blows by iron nuns with wooden mallets.

He remembered God told Noah:

> *Make for yourself a bell of box-wood, which is not liable to corruption, three cubits long and one and a half wide, and also a mallet from the same wood. Strike this instrument three separate times every day: once in the morning to summon the hands to the ark, once at midday to call them to dinner, and once in the evening to invite them to rest . . .*

The sound made Pandi call for his wife. "Olivia."

None of us lives to himself or dies to himself, but unto the Lord we live and die; we are the Lord's.

From wood striking wood came the primordial memory—a

future where man and woman were no longer separated or beguiled into gazing on a tree their hearts were too innocent to bear:

The Lord of Glory, very God of very God, the fruit of the tree of Eden, poured out like water, all his bones out of joint, his heart turned to wax and melted within his breast.

Over the fields and the headstones, from his ringing inner ear to his every cell, the sound of the threshing semantron winnowed the eucharistic wheat deep into the grist of Pandi's being and transfigured the wood of torment, making it green again in the midst of Mother's garden, where there was hidden a new grave where no man had yet been laid.

AND ON FRIDAY IN FISHTOWN, Tuesday's postcard arrived, saying:

> *Father Naum and friends . . . Sunday Pandi's gonna sleep in the front yard under the pavilion at the Rescue Mission . . . Send bread from home.*

There was no bread from home at the Rescue Mission. It was an address Naum just couldn't find. He told Kusheri Nastradin, "Bread from home doesn't always travel."

When Pandi sang "Bless the Lord, O my soul," no matter what language, the people sleeping on the benches around the pavilion of the homeless mission sang a strange song. He was in a foreign land where the gods looked the same but were different.

Sister Patty, the cherry-faced chaplain in the short skirt and toggle-button navy blue car coat, brought Pandi coffee in a paper cup.

She told Pandi they worked to make a better future. "We help the poor, people of color, the sexually oppressed, and those marginalized by the laws of the dominant society."

When Pandi mentioned bread from home, she said she'd check to see if he was on the list of registered guests and if any packages for him had arrived. "What's your name? How you spelling that?"

Sister just couldn't make her pen write *Koukouzelis* no matter how slow Panteleimon spelled it. She looked at his 1989 Fishtown Library card and said it just didn't get the job done as far as ID went. "But you're welcome to stay anyway, Pandi," she said.

So he thanked her for the coffee and said he understood. Bread and beds and all the other stuff was only for those who registered with a proper photo ID.

He wasn't sure he woulda eaten different bread anyway.

Pandi slept on the benches out in the pavilion with the rest of the breadless not-people—people who were nameless 'cause they didn't have IDs.

In the morning before light, Pandi rolled out and eased down the road, hoping he'd run into Sister Patty's better future and praying not to sexually oppress, dominate, or push anybody into the margins along the way.

ON FRIDAY IN FISHTOWN, Tuesday's postcard arrived, saying:

> *Father Naum and neighborhood friends, Sunday Pandi will arrive before dawn at the monastery on the island and walk from there to the Pacific Ocean. Send bread from home.*

The bread made it to the monastery, but Pandi never did.

He saw the man in the orange shirt, but it all happened too quickly. There was nothing Pandi could have done to stop the man pummeling the old monk with the long white beard.

A monk filling his tank—maybe it was the oddity of seeing something so out of place at a gas station convenience store.

The black *riassa*. The *klobuk* headgear with the hanging veil. Maybe it was the cross around the abbot's neck that enraged the man in the orange shirt.

Pandi had heard what happened to Father Abraham, a priest back home. Carjacked. Dragged into a lot over in Camden. Laid in the dirt. Told by one of the teenagers, "Guess God is gonna forgive us, eh, Father?" The pistol, close range, to the back of his head.

One bullet just grazed his skull. The other through the back of his shoulder and out the front.

The three laughing banditos so crunked up, they misjudged the fullness of the priest's beard, and Father Abraham had the sense to play dead.

After he recovered, Father Abraham made a visit to the carjackers to try and make sense of what had happened. None of 'em did anything other than shrug.

Pandi stood on the rise above the Pacific and said to the young monk who'd driven him, "It won't only take me a minute."

The monk walked back to the car. He said, "I understand."

Pandi refused to go down to the water. He said, "I ain't puttin' my feet in the Pacific without Olivia."

Then he said to the pull of the Pacific, "Let me go home."

The monk who drove Pandi to the airport told him, "You

know that orange man was at five different churches, none of them Orthodox, and received five different communions that same morning. When he saw Father Abbot in the gas station, he was headed to our monastery to try and make it number six."

"How's Father?" Pandi asked. His heart was still pounding.

"Good," the monk said. "The ringing in his ears was only temporary. He went to the jail to see the man to ask his forgiveness, and he sends thanks to you for helping him up."

"*My* ears are still ringing," Pandi said.

The island monks returned Pandi's unopened bread package to his Fishtown address and enclosed a copy of *The Way of the Pilgrim*, a prayer rope, a special edition of the *Little Philokalia*, an *Orthodox Study Bible*, a collection of Orthodox short stories called *Big in Heaven*, and a pound of roast coffee blended specially for the monastery.

PANDI THOMO DID EVERYTHING BACKWARDS. He couldn't wait to say he wasn't happy to be back at Saint Alexander's in Fishtown.

At coffee hour after Liturgy, Pandi told Naum, "Nothing like bread from home."

Then we remembered the first time he led her into church. His Olivia. Holding her close.

The first time someone said, "She's blind."

The first time someone said, "She is."

Some smiled but would not admit they were bewildered by the pairing.

Others wondered in a way that left them unseeing

Why would such a handsome boy
Want to wed
A bride who couldn't
What?
See
Appreciate his appearance
Compliment the beauty of his countenance
Only feel his movement
Only touch him in the darkness
Surely
She could
Hear his voice
Receive his kiss
Delight in his presence
Be immersed in his life
Inhale the scent of him
Share his bread
But
Would she ever really
Know him
As he knew her
And what about the sight
Of their children
Can a blind bride
Bear children
Who see
Questions—questions—questions
Questions
That made some of us ask

And some of us stop asking
Who it was
That felt their way
Questioning
In such darkness
Some remembered her funeral
When her eyes no longer seemed that much to matter
Some other sight
Rose up that day
In Olivia
And
in some of us
The people
Who sat in darkness
Have seen a great light
And upon those
Who sat in the region
And shadow of death
Light has dawned

Pandi unwrapped bread from the package the Pacific monks had sent and placed a dried cube in Naum's palm.

Naum made the cross.

The bread was hard. The bread had a nut-like crunch. The bread was alive with a fermented yeasty goodness.

Meaningless
Words
Were unpronounceable
On their tongues

So Pandi Thomo
Who did everything backwards
Our Pandi
Began to sing
"O Taste and See"
And Naum
And all of us
With him

The Standing Priority of Covenants

JACK STANDING JUST COULDN'T GET IT RIGHT.

He was proud of his name. Jacob Yaqif. Jack Standing in English.

Upright and ready to fight over any scrap or rag.

Jack, according to Jack, was correct in all his outward forms and interactions. Yaqif was certain there was no way Jack Standing could be wrong.

Every morning the middle-aged four-foot-eleven overweight man with the big feet cursed the bathroom mirror as fewer and fewer thinning gray strands were available for allocation across the barren regions of his head.

His American wife, Rita? "Not even worth bothering."

Yaqif smiled at Sakhr, the Rock, grinning back at him. "I pin her and her arguments, not even a sweat drop, to the arena floor with a finger."

He blamed the priest at Saint Isaac of Nineveh, the Syrian parish.

"The combat arena of this marriage into which *you,* Abouna, have fallen me to."

That was Jack.

Banging on the back door of our neighborhood medico, Doctor Baks, demanding more Prozac, Viagra, and blood-pressure meds because of the unpredictable gusts of anger that pulled Jack inside out and left Jacob Yaqif twisting on the outside through the streets of the neighborhood like a *haboob* dust devil seething out of the Syrian desert.

And money . . . Money. Money. Money.

"If God is so rich—" Standing took a roll of bills from his pocket, round as a Kaiser roll, and asked Father Najib, "why isn't *His* kisser plastered in the place of Benny-boy Franklin on the American hundred-dollar bill?"

Abouna Najib told Standing, "You've done well since coming to America."

Standing told the priest, "America ain't done bad since Jack arrives either."

Lots of well-intentioned people in the parish wanted to help Jack Standing.

Help with his manners, his aggressiveness, and his grammar. But knowing his anger and having seen him rebuke the priest Najib, telling the man who founded the parish, who donated the land, "My English is *im-peca-tabol* . . . I learned how to deport myself in the camp on the border over there . . . And what? You? Are trying to say I spoke-ed with an accent? Who the hell are you to tell me? You and your on-and-on blabbering every Sunday are the one no people can wish to understand."

Jacob Yaqif didn't have to settle for this old-world baba ganoush. "This is America. Saint Isaac of Nineveh is *not* my only option."

Jack had heard about the other Orthodox church, the one called the Whirling Dervish.

"That sounds more like I like it."

When Father Najib quoted Saint Isaac to Jack, "Make peace with yourself and both heaven and earth will make peace with you" . . .

Jack bent his knee, lifted his big foot so they could see, and told the priest, "*Ya gazma*!" You are the sole of my dirty shoe.

Jack looked over his shoulder and laughed. "Make peace with heaven and earth!"

Pretty funny, Jack thought, for someone raised in a war zone, someone coming from their part of the world.

KUSHERI NASTRADIN INVITED NAUM TO COFFEE when they finished cleaning the church. They walked along the Avenue to Schmidt's Bakery and found a table on the pavement under an umbrella that said "Best Butter Cake in Philly."

"You know he's angling?" said Nastradin. "That man, Jack."

"For what?" asked Naum.

"Marriage."

"Marriage?" Naum said. "He's not even divorced yet from Rita."

"You'll see." Nastradin ordered for both of them when Mrs. Schmidt came to the table. "Two coffees. Two onion bialy, toasted, with smoked-salmon cream cheese, and one jelly doughnut for the priest here's dessert."

Naum said, "One of the bialy's not for me?"

Nastradin said, "Do you know what a bialy is?"

Naum let it go.

"Jack Standing," Nastradin said, "has a few very beautiful young women living in apartments he owns, where he insists on doing the repairs and maintenance and collecting the rent personally. And he has strategically drilled pinholes transmitting signals to his phone from remote digital spyware cameras."

Naum stopped short when a young woman brought the tray. When the girl walked away, Naum said, "He's a lecher."

"Yep," said Nastradin, licking cream cheese from his fingers and taking a minute to inspect the bialy. "But these are bright young women. They figured it out, these girls. Once they knew they were dealing with such a degenerate, they got together and turned the tables and digitally videoed Standing videoing them."

When the waitress asked, "Anything else I can get you? Going off shift now."

Nastradin looked at Naum.

Naum said, "Nope."

Nastradin handed the young woman a five and said, "Thanks, Miranda. You're the best."

"It's too bad they had to endure that in the first place," Naum said. "Really, breaks your heart. If they were our daughters, or sisters, or wife or mother."

"Yeah, but let me stop you right there, *Prifti im*. These kids don't need no man to protect them. Not these girls. They took action. Some people might say it was like entrapment or blackmail, what they did. I say it was justice."

Nastradin started on bialy number two.

"Why?" Naum wondered. "What they do?"

Nastradin said, "They hit him where it hurts."

"His conscience," Naum said.

"That's what you think?" Nastradin said. "They broke his piggy bank, what I heard."

When Jack's wife, Rita, an American girl who wouldn't put up with walking three steps behind Jack, found out, she maxed out their credit cards, cashed his bonds, and walked three steps ahead of him to cash it all in at Fishtown Savings and Loan.

When Jack came crying to Naum, he said, "Thank God I am a property millionaire."

Naum said, "What does that mean?"

Jack said, "Come, see my properties. Bless them. I can pay you. Baksheesh, maybe you understand?"

Jack Standing thought a blessing might keep Rita from taking his properties too. Between her and the child support, Jack figured there might be a way to make a deal with God if he could sweeten Abba Naum and entice him to do the magic priests get paid to do.

"I'll come," Naum said. "But understand, Mister Standing, money has nothing to with it."

Jack swung the alloy wheels of his silver-cream '99 Corvette in front of the church, leaned over, popped the passenger door, and motioned Naum to lower himself into the low black bucket seat.

First stop was a three-story 1920s tenement under the Tunnel on Kensington Avenue, just off Huntington El stop.

Jack got a call. Told Naum, "I must take," waved Naum to a spindle-backed speckled blue bench in the hallway, and quick-stepped out under the El so the trains rumbling overhead would drown out him cursing his lawyer.

"A class A1 misdemeanor, and *how much* am I being sued for?

Emotional damages? Stress? That makes no sense. I'm the one who's damaged and stressed!"

Kim Taylor came down the stairs, saw the man on the bench, and said, "Hello."

She put Naum in mind of an Ethiopian icon of Saint Verena.

The first-floor door opened.

Two girls stepped into the hallway, and one said to Kim, "The creep is here." That was Valerie.

Naum smiled at the girls. He said, "Doing all right?"

The third girl said, "You're the priest who comes in for jelly doughnuts."

Naum said, "You work at the Schmidt's, and I know you from . . . ?" He'd seen her in another setting too.

"Miranda," she said. "From the community college. You spoke to our survey of religions class."

"You're not here with him?" Kim, the first girl, said to Naum, looking out at Jack, waving his hands in the air like a crazy man.

Kim on the top floor.

Miranda on the second.

Valerie in the first-floor apartment.

They put it together.

Jack Standing was spying on them.

But Kim, Miranda, and Valerie were a generation ahead of the man they called Jack the Whack, and they recorded him recording them.

"I'll let you live rent free," Jack pleaded. "Don't tell my wife."

They had no intention of telling his wife.

They got a lawyer and went to the police.

They didn't need a coalition or group-speak therapy to tell them they were victims.

Our neighborhood kids weren't snowflakes who needed a safe space to hug their teddy bears.

Kim said, "He's lucky we didn't beat his behind . . . on toppa flippin' the script on his perverse old ass."

Miranda showed Naum, on her phone.

Seeing Jack . . .

Naum wanted to get on record. "I've only known him a short time." Naum wanted to jump on the El and ride to the end of the line. "I didn't know. For what it's worth, I'm sorry. Anything I can do for youse . . ."

When Jack came in and saw them talking in the hallway, he said to Naum, "Don't listen to them, they were born with twisted tongues."

Miranda held up her phone and started videoing the crazy man.

Naum said, "Jack, I'm going back to the church."

"Why?" Standing said. "Because of these *bashshaak* (liars) camels?"

Naum waited, looking to the women.

They could tell he was worried for them.

He needn't have worried about them.

The way they stood looking at Jack?

They were more like daughters who were worried about Naum.

Miranda stopped recording. They went into Valerie's and closed the door.

"You need to come see me at church." Naum was walking out onto the avenue.

"Where are you going?" Standing was shouting.

"I'm taking the El," Naum said.

"Why? I'll drive you."

Naum kept walking with Jack shouting after him. "All I want from you is a letter saying I am divorcing that American *sharmuta* (slut) and the Church is guaranteeing that I am free to go to the old country and seek a young bride who will know how to treat a man."

Jack followed Naum down the pavement. "And," Standing said, "I want you to be a character witness for me in court."

Naum turned and said, "What would I say in court? I hardly know you. You've only been to our church twice. Father Najib says you tried, but your anger got the best of you. And now this?"

Jack said, "I don't come because I'm busy."

Naum said, "Too busy, Jacob? Too busy with things that are killing your soul. Your chances for an inner life. The way you relate to God and to people? Too busy for Christ our Savior to pull you out of your self-absorbed swamp? And far as the character thing goes? That's the only thing I *might* be able to address, but not with the court, with you. But that depends on you, man, doesn't it?"

Standing stopped chasing when Naum crossed against the light at Lehigh Avenue.

Jack Standing twirling in a whirlwind.

His ears turned cauliflower purple.

His eyebrows dipped toward his nose.

He stood on his toes and cracked his knuckles.

Then he forced a smile up to his face from the soles of his silver shoes, like a baby turning a burp into smile, and called across the four lanes of busy traffic, "Well then, so this means you won't be talking to my lawyer. You could do that much, you're a priest. How much? That's it, baksheesh, am I right?" Jack stood there making the money thing, rubbing fingers and thumb. "How much?"

Six months later, Rita obtained her divorce settlement, and Jack was living over a bar in one of his single-occupancy rental properties with his brother Tamoush.

Tamoush was used to the rooming-house squalor.

Jack was not.

It was winter when Standing came to see Naum again.

His shoes were stretched-out silver leather slip-ons. No way his loafers went with his summer-weight powder blue seersucker suit. The man had stain for matching stain, blotches down the front of his shirt and along the length of his stubby clip-on tie. His pants were just short enough so you might think Jack was showing off the see-through socks that barely covered his ankles. His pants testified that Jack didn't own a belt.

His hair hugged his head, slick, slack, and trolley-track flat. Razor nicks connected the dots between his neck and chin. No overcoat. Jack wore sunglasses and couldn't stop shivering during Orthros and Liturgy.

At coffee hour he told Naum, "I almost slipped on the ice coming into your church today. I should sue."

Naum said, "Jacob, you look tired."

He said, "I came on the bus. Tamoush, my own brother, stol-ed my car to Atlantic City."

He tried to hand Naum a Final Judgment for Dissolution of Marriage document from the clerk of the Family Court on Arch

Street, along with a few rumpled pages describing his financial obligations in the settlement.

He unfolded a handwritten letter he wanted Naum to sign.

It explained, in Jack language, how women and the whole world were evil children of the serpent and had ruined the garden of his life.

He needed Naum—or even better, could Naum persuade the bishop—to sign the documents he prepared that stated Jacob Yaqif was free to marry and had the blessing of the Church to seek a bride in the old country.

"I'm done with these women who don't know their place in the covenant," Jack said.

"Jack, come and have a coffee with me," Naum said. "You could use a coffee. Just me and you. You keep your private business private. I wanna understand. I want you to tell me how you understand a covenant."

"You think I don't know *covenant*, me?" Jack said. "I understand a contract. I know quid pro quo. I know a thing or two about agreements. I'm a businessman. I look like a sucker to you? Not Jack. No way. Jack helps Jack. And you know who helps Jack? Jack, that's who."

Naum asked, "How much of the New Testament have you read? Not judging. Just trying to clarify . . . trying to understand where you're coming from . . . find out if we're working out of the same book."

"Same book." Jack thought it was funny.

"How about the Hebrew Bible?" Naum said. "The Old Testament."

"Jews?" Jack's intent was in his eyes.

Naum said, "I kiss the hand of the Jew. My Master. His Mother. The Apostles . . ."

Jack cut him off. "They were Christians."

"Jack, we worship the God of the Jews . . . We're the wild branch grafted into the covenant," Naum said.

Jack said, "You, maybe."

Naum decided to come back to the covenant. "Jack, a covenant is more than a contract. More than quid pro quo. More than a deal. A covenant is an acknowledgment of the truth that we're all related. We share one human reality. Share the same human nature."

"So I'm related to those Israeli pieces of . . ." Jack was heating up.

Naum cut him off. "Jack, there's a priority of covenants, too. When you were a boy, it was you and God, and then you and mommy and daddy.

"Then when you got married, it was you and God, and mommy and daddy moved to third place. And you and your wife were in second place.

"Then when the kids came . . . it was you and God, then you and your Rita, then the kids in third place, then maybe your parents, then maybe the job or whatever. You know your own family order, Jack, your priorities."

Jack said, "Yeah, but not what you're talking."

Naum said, "Why? Your wife and kids always gotta come first. You gotta put them before you."

"Makes no sense," Jack said.

Naum said, "It makes sense if you're following Christ. And if you get that priority of covenants out of order, Jack . . . And some priests do. I did. End up putting the parish before the family. Forget you were married before you were a priest. Everything starts going wrong."

Jack Standing said, "What about my papers?"

Naum said, "I spoke to the bishop. He said talk with you. Try and find a way to get you back in communion."

"Then he'll sign my papers? How long's that gonna take?" Jack said.

"It may take a while. Maybe a year. But if we can reconcile you to Christ and the church community, the bishop himself may even be willing to write a letter blessing you to marry again."

Jack said, "A year? You and the bishop must be outta your minds. Like Jack Standing has a year? What I need, I need now. I purchased my travel. Arrangements have been made. There's a bride waiting."

Naum said, "C'mon, Jack, please, work with me."

"Please my ass." Jack was up from his seat, shouting. The entire hall was watching. "You don't know anything about real life, you or the bishop. I read enough Bibles to know I can get a better deal with the Protestants . . . Or maybe I'll become a Muslim. There's a group of men who know how to make women know their place."

Naum wanted to hear Jack out, maybe talk him off the ledge. He said, "Jacob, talk to your cousin Naum."

"You?"

Both hands on the table. Jack looming over Naum.

"No cousin of mine is related to Jews. You and that Jew rabbi at the synagogue across the street. Or your chummy buddy at the African church. What? You think I don't know? Or those cursed man-haters who took me to court . . . You wanna know Jack Standing's priority of covenants, the Standing priority of covenants?"

Pounding the table.

Jack said, "In first covenant place, me. In second place, me." He sponged his doughnut up and down in his coffee, turned his cup upside down on the table, mashed the whole mess through his fingers with both hands, and said, "And on the third base . . ."

Jack Standing just couldn't get it right.

"Me! Home-run Me! American Tocqueville-loving Me. Life must be lived with home-plate-stealing courage. Me. Fist-to-chest, don't-look-back, take-command Jack. Sliding in the plate kicking dust in your face Me!"

Madeline, Carol, and the women of our Teuta Ladies Baking Society came to stand around Naum.

Jack Standing threw up his hands. Exasperated Jack hit the door running and slid like Hans Brinker across the icy pavement in his silver loafer slip-ons.

Standing Jack Yaqif, cold and alone on his back, craned his neck at the wire basket trash can chained to the wooden telephone pole at the bus stop in front of the church.

Cousin Jack got up and stood standing.

Ready to fight over any scrap or rag.

Confessing Dreams

It would be better to tell this story in a daytime café.

It's about a boy who loved a girl and the girl who loved him. She was Christian. He was an Ottoman Janissary.

Someone in their village was hired to kill the bishop. They killed the bishop and the people colluded in a cover-up.

An anathema was pronounced. The village burned three times to the ground.

The people fled to America and settled in Philadelphia. Most of them in Fishtown. Even in America, many of the people remained afflicted.

Naum sat at the kitchen table and heard the story of the curse. The boy and girl had grown old living like brother and sister, and now before they died they wanted to marry. She was in her early eighties. He was staring into whatever teeth ninety had left.

It was at night when they told Naum. He would have preferred never to have heard it, or at least to have heard it in a daytime café.

In her kitchen the old woman said, "For years I live secretly with this old man. You are the first to know our secret. You the priest we love. We trust your face. We can tell you love us too and so we tell."

In America, their house was a cottage not far from the Delaware River, in a part of Fishtown called the Gardens. Every Sunday they walked to church.

IN ALBANIA, when they were young and he first saw her . . .

The girl at the market blossomed in his earthen heart. Watching her breathe gave life to his soul. She embroidered every stitch of his being as brightly as the potted red flowers that colored the windowsills and doorways of the white stone house where she lived.

How could he ever hope to know this girl? She was a Christian. He was a Turk.

"But am I?" he would argue with himself. He would tell himself, "When Shën Pali [Saint Paul] comes to Albania, we say yes. Can I help it if my ancestors say yes again to Murad the Sultan? Maybe I do the same. See Allah or see the sword. Maybe I would become *timarioti* who every year pays tribute for land sultan gives.

"Am I so brave as to resist? Immune, me, to bribe? Did I of my own will join the Janissaries? Yes. Was me. Was me look at her."

And the boy had not gone unnoticed by her.

From the first time she saw him in the spring, the young girl knew every detail of his face. His eyes. His hands. His gait. She could tell the sound of him without even looking when he was circling and slowing in front of her window.

More than once she overheard him chastising the Christian men in the market, turning to see if she noticed. "You push your women to work so hard in the fields." He was trying not to let her see him looking her way. "You drive them too hard."

But she never let their eyes fully meet; she seemed to be more attentive to her mother's marketplace bargaining. It made the boy feel less interesting than an eggplant.

His heart chanted when he saw her.

A wife of noble character who can find?

She is far more precious than rubies.

By early summer, after Pentecost, her thoughts were always of him. She worked with her mother and the other women of the village, laundering the heavy *qylym*, quilts and rugs.

"We washed them at the river with wooden paddles. We spread them on big rocks to dry all morning in the sun.

"Each time I looked into the deepest current of the river, I swear I saw his face. Each time I heard the river's voice, I swear I heard the boy calling me by name. I wove a basket of my love and set it on the water with the remembrance of the boy hidden inside. I knew then I would never love or marry any other man."

By feigning to be mentally feeble she rendered herself an unsuitable match for any man her father might propose. "Then my mother would gently rouse me from my daydream. We would gather the blankets and by sundown be returned to our home and to my father, whose sad heart I could see each time he looked at me."

There were days when the boy was able to watch at the river. Days when he would walk by her house as evening unfolded and obscured the pathways of the ancient rutted lanes that led to her father's house. But not so much as a sigh would he permit himself as he prayed in the night by the window where she slept.

When they saw each other again, the morning lent no light to the hope they kept hidden in their eyes. But messages were exchanged nonetheless. Coded exchanges in gestures so finely drawn and movements so exquisitely slight as to be untranslatable by any but the two.

The old woman was called Asenath. She told Naum, "The old man, *he* tell, no me. I set table. Spread linen cloth. Good one. Cream color. Use on Sunday. I make myself. Crockery. Cups and saucers. Sugar bowl and spoons. Teapot on stove.

"I am nervous. The priest remove coat. Hat. I take. Hang up. He has walking stick. Lean stick against door. 'Peace be with this house,' priest say and sit beside table and make cross, three times."

"You know I was *mysliman*," the old man told Naum. "I was baptized to Christian, but you never ask me why. Or who baptizes me."

Naum said, "Thomo, I thought you became a Christian because you loved the woman."

"No, I love woman. But that's no why I become Christian. When I become Christian, I swear I never marry. I could tell she love me too, but I was afraid to be sure. Then when we come to America and when parents die, we have no one, and so we vow to live together like brother and sister.

"I keep room, from here two blocks, at boarding house. I ask de Got, show me a sign of blessing to forgive my vow to no marry.

"Then you come and we feel we trusting you. Albanian. Like us. We know your name. We asking you, Urata, marry us. But first we want to make confess. Confess a dream. Prifti, is possible?"

Naum said, "Tell me."

"Is so long, long ago, is like confessing a dream."

Thomo Ziu, the old man, told Naum, "Papa Kristo Negovani, the priest. I remember him. He make school in his house. One hundred children, more. Adults too. Teaching, Papa Negovani is, to read and write Albanian. Preaching for first time ever, Albanian language in Divine Liturgy.

"Other bishop no like. Say God no understand Albanian. Say to people, I take your sins on me if you no speak Albanian, learn instead *koine* letters. *Was në Shkurt*, February 1905. I am remembering his name, Karavangelis, this bishop in Kastoria. Sending men. Men kill Papa Kristo."

Naum had heard of a priest called Stathi Melani who was taken from the altar and beheaded on Christmas Eve for celebrating the Liturgy in Albanian.

Thomo Ziu said, "You know us. Can no let this go."

The old man told Naum, "Photios is another bishop against Albanians. Hates Albanians. No like our ways. Our language. Okay. He like his way. His country. His language. Maybe no kill bishop for this. But for Papa Negovani . . ."

Bishop Photios was assassinated in September of 1906.

"They arresting many Albanians for this, me too, but Turks release, say me, go. You go."

Naum looked at the man. A curious man. A man with no formal education but never without a book. Thomo Ziu paid tithes to three Orthodox churches in our Philly—Greek, Romanian, and Albanian.

Summertime in the Gardens, Thomo and Asenath kept their secret rendezvous almost every day. When she didn't answer the door, Naum knew to check in the garden plot back of the cottage.

Asenath in a faded lavender frock. Hands and shoes moist with soil. Wiping her forehead with the back of one hand. A thick bunch of *bosilok* (sweet basil) in the other . . . Or, some days, flowers, all colors, on long green stems.

Naum asked if it reminded her of the village.

She said, "Village? Mud. Houses of mud. Some wood and stone. Church is stone. *Xhami* [mosque] too. All white. And never visitors in our village. Or few. Very few."

One winter, travelers from Romania came to the village to visit relatives. All night they drank raki. Near daybreak, Antony, the oldest, said, "You are fools. Your loyalty is not with these Albanians who call you dirty sheepherders. Or with these Greeks who call you dirty *choban* and force their language and culture down your throats. Romania is your true home."

"What are you saying?" his Uncle Dimitru wanted to know.

"What am I saying? I'm saying, free yourself from the local Phanoriotes bishop, who is a puppet of the Porte, of that pinch-faced Hamid in Istanbul. Stop paying this sultan *piskes* [bribes]. We are shoving the sword of Osman down *their* throat. Come, join under our Romanian bishop, who is free from this Turk. The bishop will by his diplomats protect you. And reward your bravery and loyalty to the land of your ancestors by returning to you an honest portion of every pound you pay in ecclesiastical tribute."

Uncle Dimitru wondered to himself. Never mind the fact that the Vlachos have been in Albania five hundred years. Seen Romania only in dreams. "How would we do this?"

"Do what? Get rid of the sultan's bishop! Get a Saracen to shoot him. He may say it's *haram*, what is forbidden, but what is forbidden if you can show him it will be a benefit to others? He may find justification. I mean, what is it to him for a Christian bishop to die? Some of them twist the Koran like some of us twist the Bible."

Thomo Ziu told Naum, "I was a foolish man, Urata. I vowed in my misery, if I couldn't marry Asenath then I would never marry. I would live the life of a *kachak*, a bandit thief, and care for nothing.

"Life seemed worthless. Life was worthless to me. Then one night when I'd been drinking too much raki and the crowd was rowdy all around, someone proposed my name to the fancy-dressed Romanian visitors across the room, and their challenge bent my rage toward the target they proposed. Toward a man I did not know. Toward a man I'd rarely seen.

"A rifle? Sure. What the hell was that to me? Some of our women were better shots than their best men. Everyone who had been in the sultan's Janissaries brought back their trench gun and a pouch of eighty-millimeter ball shot.

"But what did I care about their money? It was haram to me. I just wanted to assassinate my hopelessness. What better way for a kachak to begin his end?"

Thomo Ziu said, "He was beautiful, this bishop. Maybe holy

man. Blood from his black riassa soaks cloth. Dark wide circles. Wet. Sticky like pomegranate. Sticky on beard. His head slump-ed on his chest."

Thomo Ziu said, "My name was Qamil Fuzulli. I was seventeen and still a boy."

Asenath didn't lift her head or raise her eyes from the table when she spoke. She toyed with the dish towel in her lap, twisting the ends around her fingers. She was in the village square that day. "He is walking toward me, bishop. Smiling. Deacons with him. Then rifle. Loud behind. People running." Asenath whispered. "Lying on ground, bishop. Looking at us."

She looked at Thomo and said, "Someone warn. Say, Bishop, no come."

"He come anyway," Thomo said.

"But he no do." The old woman lifted her head toward the old man. "Thomo no do, Urata. No shoot bishop."

Thomo Ziu sighted down the barrel but when he saw the Panagia, the icon of the Mother and Child, and the cross . . .

She said, "He cannot do. Another takes rifle."

For what seemed like a very long time, except for the whir of her kitchen clock there was no sound in the room.

Thomo Ziu said, "I'm no confess for other. The bishop bless me. Him say me, I forgive, and say, I pray de Got bless him who. . . But he never finish."

A FEW DAYS LATER, Asenath and Thomo were married. Just three of them in church.

After, they went with Naum to Betty's for a weekday breakfast.

The old man told Naum, "Village burn, twice, after bishop killed. Then third time, everyone come to America."

Maybe they came partly to escape the curse. And maybe they did escape the fire and the ashes and the village made of mud.

The Greeks who lived in the village called the area Vori Ipiroti, Northern Epirus. To the Albanians it was Southern Albania. Naum didn't know what the Romanians who lived there called it. But he did notice there was something disquieting that united our people. Perhaps their disdain for one another. That familiar-family disdain shared in blood by those who many times want the ones they hate to love them.

Naum noticed that in the Orthodox section of Palmer Burial Ground, on all the gravestones of the people from that area—no matter what they called it—the gravestones said, *Born in Albania.*

There weren't a whole lot of the villagers still in Fishtown, but Naum didn't know of one family from the village who . . .

Well, odd things. Stuff beyond sickness and accidents, stuff that defied all the actuarial odds. Unexplainable undercurrents that kept pulling people down in the rapids somewhere between the American dream and whatever hopeless nothing they conjured up in the night to fend off the vendetta's curse.

But there *was* no escape.

Every one of us knew somewhere deep we'd all be returning to the village of mud through the gates of Palmer Burial Ground.

Naum the priest would never let himself make too much of it.

Everyone had their version of the curse. Their why. Their who. Some denied it ever happened.

NAUM PUT HIS CAP ON. Buttoned his coat. Took his walking stick and kissed them goodnight. They were at the window. Watching like a frosted portrait of his grandparents in a faded frame. He knew they would stand there watching till he was out of sight.

Evening was coming on. He stopped at the corner. A fine dry snow was being sifted on the wind. It made circles around the streetlight, which blinked like a projector with a bulb gone bad.

Soldiers and sultans, missions and motives, bandits and bishops, a sad vendetta story with no ending. A long sequence of faces and events came to life and flickered across the snow-twirled sky in a confessional dream.

The forging of the bullet
The felling of the tree
That gave stock to the rifle
The boring of the barrel
From ore mined long ago
In the fertile damp caverns
Of Cappadocian graves
The face of an unknown assassin
The taut sinews of the arm
That wrenched the lives of generations
From the hands of Thomo Ziu

It was at night when they told Naum the story. He would have preferred to have heard it in a daytime café, or never to have heard it at all.

Behind the Wall

THE DAUGHTER. LYUDMILA. From when she was twelve, she broke her mother's heart.

"I hate people. I hate you. I hate everything. I hate myself."

In the old country, Lyudmila's mother, Lyubov Balitzskaya, went to university to study economics and graduated with honors. English as a second language was discouraged. Too many lies from America. So French was a good second choice.

After, she was assigned a prestigious job at a state art gallery, working in close collaboration with Priska Boyko, an art historian. Together they appraised the value of a work, and together they set a price range. Perhaps a Soviet-era painting of Lenin, or a lithograph of Felix Dzerzhinsky, founder of the Cheka—the secret police, principal devil of the dreaded red terror.

When explaining value range to a potential buyer, Lyubov spread her finger and her thumb. "No more than this. No less than this," indicating the space between. Touching finger and then thumb with a ballpoint pen given to her by a visitor from America.

The man with the glasses told her, "Keep the pen. They're a dime a dozen. Won't clog. Won't leak. You're gonna like it."

"I know Mister Armand Hammer makes the pencils," she told Priska, as she wrote her name in the smooth blue ink on the coarse gray paper they used in the shop. "But who is this Bic? Is he the nice man who gives me such a pen?"

"Ah, Lyubov," Priska said. "Your name means love and you have written it out so beautifully, but you think you have to love everyone because this is your name? No, Lyubov. Behind these little trinkets from the West is hiding sinister motives. Didn't you see his glasses? Spy glasses. Is there something wrong with our dipping pens, my naïve friend?"

"No, of course. I love our fountain pens better," Lyubov said to her colleague. "And Priska is a good name too." She wrote Priska with her new Bic and said, "The name of Saint Timothy's grandmother."

Priska thought to herself, "No wonder Lyudmila, the daughter, runs away from this mother. A dunce and a religious nut."

Priska was the model, the ideal emblem, the happy worker in the vivid three-color propaganda posters. The girl in uniform wielding a hammer and embodying the Soviet essential of what it meant to be a woman, which, Lyubov said, "was the uniform of feigned masculinity on the outside and a radical hysterectomy of her feminine heart, party-programmed and Soviet-hardwired on the inside."

Said it to herself, quietly, in French.

Lyubov showed the pen to her husband. "Mykhailo, let's leave here and move to America."

He said, "No, Lyubov. You go. And take our daughter Lyudmila with you. You know you will need money, and, my dear love . . . The English you studied secretly will no doubt translate, but your profession will not. There, my dear, they have all the pens and fine white paper you want, but they do not have the state subsidizing political art for you to appraise at prices they set and tell you is the range. Besides, our store is doing so well here near Poshtova, especially out the back door."

She knew what he meant. And she knew he was right.

Mykhailo was sad. What husband wouldn't be? But he was willing to sacrifice. What husband wouldn't?

His wife, good Lyubov, had been sick many years. Maybe in America the doctors could help.

"Just for a time," he said, "until you are established. I will stay here and send money, and then, when you and Mila are settled, and we have her away from these bad influences . . ."

Godlessness. Poverty. Inequality in housing, in education, in medical care, jobs . . .

Substance abuse. Suppression of free thought and speech. Absence of traditional morals.

Life as nothing but political economics, and in the end, meaningless, the life we now have here.

Mykhailo wanted to weep, but not in front of his true and only loves, his wife and daughter. "Then I will come."

Mykhailo thought to himself, if two birds are free, even the one behind the wall feels somehow free.

Priska Boyko practically spit coffee in her face when Lyubov told her she had applied to emigrate. "Well," was all she would say. What else could one say to such a weakling, to such an excuse for a woman?

During her last week, Holy Week, Lyubov went to church

every morning and evening, not missing one service. You think it was easy in those days?

Once she swore she saw the famous writer Aleksandr Solzhenitsyn. And maybe she did. Of course she never read any of his works. It was not permitted, in their language.

A woman like her? Probably never even knew his written work existed, or that it somehow might be obtained . . . Well, that is according to Priska. Not that an art historian of the stature of Priska Boyko would read such dreck as *One Day in the Life of Ivan Denisovich*.

IN AMERICA LYUBOV FOUND A LITTLE CHURCH, poor, with a modest building only a few blocks from her home, in a neighborhood the American people called Fishtown.

Lyubov didn't know why they called it Fishtown. Or why they changed the time on the clocks twice a year. Once she was late to church. Once she was very early.

It was a homemade church. Almost like a church in a Young Communist camp, with hand-me-down icons and plywood crosses painted gold. Not at all like the temples dedicated to God at home.

At home, the churches—the ones that were still open and hadn't been desecrated—looked like palaces, and the people lived in shacks. Here, Lyubov thought, it was the reverse.

In the Fishtown church, there was a thick outside wall of old gray fieldstone that had been turned into an iconostasis by the men of the parish, who punched holes in the stone for the Royal Doors and the deacon's doors. They built a shed of wood sided with vinyl to house the altar area and topped it with a slanted plywood roof, covered with alternating asphalt shingles of gray-black and pea green.

Lyubov said Priska would have described it as either pretty or rustic, but not both, even with the tall three-bar wooden cross painted flat gold and appended to the side with large black brackets.

No, she wrote to her husband, *little Saint Alexander the Whirling Dervish Orthodox Church didn't have much in the way of cathedral accoutrements. And, Mykhailo* (she knew he would smile when he read it), *with a priest everyone called Naum, not even bothering with Batyushka. A smiling Father behind a gray beard anyone could tell he trimmed himself in a mirror with no overhead light. Were there no barbers in this Fishtown?*

But he loved my cooking, Mykhailo, this priest, and was so happy when I invited the American workmen, the black men fixing the street, to come in and see the home blessing, and eat with us, and when I made them all wash their hands at the kitchen sink, they told him I had them in for lunch every day since they began work, and so I did, when the priest visited; and complained with a smile when I saw him again, how garlicky good were my potatoes and carrots and sausage and my special pudding cake. He said his Matushka Greta wouldn't kiss him for the garlic, but she loved the cake I sent . . .

This Albanian priest, wearing vestments half a century old with sleeves shredded from being rolled up at baptisms and Epiphany water blessings at the river, and an epitrahelion thin enough to strain gnats—a biblical reference Priska Boyko would have appreciated if she had known it, and maybe she did.

But Lyubov, who was never permitted to read the Bible, if she wanted to keep her apartment and job, she knew the Scripture.

And with such a priest and such a place, Lyubov wrote to her husband, it could only be an honest church with honest faith. Who would feign faith in such shabby dress?

And this priest introduced her to Doctor Meggie from the former Soviet Georgia, who said she could help Lyubov with her women's issues. Doctor Meggie told Lyubov, "Twelve years is long enough to suffer."

So there, Priska.

But America, for her daughter, for Lyudmila?

Godlessness. Poverty. Inequality in housing, in education, in medical care, jobs . . .

Substance abuse. Suppression of free thought and speech in her university classes. A passing grade required the *right* answer in America—who would believe such a thing?

Absence of traditional morals. Life as nothing but the economy of politics, and in the end, even that seemed a meaningless charade.

And twelve years later, the same antagonistic reaction, except this time in English. "I hate it here. I hate the people. I hate you. You, my mother, *trafficked* me here. I hate myself."

"What is freedom to you," she told her mother, "is chaos to me. I'm allergic to this crazy so-called freedom."

Being free to choose became like a toxin to the soul of daughter Lyudmila.

"What kind of people stand in an aisle of over two hundred different kinds of breakfast cereals and say, 'There's nothing here'? How many different kinds of peanut butter do you need?"

Lyubov knew where this led, that a child should consider taking her own life. Those who lose sight of God lose sight of the world and everything in it.

Her daughter was screaming in the aisles, people were turning, afraid. "Turns out your choice and your freedom is no freedom at all. It's a store full of illusions, just one more thing we are forced to play at to sustain this stupid existence none of us choose to begin with. I didn't ask to be born. You call that a choice? To hell with you, your freedom to choose and your free will."

Every appetite popping into Lyudmila's twenty-four-year-old head became her master. "Heroin is not addictive, Mother, if you snort it." Every desire that presented itself in the mirror of her cravings ruled her day and buried her in the grave of her cravings.

Lyudmila told her mother, "I am lost in this endless American festival. I am being eaten alive by my own appetites, Mother, one bite at a time."

Lyubov was a stranger in a strange land, not knowing how to comfort her child without crying. "Your crying makes me wild," Lyudmila said. "And am I pursuing slow suicide, or it is pursuing me? Something is wrong with me. I have become incapable of being satisfied or happy."

Each desire fulfilled upped the ante—demanded more with each subsequent indulgence, devoured her in tiny bites, then turned and mocked her to her face, spewing less pleasure and more pain every time the digital touchscreen offered her the option to hit it again.

She OD'd twice. Was at the ER so many times the nurses knew her mother's number by heart.

Find her sprawled on the same Kensington Avenue stone slab

step every time. "Her again." The police under the Tunnel radioed for the ambulance. "Yeah, the vampire kid again, the foreign one. Shootin' her way to Palmer Burial Ground one dirty needle at a time."

Detoxed on the prison unit. Got out. Went straight to the Criminal Justice Center, 1301 Filbert Street, Room B-3, and filed a PFA, a protection from abuse complaint against her mother.

Her mother couldn't get in to see her up at CFC prison. Lyudmila refused to put her mother on her visitor's list. "Just tell the bitch to put some money in my commissary account."

When Naum went to see her, she told him, "I ended up choking on what amounted to nothing every time I swallowed."

How many times a night did she get in and out of cars with strange men to earn an edge on her addiction? Naum didn't want to know.

Most girls did eight to ten bags a night. The boys, twelve to sixteen. One-inch by one-inch functional ziplock baggies. Ten dollars a pop.

He was surprised she met with him. The unit was large and noisy and smelled like whatever the trustees in orange jumpsuits and shower shoes used to clean the institutional green deck and red metal-mesh benches bolted to the floor.

Some long-ago inmate had painted a junior-high art class mural of people-faced deer and crack-high bunnies in a meadow of marijuana on a long, low cinder-block wall. Visiting families posed together in front of it for pics.

Couples doing things behind their backs the guards thought were funny and might've pretended to miss, but the kids and people at home wouldn't miss it or think it was anything but sad when they finally got a peek at the pixelated prints.

"No touching. Face forward." The guards were in no mood. They told Naum, "You're not gonna be told twice." Then a momentary sympathy: "What are you, her dad?"

They sat together. Both rigid. Faces forward.

Her tattoos and the piercings, the eyeliner permanently etched in, the ragged, razored hair dyed shoe-polish black, two inches of blonde roots, fingernails bitten to the nubs and paint-chip black.

Even with all the camouflage—despite the hairline fissures and cracks—the deeper beauty of this kid's *pysanky*-bright soul managed somehow to remain untouched and, it seemed to the priest in Naum, in no way desecrated beyond hope.

Even though scars stood up and testified with an oath to each criminal injection, witnessed to every foul predilection, to every incidence of abuse, self-inflicted and otherwise . . .

Wounds deep and no way denying the truth of each vicious incident of hopeless resignation that brought the precipice of life without meaning closer to the aglets of her knotted black shoestrings . . .

Even though and even so, Lyudmila remained sitting upright, looking forward, hands folded in her lap, inside what people call the belly of the beast, staring out of sideway eyes . . .

A pinpoint of light from the last time she held a paschal candle and said the words . . .

Blue eyes, same as her mother, looking straight ahead, waiting for the response from old Naum, the homemade shabby priest.

"And I blame you," she told him. He knew she meant God and the Church. And he knew she wanted some kind of answer.

"I refuse your theories. I want a real answer," she shouted.

The officer came over. "What?" He didn't like Lyudmila raising her voice.

"Can I show him this?" She took a paper from her oversized orange jumpsuit, an official diagnosis on stationery from the prison psychologist. "He's a priest."

Abnormal body posturing and facial expressions.
Abnormal tone of voice and avoidance of eye contact.
Behavioral disturbances with flat or monotonous speech.
Deficits in language comprehension.
Inappropriate social interaction.

Lyudmila asked while Naum read, "Is that evil?"

Naum knew nothing about ASD. He'd never heard of the Autism Spectrum Disorder. He said, "I don't know how to answer."

"Then what good are you?" Lyudmila wasn't mean, just flat matter-of-fact when she said it.

"All I know is I'm here," Naum said. "For now, that's all I know."

Naum felt strapped to the bench, his own inquisitor, trying to sort out some sane, loving response in the middle of a prison visitors' unit, and all he knew was, "This daughter still wants her mother. Just some part of her's broken and doesn't know how."

Then Lyudmila said, "Do you know I got a restraining order against my mother?"

Naum said, "No."

"To protect her . . ." Lyudmila was beginning to fidget in her seat. "From my harming her."

Naum said, "Because you love her?"

She was quiet when she said, "Is that evil? Am I?"

Naum wanted to take her hand. It was not permitted. The black-bordered loud red sign said so.

Would Lyudmila have welcomed it if he did? Probably not.

He kept his hands folded in his lap and said, "Sometimes all we can do, Lyudmila, is something like what you've done, even if other people don't understand right away. Maybe, eventually, they will."

Her mother, Lyubov, was surprised on Sunday when the homemade priest asked her to read the Gospel lesson in her language. This would never happen in the old country. But today there were so many visitors from her country—why were they coming to an Albanian church?—but how could she say no?

He was so sad, this Father, when he told her after liturgy, "Lyubov, I did see her. But . . ."

"No worries," she said. "The Gospel you gave to me to read makes me to hope. Our Jesus says to my daughter, *Talitha, cumi*, and to me, don't be afraid, daughter, and so I am not afraid no more today. Am I, good Father?"

Lyubov had read at the homemade stand, in front of the homemade iconostasis punched through the thick cold wall of gray fieldstone that was like the wall of her daughter's prison, a thick impenetrable outside wall without doors for deacons or Royal Doors, a wall through which nothing and no one could pass, except perhaps an angel.

Or maybe she was as Priska said: "Ah, Lyubov. Your name

means love, and you have written it out so beautifully, but you think you have to love everyone because this is your name?

"No, Lyubov. Behind these little trinkets from which the West builds its walls is hiding sinister motives. Don't you see this priest? Have you put on his glasses? Spy glasses. Is there something wrong with you, my naïve friend? Can love pass through a wall?"

Lyubov and Lyudmila, mother and child, the first and most intimate of communities, bore their scars together: the twelve-year ailment of the mother and the suffering of the daughter from when she was twelve, together on either side behind the wall.

Keep the Change

Part I

Summer in the Neighborhood

NAUM HAD TO BE IN CHURCH early that day, and he wanted to have something on hand for his visitors. Walked to Fufari's Philly Soft Pretzel Bakery on the Avenue, bought three dozen soft pretzels right out of the oven. Still warm.

Said to dude behind the counter, "Better give me another dozen, Stevie."

Stevie said, "Here's one on the house, Padre, for the way home," and nodded Naum to the mustard, yellow or spicy brown, in plastic squeeze bottles at the end of the counter.

Naum figure-eighted the spicy brown, extruding the mustard like cursive script, following the chewy bulky body over the crisp salt-brown crust. He stuffed his cellphone in his breast pocket and said, "Got a Black Cherry Wishniak?"

Stevie pointed to the red coffin-box Coke cooler. Glass bottles, wet and cold and bobbing up to their necks in floating ice.

"Ah." Happy Naum. Put a hundred-dollar bill on the counter and told Stevie, "Keep the change."

Stevie looked at the bill. Naum said, "Guy at a baptism gave it to me, said do whatever I want with it."

Frank's soda and a morning pretzel. Carbonated fill-ya-up. Pretzel yeast rising in your insides. Called a belly-buster in our neighborhood. Get 'em on the morning walk to school. Keeps kids fully expanded till lunchtime.

Summer morning, walking back to the parish. Not quite hot, but Naum could smell the heat coming up. Waved across the street to Tio Daniel, the owner of Vera Cruz, out washing down the pavement with bleach water. Get rid of last night's stench outside his Mexican corner restaurant, named after his hometown.

Tio Daniel—*el viudo*, the widower—and Lea, the do-good social worker from the Youth Agency Outreach Storefront Drop-in Center on the Avenue, right next door to Daniel's Vera Cruz. The do-good girl who told the neighborhood kids, "Don't give up. Never give up. You gotta keep on trying. You gotta believe in change. We can change our neighborhood, if *we* can change ourselves."

The two of them out there every morning sweeping up broken *cervezas* bottles, *cheve*, what people in that part of the neighborhood called beer.

Styrofoam containers. Chicken bones. Empty dope baggies. Vomit. Used condoms and blunt spit, scooped out Philly-blunt cigars stuffed with weed.

Get high. Get hungry. Mess up Tio's steps on the overnight.

The morning drug-set shift arriving across the street any minute to set up shop, relieve the overnight crew, and start slinging. Ten one-million-dollar-a-year corners run by Abuelo (Grandfather). There was serious money to be made.

Daniel had to get down to his basement kitchen and start cooking. Working the corner got people hungry.

Out there, waving the hose, Daniel saluting Naum with his broom. The mist from the spray making morning sidewalk steam. Tio called across the street to Naum, "*¿Cómo amanecio usted, jefe hombre*?" How you doing, boss?

Naum, squinting in the sun, nodding, saluting with the soda bottle. "*Buen dia.*" Balancing the soda and the oversized heavy-duty brown paper sack, pretzels skyscraping out the top. "You two want a pretzel?"

Lea asked Daniel, "Tio, *quieres un* pretzel?"

Shook their heads and almost laughed when they heard his cellphone ring and watched Naum twisting to reach it, tilting the overloaded brown paper sack. A single fat pretzel bounced to the pavement. Lea and Daniel smiled at each other, watching the old priest bend down and kiss the pretzel up to God.

Lea, the blonde do-good girl with the long legs and the short skirt, smiling, waving Naum bye down the pavement. Same thing every time they saw each other. "Hey, Father."

"Hey, Lea." Naum had to give her credit. Talk about faith. Girl like that, like she was gonna broom up all the problems in the neighborhood and tie them up neat in her bulky black trash bag.

If the girl only knew what she knew.

She'd been raised in that church out there. The APOSTLES. The busload coming today to visit Naum. The Apostolic Protestant Orthodox Society of True Latter-day Evangelical Saints.

People said it was a cult. When Lea got old enough and bolted, she said it too. Naum wasn't so sure. Not now, anyway.

After a time, Lea found a job at Good and Plenty Candy factory, Sixth and Susquehanna, and started nights at Philly Community College, when it was still in the basement of Snellenburg's Department Store down at Eleventh and Market.

Girl was pretty sure she'd had her fill of religion, but it put her over the edge good when one of her professors, Felicity Cadbury, explained Docetism. Said religion wasn't real anyway.

"All phantasm," Professor Cadbury told the class. "Or maybe, Christ's body, if it was real, was sort of real, but made of some extraterrestrial or celestial material not subject to our understanding of physics, and so he only appeared to be real, only appeared to suffer and die."

Professor Felicity said suffering was only what *we* thought it was—the resurrection, suffering, *all* that—something that only appeared that way to us, in our minds. Nothing really changed. The only thing that changed was the way it appeared to us.

But Lea had seen suffering. Real suffering. And to some extent, the girl had known the truth all along. Knew it Ivo the Prophet style, up in her face, with her parents pretending what he was doing was something good, something holy.

Why bother with a God who's pretending?

There were days when Lea wanted to ask Tio Daniel what he thought.

Tio could tell by the way she talked to the kids working the drug set that she wanted things to be different for them. He knew she wanted to change things for the better, for the kids and for herself, and when she'd hint at it, he'd stop sweeping, make a circle and bless the air with his broom, give her that sad Tio look, and say, "*Es bueno hablar con La Mujer.*"

Talk to the Woman. It's good to talk to the Woman. *La Mujer que se mantiene fiel* . . . The Woman who stays true.

Lea transferred to Temple University. Figured she'd replace religion with social work, give that a shot at fixing up our neighborhood and maybe her life. Got her MSW, master of social work, in less than five years. Not bad for a kid homeschooled in a cult. Not a bad paycheck either.

Found a two-bedroom on Almond Street. Tacconelli's Square Pizza just around the corner. Stocks butter pound cake Bakery just down the street.

Walked up past Mother of Divine Grace every morning to Allegheny Avenue. Hopped the #60 trolley to work. Couldn't'a been sweeter or more savory, being out on her own, living whatever reality she wanted reality to be.

Times though, nights mostly, when that sweet two-bedroom went sour and shrink-wrapped around her. Nights when there was no pretending the empty pizza-stained cardboard containers and butter-brown wax paper cake wrappers took up anything more than space in her trash can. When her two-hundred-plus channels and internet-connected social-media network morphed into two hundred channels too many, and the irony of *live-streaming* in a dead-end bed started to hit her as sad and sardonic and damn silly. Digital-on-demand got pathetic real quick.

Sometimes at night, especially in the winter, when it got dark early, when she had a cold or didn't feel quite herself, when there was no one to even make her a cup of tea, she'd stare at the ceiling and think about maybe talking to that priest who walked by, the one with the beard. Then she'd change her mind and turn toward the wall.

She couldn't believe it when she heard her parents and almost two hundred other followers of that dumbass Ivo had decided to get together and give it another try.

Lea heard a busload of their kids were coming to visit Naum. The Apostles' new leader wanted the kids to see a traditional Orthodox church. She thought about Naum and said, "At least they're going to see somebody normal, sort of."

Naum knew it wasn't gonna be the usual neighborhood school visit, like the kids from Monsignor Truen's Saint Veronica's, kids getting ready for first confession and communion. Or like when Professor Golden from the college brought sixty students every semester from his religion and philosophy course.

Earlier, under the Tunnel, Naum told Professor Sergei Golden, "I have the Apostles coming today."

Sergei admitted, "It was me who . . . me who sent them, Naum. I knew you'd open the Father's box, show 'em what's inside. I mean, who do we blame but ourselves if we don't at least offer to show them the inheritance. It's just as much their calling. I mean, if someone takes them in, makes them a true friend. There's been big changes there since Ivo the Prophet took off and Bishop Harry took over."

At home, Naum asked Greta, "You seen my overalls?"

His wife said, "You look on the hook behind the garage door? Hanging with your hat and your work boots." She didn't have to ask why he wasn't changing into his cassock that day.

A yellow school bus rolled up to the door of our little Saint Alexander the Whirling Dervish Orthodox Church. Bold red letters, two feet high, APOSTLES, on the side. The kids were singing what sounded to Naum like, "Bringing in the cheese . . ."

This was a polite group of kids, reverent, making the cross, walking into the church, in from the bus, two by two, kissing the icons, making prostrations, cupping their hands, asking Naum for his blessing.

Bishop Harry, in a Carhartt work jacket, worn-out dungarees, redheaded and robust, wearing the same steel-toed putty factory boots as Naum, took off his cap, smiling with his hand out, said, "Thank you, Father, for letting us come today," and he kissed Naum's hand.

Naum said, "I got pretzels for the kids."

Harry said, "Thanks, man. I wanted them to see a real Orthodox church for a change."

"You want a pretzel?" Naum said. "I got one left."

"Yeah, Father, break me off a piece."

"I did drop it on the ground."

"Makes it taste better." Harry had that kind of smile.

Naum, standing there in his bib overalls, looking at a brother—a brother on one level, the potential to take it deeper—shaking hands, sharing a pretzel.

Harry said, "Be better with mustard."

Looked like Harry and the Apostles were changing.

Standing with Harry, some part of Naum praying for Lea.

She'd been raised in that church. The APOSTLES.

Smiling, waving. "Hey, Father."

"Hey, Lea."

Naum had to give her credit.

If the girl only knew what she knew.

Talk about faith.

Social work would change. Nothing wrong with that. All the sciences grow and evolve. What's considered true and thought to work this year might not be the same next year. Improvement's a good thing, ain't it? Thank God for scientists and science.

Social work policy and procedures manuals were bound to change, and Lea would change the work, and the work would change Lea.

If she hung in helping people long enough, she'd find the one thing needful, the difference in change between the transient and the true.

To Naum, change was like the Delaware. Winter mornings he'd sit bundled on the shore in Penn Treaty Park and watch the cold gray water whitecap in the wind. Never the same river twice. Blink and he could hardly remember what just curled by on the current in his eyes.

But that big rock in the middle? Been there unchanging since Naum was a boy. Like that since before his father's time. Before Penn shook hands with Tammany, Chief of the Lenni Lenape. Unforgettable, unchanging, immovable in the current, like an enduring truth in the flux and flow of human forgetfulness and change.

Far as Naum was concerned, you could keep the change, that kind of change. Finding the one thing needful, sorting the transient from the true, all Naum knew was our Master, Jesus, the Christ. He only is my rock and my salvation, the same yesterday, today, and forever.

Part II

Tio and the Woman

LOCKING UP. Pulling down the iron window grates. Hooking in the ancient padlocks. End of a long day sweating in that cellar kitchen. Almost dark. Cheve—paper bag sopping the sweat off the slick cold bottle inside. El viudo, Tio Daniel dragging home to his studio apartment over Abuelo's tire store.

Getting too old for this, for these long days and this little bit of money. Wanna see my babies. My sister. Be home. My Vera Cruz.

Holy Name. The bells started calling people to evening Mass.

Tio Daniel slowed his walk and made the cross.

A dark-skinned Afro-Caribe woman with a head covering said to him, "You should come in. Light a candle."

He looked at her.

She looked like his *abuelita* (grandmother), but sexy, for an old *chica*.

She said, "Help you, so you not feel all alone with those troubles you carrying."

After Mass, he stayed with the Rosary Society Ladies for supper. He read the brochure the woman had given him, the one about the Image of Our Lady of Guadalupe, and fell asleep in the back pew staring at her icon.

La Mujer—the Woman
No sleep like church sleep
Where the seed of the Word
Seeps into the garden of your heart
Estaba sano y salvo

Safe and sound

Tio

The brochure open on his chest

Rising and resting with every settled breath

The words seeping

Al jardín de su corazón

Into the garden of his heart

When Tio Daniel woke, he stayed, had a coffee with the ladies and Monsignor, and helped with the cleanup.

After, he sat in the church, looking at her, Nuestra Señora de Guadalupe. Her, the Woman who stays true. Sat looking at her. Her looking at him.

Tio Daniel never questioned the reality of ecclesial life. When Lea asked about it, he told her, "I don't go to church."

"But you go to Mass almost every day," Lea said.

"The church is in me, and I am every day out here, so I am not going to church. I am living the church, me and my Alma, and the church is living us."

He never said so, but Lea knew what she knew. Tio's Alma, his wife, the love of his youth, was always in front of his eyes. The world might be broken in pieces, but in their love there was no change.

Part III

Artos

THE PROFESSOR SAID, "I heard. They're a good group. The new leadership, primarily the guy who replaced Ivo, guy they call

Bishop Harry, began to read church history, like Eusebius, *History of the Church*. Somehow found the writings of the first- and second-century Fathers, people who'd been disciples of Christ or His Apostles. Saint Irenaeus. Ignatios. Saint Polycarp . . . People consecrated bishops by the Apostles.

"And then," Sergei said, "when Bishop Harry and his buddies get up to the third and fourth century and encounter Athanasios, it starts to dawn on them that the New Testament is *not* the founding document of the Church . . ."

Naum said, "How 'bout that?"

Professor said, "And I visited their place. You should see it. Artos, they call it."

Naum had heard about it.

"You gotta give 'em credit, Naum," Sergei said. "These guys have made an effort. Visited numerous Orthodox temples. Seminaries. Monasteries. Traveled to Mount Athos. Made pilgrimages to the Holy Land. And Naum, these people are a church supplier's dream. Liturgical books. Vestments. All that stuff, for more than ten years now, buy by the barge load. And they love to *dialogue* with us, with the Orthodox.

"You should see these people, Naum. I really think they're true believers. They pray for their pastors. They tithe and give money to support the work. They seem to live what they confess. They don't just *go* to church; they build their lives around the church."

Sergei said, "They have an ecclesial world view of reality. They help each other selflessly. Pious lay leadership. Know the faith. People known around the neighborhood for their compassion and good works. Got their own schools. Their bishops, Naum, are actually—not just with a verbal wink—*actually* approved of and recommended by the people, from among the people."

Naum was listening.

"I saw them, from the bishops right down the line, when this young grocer died, one of their folks. They all took turns pitching in and manning the store for his widow. Whatever it took so her and her kids wouldn't lose their livelihood."

The APOSTLES had grown to over six hundred members.

Sergei said, "They purchased more land on the river and built a domed cathedral in the center. There were cedar-shingled homes, a school, and businesses arrayed around the cathedral in wagon-wheel fashion.

"Their own water-driven power generation plant. Spiral-shaped wind turbines making electric. Solar panels everywhere. Got chickens and livestock. Grow their own veggies. Got an orchard and vines. A medical clinic. A print shop. Various merchants and service-oriented shops. Computer and IT service providers, all known for the excellent quality of their work."

Professor told Naum, "These folks never have to shovel or plow their streets. Steam pipes from their central steam power plant on the outskirts of the village carry heat via underground conduits to every building and warm the byways just enough so that snowflakes melt when they hit the ground. Can you believe it?"

The collective grew wheat and bought other grains and supplies, prepared it at their mill, baked the stone-ground products in wood-fired ovens, and sold them all over the area.

Naum had seen the trucks. ARTOS BAKERY.

Barenbaum, the grocer under the Tunnel, told Naum, "It's so

good, Naum. Every restaurant and retail guy within a hundred miles can't get enough. Sells out, gone every day by noon."

When the Artos community gathered for Vespers at their cathedral, the thick wooden beams arching high overhead, every member, from the oldest to the youngest, was in attendance.

The professor said, "It's true. I was there. It was wonderful. And okay, maybe they tried to justify singing 'A Mighty Fortress Is Our God' when I asked, saying it was a national tradition, like the Russians or the Greeks . . ."

Naum said, "Yeah, but heading in the right direction, right?"

Mailings the APOSTLES sent to the bishop's office ended up in what the chancellor called the *flake file*.

The old guy, the Prophet Ivo Dye, who founded the group? He was gone. The man with the long hair and big dark beard had finagled a sizable site up on the river near Pennypack Creek and the old Baxter Trail.

Naum never understood how otherwise sane people ended up pooling their resources, blending their families, and living in tents and shacks out in the woods.

People said strange stuff went on up there. Every kid was the Prophet Ivo's kid. Every wife was Ivo's wife. Until Cairo, the prophet's old lady, died and the prophet told the faithful, "Leave 'er on the bed and in three days I'll resurrect 'er."

Three days later, three hundred people had a lot of choices but not a lot of options. Turns out everybody's money was Ivo's money, and the Prophet Ivo Dye was gone, up and away without a shout.

Part IV

Something in the Girl

SUMMER MORNING.

Not quite hot. But he could smell the heat coming up. Tio Daniel, the owner of Vera Cruz, el viudo, the widower, feeling his Alma, out washing down the pavement with bleach water. Get rid of last night's stench outside his Mexican restaurant he called after his hometown.

Daniel and Lea, the do-good social worker from the Youth Agency Outreach Drop-In Center, the storefront on the Avenue right next to Daniel's restaurant.

Out there, the two of them, him waving the hose, saluting the new day with his broom. The mist from the spray making the morning sidewalk steam.

Talk about faith.

Girl like Lea, like she was gonna sweep up all our neighborhood problems in her broken-glass bag. Girl was gonna make a change. Knew what she knew.

Something in Lea the survivor was getting to the point where she finally had enough of having enough with religion.

It wasn't the institution, was it? It was people. Self-ordained, self-contained individuals who were less than persons, selfish individuals who screwed things up and rendered faith unreal.

Something in the girl
Would not let Lea the woman doubt Jesus was real
Was true—was the same
Some inextinguishable
Fight in the child

Refused to let
The grownup
Give up
And lay down her heritage
Some stubborn
Spit-in-your-face
Innate defiance
Said hell no
To letting her relinquish
The hope
That there was more
That she wasn't alone
That He still loved her
Same as He always did
Yesterday
Today and forever
And because He first loved her
How could she not fight for the gift?

Something in the kid homeschooled in a cult, the girl who told all the neighborhood kids, "Don't you give up. Never give up. You just keep fighting . . . If we can change, *things* can change."

Summer morning. Not quite hot.

When Tio nodded in that direction, Lea saw Naum across the street.

Naum, squinting in the sun, nodding, saluting with the soda bottle. "Buen dia." Balancing the soda and the oversized heavy-duty brown paper sack, pretzels skyscraping out the top. "You two want a pretzel?"

"No. But thanks, Padre," she said.

Lea, the blonde do-good girl with the long legs and the short skirt, smiling, waving Naum bye down the pavement. "Hey, Father."

"Hey, Lea."

Talk about faith. That same stubborn toughness wouldn't let her play nursemaid to any doubt.

Tio watched her circle her broom like a blessing in the air and lean it on the bleach-wet wall, crossing over, calling to Naum, "You know what? Hold up, Padre. I changed my mind."

When she got over, the part of Naum his mother kissed up to God wanted to ask, "About the pretzel?"

But Lea knew what she knew. She said, "Yeah, Padre, that's what I'm talking about, give me a pretzel . . . Not that one."

Bermuda Report

THE DARK-SKINNED WOMAN who ran the teen homeless shelter under the Tunnel called Naum. She said it was important.

"Nope." She couldn't talk about it on the phone. She said it involved her rehab manager, Elisa.

Naum said, "Okay, Corrine. I'll come." He wondered what Elisa was doing in Bermuda.

Two of our Teuta ladies were in the hall that morning baking *meshes*. Madeline said to Carol, "Nothing makes a place smell like home more than baking holy bread."

Naum was on the front steps of our Saint Alexander the Whirling Dervish Orthodox Church. He was looking out past Donahue's Funeral Parlor toward the trees and hedges around Palmer Burial Ground.

Carol looked at Naum and then at Madeline.

Madeline could tell. She saw the newspaper folded on the step. Carol finished locking up and motioned to Madeline. They sat on either side of Naum.

Corrine, the shelter manager, gave the paper to Naum without a word. That's all she could do. She had to walk away. Naum didn't open it till he sat down on the steps of the church.

Carol unfolded the newspaper. She said to Naum, "I remember her. You spent all night out there looking for that kid. Comes a couple times a year now, got a grown daughter, right?"

Out there.

They call it the Tunnel. The beat Elisa used to work on a stretch of Kensington Avenue under the El. Elisa called it the tunnel to hell. Especially on dark or rainy days. Call the boys and girls who work under there Tunnel-boys or Tunnel-girls.

Functional square-inch ziplock baggies full of the most potent forget-about-life-poison a person in pain could ever pump into their veins.

Eight to ten bags a night, Tunnel girls. Boys, twelve to sixteen.

In and out of cars. Eight, ten, twelve times a night. Ten dollars a pop. Oral. Quick. Cheap.

Out there hidden in the open right in front of Billy Penn's Shackamaxon eyes. And of all the girls who ever went down under the tunnel of hell, our Elisa was one of the few Billy Penn saw make it out.

Madeline said, "Elisa's mother must've called every Orthodox church in the city that night."

"The mom's an OR nurse. Am I remembering that right? Poor thing," Carol said. "I see her in my shop sometimes."

Madeline sighed. She said, "Yeah. She did get Naum that night. Eventually."

Naum went out there and got lucky. He found Elisa.

Short, tight outfit. Piercings. Tattoos. Jet black hair. Doc Marten combat boots.

Carol said to Naum, "Do you wonder how that happened? How you ended up finding her. What made her decide to come with you?"

Naum said, "I can't remember why she agreed to come. All I know is it was just getting light and she came and helped me with the Clergy Brotherhood meeting."

Elisa finished school. Got her daughter back. Did good. Damn good.

Many a time Naum would go to see Elisa under the Tunnel. But it was a new day under the Tunnel for Elisa. With a new sky. Wasn't it?

Naum got buzzed through security at the teen shelter the first time he visited and asked the receptionist for the rehab manager on duty.

And there came his girl. "Elisa," he said. "Kid, ya look good. How's your little girl?"

Elisa stood there looking like a person just shaken from a dream. "Father Naum. She's in college. About to graduate. You remember her name? C'mon now, you baptized her."

And damn if he didn't pull it out of somewhere. "Dayna," he said. "First time I saw her she was four or something. I remember her being so proud 'cause she could double-knot her shoes."

A constant movement flowed through the lime green cinder-block hallways of the rehab. Clients and staff stopping to ask Elisa, the veteran clinician, what about this? When? How much? Why me? Why? Why not me?

Naum couldn't figure what was worse, the disinfectant smell or whatever infectious ether it was failing to deal with.

Elisa noticed. Not much got by our Elisa. She said, "Let's go out. I gotta have a smoke."

They stood on the pavement under the El, smiling over trifles that were neither here nor there, just so they could fend off the notion that Naum had come only because he wanted something.

Then he said, "I remember you going over that fifth-floor balcony."

"Yeah, I was going for a smoke that night too."

Sweaty summer evening. A recovery meeting in the project high-rises. Naum said, "What the hell were you thinking when it happened?"

"What was I thinking? Damn if I know. I leaned over to yell at my Tommy to get the hell up to the meeting and over I went. I'll tell you what I was thinking. At about the second floor, I was thinking, this is gonna hurt."

Naum wanted to hug her. She knew it. She got close to Naum and said, "Still afraid to hug me?"

He circled her with both arms. Elisa was looking up at the old priest like some kind of father she hadn't seen since once upon a time. Naum wished he had a daughter.

"'Member why?" she asked. "Why you wouldn't hug me? I had that thing put in me. From that crank doctor working the Avenue. Supposed to be instant detox. Looked like a black chewing gum pack. Six hundred dollars. You know how long it took to earn that out here? Ripped off so many of us. What a scam. And damn, Naum. Here I go, *knowing* the instant detox thing is supposed to block the junk I'm shooting. So what do I do? I double up. Shooting more. Twice, three times the dose. And then instead of instant detox it was instant OD. Instant see ya later, Elisa."

Naum opened his arms and looked at Elisa.

"Thank God you found me in that lot. I was dying. You picked me up and carried me out. You saved my life, Naum . . . And I gave you scabies."

He ignored that. Naum said, "Yeah, I was yelling, hoping somebody would hear . . . 'Call 911. Call 911.'"

"That was funny," Elisa said.

"Yeah, maybe now."

"'Member what came?"

"A red hook-and-ladder," Naum said. "I was looking at them like, what the . . . ? Guys in long fire coats and helmets and gigantic boots with axes, big gloves . . . Lights and sirens going. I said to 'em, 'She ain't on fire.' They told me, take it or leave it. You limp, crying in my arms, saying, 'Yeah, but it does burn.'"

Prifti Naum didn't want to hurt her with his memories. Didn't want to tell her that when he handed her over to the fireman, the emptiness in his arms, where he'd been holding her for what seemed like a damn long time, was a void he still had, and knew he always would have till God came to take all of us in His arms.

"You almost cost me my marriage, girl," he told Elisa.

"Yeah, that's why you're afraid to hug me," she said.

"You had scabies, bad, and I got it. My Greta couldn't bathe for forty-eight hours. I took that stuff home. Had to apply that lotion every twelve hours to get rid of those microscopic critters making scratch lines up under her skin. And mine."

Elisa said, "I'm so sorry. Tell Priftereshe I'm sorry."

"Go ahead. You can laugh. It's funny. Now," Naum said.

"Tell you what I remember," she said. "Tal. You remember that guy, Talford Lee. With you on the ground and his boot on your throat. Telling you, 'You working with these crack whores and night-birds . . . You come around here again . . .'

"They sure as hell didn't want you here," Elisa said. "Not even a little bit. When you first came down here trying to find me and kept coming back. They told all of us out here we were gonna catch a beatdown and they were gonna kick your ass."

"Tal lived upstairs over the Outreach storefront, next to Tio Daniel's Vera Cruz, right?" Naum said. "Where Lea works."

Elisa said, "Yep. Tal was up on the third floor."

"He used to open his window and hock up a big green loogie and spit on me every morning. A large slimy glob of spit mixed with nose snot and mucus blood, coughing it up and hocking whatever was in his throat."

Elisa said. "He ever getcha?"

"He got lucky," Naum said.

Monday morning. End of July, beginning of August. Humidity. Steaming heat like a jungle. Naum came early through the abandoned houses and rubble lots and could smell it down the block.

Elisa said, "I remember. I was sitting on the Outreach steps. You used to walk through the lots where we slept, singing, some kinda church chants, carrying Fruit Loops and Count Chocula. Knew we were craving sweets. Get us to come sit on the storefront steps. Get us to talk with you."

No mistaking the smell that Monday morning. Naum looked up at the third-floor window and said to Elisa and the girls, "Where's Talford?"

Elisa said, "I haven't seen him since he took Erin up there Friday night."

Talford Alvin Lee lived on the top floor. His window looked right out onto the El platform. Tal left his curtains open on purpose. When the train stopped . . . Tal walking around. No towel. A one-room single-occupancy kitchen-combo-sleeping area with a shared bath out in the hall. A Jack Standing special.

That morning Naum said to Elisa, "You still got warrants?"

The Tunnel crowd told Naum they'd been up there knocking all weekend and it was getting weirder and weirder. Tal's place all locked up tight.

Naum told them they'd better go.

Three young cops came. Cisco Kid with her hat on and two young guys. Gagging their way up three flights of dark narrow steps with Naum following.

Inside, the place was like a pizza oven. T. A. Lee was facedown at his kitchen table. They were wearing latex gloves. Cisco Kid stepped to the bathroom and didn't come back. Bilious liquid crawled to the latex cuffs at their wrists. Talford Lee was being lifted to pieces.

Naum told the two young officers, "Sorry, fellas, I'm out." Retching. Peeling off gloves. Dropping them on the floor. "Man's been baking all weekend . . . And I know, pretty sure, he's been with at least one girl, told me she's HIV positive."

The people from the ME's office had face shields and full body suits. Naum watched them load Tal into a bag, zip him up, and bounce his behind down three flights of stairs.

Seemed like another lifetime.

Never get that smell out of your nostrils. Even now on the pavement with Elisa having a smoke under the Tunnel.

Naum said, "I did try with him, with Talford."

She said, "You tried with everybody. Don't feel too bad, Father. Ya saved me and I love you. I wouldn't be here if it wasn't for you. I owe you my life. My daughter too. I told God I was gonna kill myself that night . . . I was serious. I had a loaded needle and I'd had enough. And then this man in a big beard sits down next to me."

Neither one wanted to take that any further. Both knew why.

"Know what I remember?" Naum said.

"Go ahead and ignore me," she said. "What I said about God."

Naum said, "What I remember? The night I'm sitting on the steps out here trying to get to your Tommy and looking up to see you cursing some guy in a car. Spitting at him in his window."

"Yeah, yeah," Elisa said. "He wanted me to do stuff I wasn't into and didn't want to pay me. I mean, in those days, if I was gonna go wild on your ass . . ."

"You walk around the front and the bastard puts it in gear, knocks you down, and I'm getting up and running, yelling at that creep rolling over you . . . You lying there, and then I see the backup lights go on and he goes over you again."

Elisa said, "It only looked like that. I rolled, Father. He missed me . . . at the back-up."

"I was banging on the car, but he got away before I could stop him or get a plate number."

Elisa took a final drag and said, "And my Tommy, my baby's daddy, just sat there." She dropped the cigarette to the pavement and stubbed it out with her toe. "My so-called husband, who

OD'd on the American Street tracks, had me out here supporting both our habits."

Overhead an El train was grating to a stop. The programmed female announcer voice was saying, *Doors are opening.* The sound of passengers detraining. *Doors are closing.*

The electric engine whir and metallic stress whining two stories up above on ninety-year-old tracks strained the thick old iron beams right down to the cracks in the grime-creased pavement.

Arm-in-arm with Elisa, getting buzzed in at the rehab door, Naum asked her, "You wanna come and speak to some of the younger ones at the church?"

She said, "Yep."

He didn't know why it felt like a last kiss.

AFTER THE BROTHERHOOD MEETING that first morning at the church, the time he'd been out all night looking for her, she told him, "I'm tired, Father."

He said, "You wanna take a nap in the back, you could. You'd be safe here. There's cushions on that bench in the back of the church."

She said, "Near the icon of the blind lady?"

Naum said, "Yep, Saint Matrona of Moscow."

The Teuta Baking Society ladies came in that morning.

Nothing makes a place smell like home more than baking holy bread, and if Elisa had any regard or embarrassment or anger about her situation, she didn't show it. She passed out on the bench.

Father Naum asked Madeline to go in and cover Elisa.

But now it was a new day. With a new sky. Wasn't it?

Carol unfolded the newspaper.

The dark-skinned woman who ran the teen homeless shelter under the Tunnel called. Said it was important. "Nope." She couldn't talk about it on the phone. She said it involved her rehab manager, Elisa.

Elisa.

In Bermuda.

Carol smoothed the newspaper on the steps.

THE BERMUDA ROYAL GAZETTE

Woman's Body Found 8 Miles from Hit-and-Run Site

Bermuda Reserve Constabulary found a moped abandoned on North Shore Road, near Cottage Hill Road, Hamilton Parish, at about 1:45 a.m. Saturday.

A spokeswoman for the constabulary said it appears the moped was rear-ended while driving westbound.

They found the body of the woman they believe was driving that moped eight miles away from the site of the moped crash on the shoulder of Up and Down Lane off Berry Hill Road near King Edward the VII Memorial Hospital.

She was taken to King Edward VII Memorial Hospital, where she died.

"That's bizarre," a local man said. "That just doesn't seem very possible. But given our roads, the tourists, the sand and mud, the oil on the roads, our left hand drive . . ."

A constabulary spokeswoman said they are still trying to

figure that out. "Maybe it was someone trying to transport her to a hospital. I don't know. That's just crazy. I don't see how it could happen."

A nearby resident, who didn't want to be identified, said, "It's very scary because obviously they don't have a heart if they left the scene. What kind of a person is just going about their day with no regard to what they just did to somebody's family?"

Constabulary officers armed with a search warrant found a car suspected of rear-ending a woman on a scooter early Saturday morning and leaving the scene.

According to the constabulary spokeswoman, the owner of the home where officers believed the car involved might be refused to cooperate.

On Sunday, police executed a search warrant, and a dark-colored vehicle with front-end damage consistent with the crash was found in a closed garage less than 2 miles from where the scooter was rear-ended.

The car was seized and will be transferred to the Department of Investigation for further forensic examination.

The identity of the victim, believed to be a tourist, is being withheld until 24 hours after notification of next of kin.

Madeline remembered.

She sat with Elisa that morning before the kid fell asleep on the pew in the back by the icon of Saint Matrona, before she covered the kid. Wiped both their tears. Kissed Elisa three times on each cheek. Elisa closed her eyes.

Madeline had no doubt about the deepness of the wound when the soul is maimed in childhood.

Elisa told her, "It's not something ya just move on from."

Madeline figured it could've been the beginning of the girl's spiritual ruin had things not worked out the way they did. The child herself might not even have been to blame.

They went into the temple. Carol lit the candles and the censer. Madeline held the icon of Saint Matrona, and they stood together before the icon of the Theotokos and Child.

They made the cross. They said the prayers of the Church.

Life in the Garden*

In Naum's neighborhood, there's a little stretch down by the Delaware people call the Garden.

In summertime the Garden looks like God preserved a slice of paradise, with wide grassy lawns, birds and squirrels and bushes, and every kind of tree . . . Wonderful old houses set back on what most people think of as dead-end streets.

But there's something to be learned about one-way streets and so-called dead-ends. Something we all learned from Izzy Scott and his wife, Emma, who made a life in the Garden.

The Turtle Clan Lenape Indians and their chief, Tamanend, made a blessing on the plot they called Shackamaxon, not far from what Philly people call Penn Treaty Park, right there at Beach Street on the Delaware.

Swedish farmers worked it. Then the English Captain Palmer purchased the property, and people say the old houses in the Garden are the farmhouses, little barns, cottages, and wraparound-porch two-story wooden houses still standing from the original riverfront settlement Palmer called Old Kensington.

* Dedicated to my heroes, Johanna and Scott Watkins.

Nowadays, to most of us, the Garden is just a part of Fishtown.

Everybody knew Izzy Scott was born in the two-story porch house that had been in his family ten generations. Before the Revolution. Before Old Kensington days. Izzy grew up back there in the Garden and rehabbed the old farmhouse for his bride, Emma. Man, did those two love each other. Everybody in the neighborhood wanted to help when Izzy was rehabbing the house for Emma.

Little Harry was waiting curbside outside our little Saint Alexander the Whirling Dervish Orthodox Church in his '71 Stepside C10 Chevy pickup, the light blue junkyard jalopy with the dapple-rust patina.

He leaned out the window while Naum was locking up and said, "Ya wanna see something ya won't believe . . . C'mon, take a ride with me, Padre. Do your heart good."

Harry told Naum, "Guy's wife got allergic to him—his semen and everything. Buncha us are helping 'im ta rehab his house over in the Garden."

His cell rang, and Harry got into it heavy with some guy about a 2004 Lincoln Town Car XL and left Naum to ride the rest of the way with his thoughts.

Patty was all one color. White. Hair and skin. Teeth to toes. If it weren't for the robin's egg blue eyes, the tall slim grandmother would've had no color at all.

That Sunday after Liturgy she asked Naum for a minute. "I'm celiac, and I been communing with just the wine from the chalice for years, Father. But I still get a little sick every week," Pat told Naum.

"What is that, celiac?" he said.

"A lot of people don't know about celiac disease," she told Naum. "It's not just a stomachache. It's an autoimmune reaction. The body attacks itself and does damage to itself."

Naum was a pretty good listener when he didn't know what to say. It broke his heart when Patty told him, "I wish this weren't the case. Now my granddaughter, Salome . . ." Patty had to stop.

Naum took her hand.

She said, "I've heard stories of people with celiac disease who have no reaction to the wheat in the communion bread. But not me, Father, or my little Salome."

Naum thought about setting aside a second chalice with unconsecrated wine and adding a spoon from the consecrated chalice prior to adding the Lamb. He told Patty, "Let me get some guidance from the bishop."

"Yes. That's what I want you to do," old Bishop Skender said when Naum asked for guidance.

"But Naum," the bishop said, "you keep in mind, the Body and Blood of Christ cannot harm you. Major epidemics in America at the turn of the century, when many Protestant churches went from common cup to individual cups for communion, they still had a higher rate of sickness than those churches that continued the use of the common cup. This, for us, Naum, of course is not an issue. It's not about scientific fact or study. How can Christ, who is the Great Physician, offer you that which would harm you in His Body and Blood?"

Naum had tried to think it out, and now it was dogging him again in Harry's junkyard truck.

Being afflicted with an allergic reaction to life in communion with creation . . . An allergic reaction to the primary mode of our relationship with Him and each other, to food? To food in the Garden?

I guess it's possible. I mean, look what happened with the apple . . .

At night Naum lay awake wrestling with the sheets. He was in a nasty shouting match with himself.

You don't have faith the size of a mustard seed, do you?

When you limit your reality and communion with God to two alternatives.

When you think you're canonically correct because you chose the one documented in the book.

Naum thought, Maybe my doubt is my allergy. Maybe each of us lives with our own deadly allergens, things we may not even be aware of. Naum figured he would probably *never* be fully aware.

You react in a good way to some people and things, he told himself, and you're allergically repulsed by other people and things . . .

Naum wasn't sure he understood his own mind when he thought, Doesn't my reaction to people, good or bad, reduce my capacity for being as life and life as communion?

He wondered if God had truly left Patty and Salome with only one choice because of their allergy.

Harry held the phone away from his ear and mouthed, "Sorry, Father."

Naum moved his hand in the *it's okay* wave.

Over the years, Naum had known parishioners who were recovering alcoholics, and a few people in pre- or post-surgery situations or suffering with chemotherapy treatment. Folks susceptible to relapse or infection who said maybe they couldn't deal with the wine.

People he loved. People Naum told, "We'll make a way."

Naum closed his eyes. He saw Patty holding Salome's hand. The two of them every Sunday in the communion line. He wished he knew of someone who was actually doing something about it.

Patty told Naum, "I know for some it has little or no negative effect. But our Salome has a very extreme celiac reaction to communion. When she was almost a year old, she was only twenty-five inches long, not even on the pediatrician's chart, and hardly weighed fifteen pounds. Not even near the bottom of the chart. Every gluten reaction set her back. We couldn't figure it out. After the baptism, every time we'd bring her up to the chalice . . . That's when we saw the pattern."

When Salome was old enough to walk to the chalice, arms crossed over her chest, Naum would say, "How did your eyes get so big and brown, Hershey's Kisses?"

Salome was as creamy brown as her grandmother was milky white. She told Naum, "I got my eyes from my daddy."

Getzy, Salome's dad, married Pat's daughter. Things didn't go well in the marriage. Getzy, the '92 Mogadishu Marine. Not the only black guy working at the auto scrapyard with Little Harry but probably the most dark-skinned. Took a lotta guts in Fishtown in those days. Getzy was the one Naum buried after the incident on the railroad tracks outside the salvage yard.

"So, Father," Patty said, "Do you know of anyone that has celiac that has any opinions on what we should do? I still prepare and commune every week, because I believe communion is life. But I worry about my granddaughter . . ." Pat couldn't finish.

One priest told Naum, "Tell Pat *and* Salome's mother, the Eucharist is the medicine of immortality. It's the way we've done it for years."

He told Naum to think about "sneaking the bread in on the kid."

Naum said, "How's that work?"

"Slipping particles of the consecrated bread in the chalice. And I doubt it would do a thing. It's all in their heads. And the parents nowadays kowtow to their kids too much. Obvious who's the boss in those families."

Naum said, "Father, I don't believe you'd do that. Wouldn't that be mean?"

Salome wrote to Naum when she went away to college.

Dear Father,

I remember you. I remember the other priest too. You spoke to me at my grandmother's funeral and it brought back memories, things I had inside me I didn't realize were there. I guess you could call it a longing. I haven't been to church for years, at least since I've been away at college, but I'd like to come and see you when I'm home on break. I have a question that's been bothering me since the other priest came to our house. All I know is my mom and grandmom cried a lot after he left.

Through no fault or choice of my own, I was born allergic to the physical Garden and so prevented from eating its fruit, which is the means of communion with the spiritual Garden.

If, knowing that eating the physical fruit will result in my physical deterioration and eventual death, I eat it anyway in a desire for the life of the spiritual Garden, am I committing a physical suicide that results in my being excluded from the spiritual Garden because I have committed spiritual suicide by knowingly eating that which God allowed me to know in advance would harm me?

The day Salome's letter arrived, Little Harry, Getzy's boyhood friend, came to the church to deliver five cases of beeswax candles. Sitting curbside in his '71 Stepside C10 Chevy pickup, he leaned out the window and said to Naum, "Ya wanna see something ya won't believe . . . C'mon, take a ride with me."

Izzy Scott was a member at Holy Communion Protestant Church, Pastor Cal's congregation, where they had the little cups of grape juice at their once-a-month communion service.

When Little Harry and Naum pulled up to their house in the Garden, Izzy was sitting on the front steps, taking a break with the volunteer renovation crew. They were all eating radio balls. A Fishtown thing. Alternating layers of water-ice and vanilla ice cream. Munching soft pretzels with mustard from Fufari's. A Fishtown classic combo.

Little Harry said, "Got any more?"

Izzy pointed to a cooler on a table up on the porch.

Naum told Harry, "Get me one too."

Naum sat down and asked Izzy, "How is she today?"

Izzy told Naum, "Our life is a constant crisis, Father. Emma's immune system is just totally misfiring. Irreversibly out of order. She's at the mercy of the whims of her body. This is a killer disease, Father Naum, and her form of it is a particularly vicious killer, an insane killer.

"When we first started dating," Izzy said, "she started

developing sensitivities to a lot of things a lot of people are allergic to—gluten, dairy—things that aren't all that uncommon. But her symptoms, over time, got worse and worse, and her allergies really accelerated and got way out of whack when we got married. Coupla years ago, it just blew up way out of control."

Izzy stopped eating the radio ball.

Little Harry came and sat with them. Harry handed Naum a pretzel and radio ball. "I didn't know if ya took mustard or not, so I brought it on a plate." He handed Naum the small paper plate and the cup of water-ice and ice cream. He said, "I'm gonna let you twos alone."

Little Harry and the crew went back to work. Naum sat the plate and the radio ball on the step.

Izzy said, "We've seen dozens and dozens of doctors. None of them knew what was wrong. Emma's been hospitalized so many times we've lost count. Finally we got some answers from this one doctor down at University Hospital. Turns out my girl has this thing called mast cell activation syndrome. Whatever the hell that is. Ya ever hear a that?"

Naum shook his head.

Izzy said, "But at least now we know the name of this thing, for what that's worth. When things hurt you, Father, and you don't know what they are, friggin' more bewildering than when you at least know what's hurting you."

Naum wanted to weep. Something about Izzy wouldn't let him.

"Ya got this disease and the systems your body has that are supposed to protect you are actually hurting you. Emma's suffering, Father Naum, feels to us like it's one of a kind. She has it in an exquisitely horrible way. It's a hellish experience. She's constantly on the edge of anaphylaxis, life-threatening allergic reactions."

The kid, Izzy, was not even out of his twenties. Sitting there, dog tired. Hands roughed out. Hammer-raw. Tools hanging from his tool belt . . .

"If we control her environment perfectly, her disease doesn't get worse. So my girl's been isolated for over a year. Most people, when their throat starts to close in, they go to the emergency room. But Emma's throat is always tight. Her body always hurts—that's just her normal everyday life, because these cells are identifying everything as a threat."

Izzy picked up his cup and sat slurping the radio-ball, tearing big bites of pretzel. He said, "She has a list of fifteen foods she can eat and that's it. Even those foods make her feel ill, it's just that they don't kill her."

This kid's a hero, Naum thought, an icon, a bridegroom of love.

"She's eaten the same meal two years. I make it every day. A small piece of wild salmon with carrots, celery, and steamed mashed parsnips, maybe some broccoli. Sometimes she can handle a cucumber slice or a small bite of kiwi. Those are the only things her body tolerates."

Izzy looked at Naum like maybe the priest might have an answer.

He didn't.

Naum said, "What do you eat?"

"What she eats. That's the blessing, right? Our communion. Me on one side of the glass. Her on the other. That's our relationship right now. It's a gift just to be able to share that much. We're not in heaven yet, right, Father?"

Naum wanted to tell Izzy, "You shoulda been the priest."

Izzy said, "She's allergic to everyone except her siblings. Not even her parents can get close. She gets sick when I'm around her. If I stayed around her for more than fifteen minutes, there's a decent chance she would go unconscious and I'd have to bring her to the ER. Who would ever think that just your presence would hurt someone?"

If he could've brought himself to put his hand on the kid's shoulder—Naum . . . What is there to say?

"My Emma's been hospitalized many times, Father—undergone chemotherapy, but there's still no treatment that amounts to anything. Sometimes it makes her sicker. I've cleaned up a lot of diarrhea and emptied a lot of vomit buckets . . ." Then he looked at Naum and said, "I hope I don't sound like I'm complaining, 'cause I'm not."

Naum said, "No."

Izzy said, "She has the main floor of the house: dining room, living room, bedroom, bathroom, and sunroom. I wanted to give her the best part of the house because she never leaves, and when you're stuck in one place for the foreseeable future, I want her to have a beautiful space."

Naum looked out at the neighborhood called the Garden. Somehow the infective allergen, the Luciferian notion that we can make it on our own, be a communion of one, the notion that there can be life apart from the One who is life, apart from the other, someone to love us and someone for us to love, the lie of being as individual existence . . . Adam and Eve had been beguiled, taken in by a thankless taking that dead-ended life as relationship.

Izzy told Naum, "We have her space pressurized. Drops in pressure can trigger her mast cells to hurt her. There's an air lock outside of her door, plus we installed special filtration, insulation, and seals. I live upstairs and never enter her space. I do sometimes see her through glass as she's on a couch and I'll wave to her. It's hard for me to see her because she's so sick. You know, Father, some people tell us it's all in her head."

Naum tried to breathe.

The brave young husband said, "Also, because I love her so much and I can't be with her, seeing her doesn't fulfill all those missing pieces of our relationship. We haven't kissed in about a year and a half, maybe two years. We talk on the phone all the time. We watch shows together—she watches the show on her TV and I watch the show on mine."

A sparrow landed in front of the porch, and then another and then another. Izzy broke off pieces of the soft pretzel. He said, "They come every day."

Naum wished he could ask the three little birds if they knew and prayed to God for Emma in their hopping and chirping.

Izzy told Naum, "Sickness wears on your body and soul, so she's tired. Her life hangs by a thread, and she's aware of that. Physically, her body is a disaster. She can't walk without help. She weighs ninety pounds because her body is so weak. Her daily life is full of pain and suffering. She always feels like she's breathing through a straw. Her normal level of pain is most people's highest level."

Naum knew there was a connection to his celiac communion dilemma, but couldn't concentrate or intuit . . .

The young husband told Naum, "Psychologically, she's the

world's healthiest woman. She's the strongest woman I know. She has faith and hope and takes joy in what she can each day. I'm just immensely proud of her. She's amazing. My biggest treat, Naum, sometimes I get to carry Emma. But I can only be around her for a few minutes."

Sitting in the Garden, looking at Izzy, Naum saw the icon of another communion.

Izzy told Naum, "We believe with all our hearts that God is in control of this situation, and our faith carries us. There are a million ways she could look at her life or I could look at mine and say 'Woe is me,' but that doesn't fix anything, and it doesn't lead to happiness. There are many times I've been so angry at what has happened, but I don't stay there, I don't live in that. We have joy in our days. There's sadness, too, but we move on."

When sadness overcame him, Naum could only bow his head. And when he closed his eyes, he saw Pat holding Salome's hand. The two of them, every Sunday in the communion line. He was certain now, after sitting with Izzy, there was only one life, one suffering, one priest, one communion, and one love that didn't know dead-ends or one-way streets.

Naum had wished he knew of someone who was doing something about it . . . It would have been better to show, then tell.

With Izzy, there was no tripping over any epitrahilion or fancy words. No intellectualizing. No moralizing. No canons. No obligation. No emotional sentimentality. The kid just did it. Lived it. He said, "Love is as love does, that's the blessing."

Everyone knows that oftentimes sick people cannot eat or keep things down and must be fed intravenously.

Naum wanted to draw a lifeline between this current frailty

and our earliest violation, the event where the allergen was first communicated. But even though he was sure of the way down deep in his skin, he also knew this was not possible for man alone. We were too deep in and drowning in fatal reaction to our own useless words.

Naum got up off the steps, kissed Izzy's hand, and told Little Harry he was walking back to the church.

As he was passing through Palmer Burial Ground on the way home, something got up off a bench behind a headstone and whispered in the footprints Naum left along the gravel path.

Get off the cross, Naum
We need the wood
Stop complaining
Get over yourself
It'll work out
Like you always tell us
There's a God

When Naum looked up, he saw Johnny C coming the other way under the trees and said, "John, where ya going?"

Johnny looked down at the tool bag in his hand, looked up at Naum, and said, "Now, Padre, where ya think?"

In Naum's neighborhood there's a little stretch people call the Garden, with wide grassy lawns, birds, squirrels, and bushes, and every kind of tree . . . with wonderful old houses set back on what most people think of as dead-end one-way streets.

Naum made it through the wrought iron gates of the burial ground, praying over and again, "O Christ, Great and Most Holy

Pascha, Wisdom, Word, and Power of God, grant that we may more perfectly partake of Thee in the never-ending day of Thy Kingdom."

Confess

THE PRIEST NAUM DID NOT LIKE to hear confessions.

The priest Photios Fsitsi did not like to confess.

But it was Kreshme e Madhe, Great Lent, the forty-day fasting period prior to Pascha that everybody loved and nobody liked, not in our neighborhood anyway. Father Photi felt compelled to make his yearly pilgrimage to Fishtown for his annual confession with the priest he thought least likely to remember anything he said and most likely to be lenient and non-judgmental.

After all, at that time, Father Fsitsi had heard of, but never actually met, a priest who'd made more of a mess of being a priest than old man Naum. He should never have been ordained in the first place.

"Naum." Father Fsitsi had a smartphone with extra-large keys on a simplified keypad. He showed it to Naum. "My kids got it me after we put my Philomena in the home."

He never cried publicly, Photi Fsitsi, but he often looked at the yellowed photograph of Philomena cutting his hair, before the Alzheimer's took her away and left him behind with the memory of the girl that once was.

"Look," he would say to fend off the memory. "She was so beautiful, and I had hair."

His son scanned it to his phone, and Photi showed it off and looked at it ten times a day.

Father Fsitsi had the title *nomikos*. An Orthodox ecclesial court appeals judge in matters of rubrics. Nomikos made Naum nervous whenever he came.

"Naum." Fsitsi held the phone like an Olympic torch. "See, bright, high-contrast color screen. No glasses, Naum. Day or night. Backlit, the display. You understand what that means? Amplified speaker. Has a speakerphone, listening and talking, and the compatibility with my hearing aids, Naum—are you listening?—is flawless."

They met in Palmer Burial Ground.

Father Fsitsi didn't like our little Saint Alexander the Whirling Dervish Orthodox Church. He told Naum, "It faces the wrong way."

He got irritated but covered his feelings, making a blessing over Naum when Naum said, "Maybe it's you, Nomikos, who's facing the wrong way."

Naum wasn't sure why he said it. It just came out.

The nomikos, who'd taught a course featuring Cavarnos and Kontoglou on sacred art and architecture, knew Naum was an architectural dome of empty space and not much on rubrics either. After forty years, the priest Naum still didn't know the *dikiri* from the *trikiri* when the bishop came for his yearly visit. One candleholder with two slots and the other with three . . . Why bother explaining? It drove Nomikos crazy when Naum called them the hickory and dickory. Nomikos told him, "Just forget it, Naum."

Naum looked at his feet and said, "Yes, Nomikos. I'll have to remember to forget more often."

Father Fsitsi often told the bishop, "Naum is right where he belongs," and quoted a canon about small parish and country priests not being permitted to serve in big city cathedrals. "There's a reason for Naum being where he is, Bishop."

"Thank God," the bishop said. "Tell me again what he said."

"He said," Father Fsitsi repeated, "when I showed him the new liturgy book you approved for use in the diocese, Naum the clown said, 'Is it fully rubricated?'" A clown, this Naum.

"Rubricated. He was serious?" the bishop said.

"Hierasi, if you stand close enough to Naum, you can hear the echo."

"You heard about the time he brought his vestments to be blessed and had a different color for every piece? The stole was green. The phelonion was blue. The belt was gold. One cuff was Lenten, one was Paschal, and the sleeves of the dalmatic were so old and water-stained and shredded. I think it had once been white." The bishop stopped. "Oh, and he looked surprised when I asked him, why nothing red?"

"The man's an idiot," Fsitsi said. "What did you do?"

"I told him to go sing in the choir, which, now that I think of it, is probably exactly what he was aiming for."

"With him," Fsitsi said, "you never know. You know what he told me? 'You can't tell which way the train runs by looking at the tracks.'"

"A good heart. But maybe not the sharpest knife in the drawer," the bishop said.

"With half the handle broken and a thin dull edge," Fsitsi replied.

The bishop wanted to ask Father Fsitsi, why, then, do you go to yearly confession, for more than twenty years now, with the man you say was more than likely held under sixty seconds too long the day he was baptized?

But the bishop knew.

Even though Naum always told people, "This is a one-time offer and there's no telling the bishop," the bishop knew very well what Naum was doing.

How did the bishop know? Naum told him. That's how he knew.

Years had gone by. Decades. And as far as the bishop knew, no one had ever declined Naum's one-time offer. To the bishop, it was a particularly Orthodox kind of one-time offer because people kept going back, one more time.

Naum would say to the one who had come to confess, "You will sit alone and ask God for stillness. I know you *think* you know what it is you want to confess.

"Take this." And he would hand them a pencil nub and a scrap of paper or the back of a church calendar with vacant areas where Naum cut out icon pictures to take on hospital visits. He would look at the person and say, "After thirty years of prayer, if you have three seconds of stillness, that's a lot . . .

"But today, if He grants you stillness while you're sitting here, listen. See if He reveals to you, not what *you* think you need to confess, but the thing *He* sees in you and blesses you to *know* you need to confess for the healing of your soul."

First-time visitors would squint at Naum, then nod and say, "Okay."

"This is a one-time offer. Of course, if you'd rather speak your confession, we can do that. But if you choose to sit and listen and record, confessions afterwards will be in the usual manner."

When Naum sensed that a person was too wounded even to speak . . . "Write down what He gives you. No one will see it. Not even me. Fold it. And you and I will go together to a place and burn it. Then when we make the prayer of absolution . . ."

Finishing the sentence, to Naum, would be the end of the gift and would finish the thing he never wished to be explained.

Flames curled the paper-edges. "Consigned to oblivion . . . As far as east from west . . ."

And after, at the confessional stand, under the epitrachelion, some word was always offered. Some short comfort or encouragement apropos of what had been written in whatever language or time of stillness God had granted to the one who wrote their unspoken confession.

"But I know the priest does not speak the language I wrote." People wondered.

Naum wondered.

He would never discuss openly what words were given to him under the stole. Once out from under the stole, Naum freely admitted he had no recollection of what may have been offered.

The priest with the echo in his ears who didn't like hearing confessions seemed to have no interest in being told by the one who confessed what guidance or admonition he may or may not have given, or even if what he had advised had anything to do with what was confessed secretly to God in writing.

He told them, "Our Master said, 'Where two or three are gathered . . .' He's One, here and present. You're two. I'm third. Talk to our Master. Christ is in our midst."

Some walked away without tears. Many didn't. Naum told the people, "It's better not to talk about it." People talked anyway.

The rubrical formula Naum knew consisted of relationship over rubric.

Something in him also knew each of the Mysteries—the means by which the Creator communicates His love and salvation—each of the Mysteries had two sides, a divine side and a human side. Like the two sides of the epitrachelion, the priestly stole.

"How to heal the trauma of the soul? That's the question," Nomikos said.

Was there a formula that worked every time in every instance? Naum didn't know of one, but he knew the opposite. But he wanted Nomikos to know he wished to be friends, brothers in Christ, so he said, "Speaking it is one way. Confessing aloud. The growing Church has known this way of cultivating fertile ground favorable for the seeds of healing. Healing relationships. God with His people. His people with each other."

But Naum also knew, from his own weaknesses, that sometimes on the human side of the epitrachelion, things broke down. People broke down. Relationships ruptured.

And words didn't always do it, did they?

In the multitude of words
There wanteth not sin

But he that refraineth his lips is wise.

In a world defined by
Psychology
Counselors
Notions of closure
Talking it out
Words
Even words
Like good and evil
Are trivialized and they trivialize
The coin of the realm
Comes cheap
Devalued on purpose
By the one who attempted
To entice the Word
With words
Bankrupt
Meaningless
Sad sounds
Worn-out noise

When the path of words becomes impassable, people need a different road to reconciliation.

The Word became flesh
The silent unseen
Pitched His tent among us
Audibly visible
For those with ears to see

Naum had discovered through his own suffering that nothing

clarifies the truth like seeing the icon of our plight portrayed in ink squibbles on a page.

He walked through the headstones, bending to weed the new growth that came up every spring. Reading gravestone names, saying with each petition, "Thy will, O Lord, be done on this poor earth . . ."

Father Fsitsi sat in the graveyard with his pencil and paper.

Word-icons
Emerged from the depths
Into the light of the Holy Spirit
A gift of confession
Filled his page
Symbols illumined
The truth of his inner reality
In a language
Not limited in dimension
To the earthly side of the abyss

Father Fsitsi folded the paper. He put the pencil nub into the pocket of his cassock and sat on the steps of the gatehouse at Palmer Burial Ground. Nomikos felt he had been blessed to lay aside his own notions of the sins he needed to confess. Now three things stared at him from the page.

I don't consider myself a priest.

I only act like a priest on the outside.

If I am truthful, I don't want to be a priest, or if at one time I did, it was for all the wrong reasons.

Naum noticed when Father stood. Fsitsi asked Naum for a handkerchief. Naum had one. He always carried one.

Fsitsi wiped the grave soil off Naum's cassock with the

handkerchief, tch-tching. Handed the damp, soiled handkerchief back to Naum and said, “I suppose now we have to go back to your church.”

He followed Naum through the leaves toward the stone altar in the Orthodox section of the cemetery. He became impatient watching Naum wrestle the stole from inside his cassock.

Naum made the blessing prayer and put it on. Both priests made the prostrations. Fsitsi handed Naum the folded paper.

In the chiseled alcove there was a sleepless lamp. The oil-flame lamp kept on the Table that never went out. Photi watched Naum take the folded paper, hold it to the lamp, and set it on the rough-cut stone.

The paper ignited. It unfolded across the gray stone top like a flower of flame and slowly disintegrated into red-edged cuticles of soft warm ash. Not even a wisp of smoke rose from the circling fringe.

Father Fsitsi knelt at the Table with the epitrachelion over his head.

Naum said, “There is only one Priest.”

Fsitsi said, “Amen.”

Trash trucks out in the street beyond the graveyard gates were banging dumpsters to the pavement, cable gears whining under the weighted strain.

Young squirrels pursued each other around the thick wide trunks of bark-worn trees.

A long-tailed northern mockingbird chased two bluebirds in circles through branches so sapless and thin that they rattled in the wind like dry bones because they had no leaves.

Naum, at his right ear, said to Fsitsi, "On which side of the epitrachelion does the relentless din cease?"

EVERY NIGHT PHOTIOS FSITSI sat on the edge of their bed. His bare feet did not reach the floor. He turned on Philomena's lamp, found his glasses, and unfolded the note in the amber yellow light.

Naum said there was only one sin, one confession, and One Absolution . . .

The One Absolution sat beside him on the bed and listened with His arm around Fsitsi's shoulder.

Nomikos had written a note to Naum almost two decades before with a pencil nub no doubt sharpened with a broken-handled thin dull knife.

And the idiot had kept it.

It whispered in a scribbled echo from the back page of a long-ago church calendar snatched from the brackish flow of linear time, rescued from the sequential, irrepeatable, and irreversible river . . .

And Moses said to the LORD, O my LORD, I am not eloquent, neither heretofore, nor since you have spoken to your servant: but I am slow of speech, and of a slow tongue.

And the LORD said to him, Who has made man's mouth? Or who makes the dumb, or deaf, or the seeing, or the blind? Have not I, the LORD?

Now therefore go, and I will be with your mouth, and teach you what you shall say.

THE PRIEST PHOTIOS FSITSI did not like to confess.

Naum did not like to hear confessions.

But it was Kreshme e Madhe, Great Lent, the forty-day fasting period prior to Pascha, and he felt compelled to make his yearly pilgrimage to Fishtown for his annual confession.

After all, there was a time when Father Fsitsi had heard of but never actually met a priest who'd made more of a mess of being a priest . . .

Maturity in Time

Even the stork in the heaven knows her appointed time; and the turtle dove and the crane and the swallow observe the time of their coming; but my people do not know the judgment of the Lord. *(Jeremiah 8:7)*

Sometimes in the summer people forget about church."

Naum wasn't making excuses for folks when he and Kusheri Nastradin took a break in the shade on the side steps of our little Saint Alexander the Whirling Dervish Orthodox Church.

"The allure of the Shore." Kusheri Nastradin understood.

He said, "I don't know what it is that gets you thinking about that one particular barrier island once you see the first robin and the weather starts getting warm."

"Yup," Naum said. "Disconnected from the rest of the world, that island—that one place our people love to go. Doesn't have an Orthodox church—or even a graveyard."

"Taking my two weeks right after Dormition fast," Kusheri said.

It was almost June, and every tree in the neighborhood was

vying with the bushes to come up with fresh variations on the theme of spring green. Old Prifti Naum and Kusheri Nastradin had as much eggshell paint on their bib overalls as they did on the stucco side wall of the church. Hats tilted back, sitting on the steps, drinking Orangina and eating TastyKake Butterscotch Krimpets. Finally warm enough to be outside, but still cool enough for paint to season without puddling in rivulets at the bottom of the wall.

Kusheri said, "I can see myself, sitting stretched out in the sand, ankle-deep in the surf. I can taste it. I can smell it too."

He closed his eyes and said, "I can see the whole thing so clearly, I could paint a mural of it, right here, right now, on the side of the church."

Magic-carpet Nastradin set the compass heading, scooped up Naum in his reverie, and together they rode the prevailing winds out of Fishtown to the hidden seaside garden.

To that one particular island. The one sculpted by the sea with the curve and feel and color and smell of that once-in-a-lifetime girl.

Dreaming Nastradin made them kites. Summer-colored kites. Kites without strings, dancing on divergent currents. Free and lost aloft. Two old dreamers spinning like dervishes just a few nautical miles over the horizon from Atlantic City.

Kusheri Nastradin held his fez to his head and told Naum, "Hold on, Urata."

They swooped in low over main streets spun north to south like seven-mile icing ribbons along a cake of sand. And running east and west from beach to bay, shaded seaside cottages went crisscrossing by along pleasant tree-lined avenues a mile across at their widest point.

The side gate creaked. Jessica and Rubin walked up the brick path holding hands. Jessica said, "Father Naum, Kusheri."

And they were back in Fishtown. Both feet on the ground.

Naum had forgotten they were coming.

"You forgot, didn't you?" she said.

Rubin kissed his girl on the cheek. "Wedding, Father. July sixth. A few weeks away."

It was twenty years ago, the first time Naum had seen them holding hands. The two lived next door to each other on Tulip Street. They shared a backyard and a dog they called Luan, meaning "lion."

Twenty years ago, Naum was taking his time consuming the Gifts after Liturgy on June 29, the Feast of Saint Peter and Paul. Both children came in crying. Six-year-old Jessica told Naum, "Urata, our lion died."

"A man hit him with a car," Rubin said. "Does God take dogs in heaven?"

IN LATE MAY, Jessica's mom, Edith, and Pilar, Rubin's mom, were walking the kids home from Adaire School through Palmer Burial Ground on the last day of kindergarten.

"Adaire?" Edith said to Pilar. "I didn't even know that was somebody's name. He was the guy who had the old lumberyard at Howard and Berks. Long gone now." Then she called out to the kids, "Don't get too far ahead, you two. Stay where we can see you."

Pilar shouted, "Yeah, if we can't see you we can't save you if the bad guys come out from behind the gravestones. You know they eat kindergarten kids." Pilar and Edith loved to use that line.

Jessica said, "We're first-graders now, Mommy."

"What the hell are they doing now, P?"

Edith was looking up ahead at the kids stopped under a tree just past the cemetery gatehouse. Edith said, "That girl loves rolling in the dirt better than the boys. I gotta get her home, feed her lunch, get her in the tub and cleaned up for dance class."

"Petting a dog," Pilar said. "Puppy, looks like."

The kids were coaxing a furry yellow puppy. "Mommy, mommy, can we keep her?"

Edith picked up the puppy and said, "It's a him, not a her."

"Maybe," Pilar said. "But only if he follows us home and he don't belong to nobody." She whispered to Edith, "He don't have a collar, does he?"

"But if we do keep him," Edith said, "you two gotta feed him and take him for walks and clean up the you-know-what."

"And he's gotta live in the yard," Pilar said. "He ain't living in the house. Maybe in the cellar in the winter if it gets real cold."

"They're a lot of work," Edith said to Pilar, "and I'll be damned if I'm doing it. 'Specially not once we're down the Shore for our two weeks."

The putty factory closed the same two weeks every year. Everybody who worked at the putty factory got the same two weeks, their husbands and half the neighborhood.

Edith, Lou, and Jessica, Pilar, Johnny C, and Rubin were Tulip Street next-door neighbors. They shared the same backyard and the same down-the-Shore rental property mid-July, every year since the kids were babies.

Rubin wanted to name the puppy Monster, but Jessica said Luan was better, "'Cause it means lion, and don't he look like a lion?"

Rubin said, "He does."

Early morning. End of June. Still dark and Rubin's father, Johnny C, half dressed, was knocking on his neighbor's door.

"Lou," Johnny said to Jessica's dad, "somehow that damn dog got out the backyard and some creep in a pickup ran it over and just kept on going."

"You see who it was?" Lou said.

Johnny C said, "I got my ideas."

Both families were out in the street barefoot in their underwear.

There was a lot of crying on the way to the clinic. The vet came out shaking his head. Everybody left the animal hospital feeling bad, not knowing what to do.

Johnny C and Lou were on first shift and couldn't miss. Not if they wanted their vacation-club bonus.

Pilar told Edith, "You know they're at the church doing Liturgy today for Saint Peter and Paul."

Edith said, "I got off." She worked reception. "Doctor Baks ain't due back till after the Fourth. Down Cape May taking his boat somewhere on the Chesapeake. They love them blue crabs, him and his wife."

Pilar did admin for Philly PD down at the Roundhouse. She said, "I don't gotta be in till four."

Naum was consuming the Gifts after Liturgy. Deacon Dionysios was reading the prayers of thanksgiving.

Both children came in crying. Jessica told Naum, "Urata, our lion died."

"A man hit him with a car," Rubin said. "Does God take dogs in heaven, Urata?"

The deacon asked Naum, "How do you tell children?"

Everybody in the neighborhood wanted to go easy on the kids. Everybody except Eddie Gjarper. He was a theologian. He figured he was one of the most religious guys at our little Saint Alexander the Whirling Dervish Orthodox Church. Taking up all the oxygen at study groups. Never missing a chance to quote some Greek term he had trouble pronouncing from a theology book he claimed he was reading. Only person in the neighborhood driving a snakeskin-wrap pickup.

Eddie said, "Kids might as well find out about death and get with the fact that there ain't no animals in heaven. They ain't got souls, the animals."

Naum with the kids and their moms at a table in the church hall. After they got the three of them settled down, Edith and Pilar took their tea to an adult table. The priest and the kids had coffee and yellow cake doughnuts from Schmidt's. Extra fat doughnuts robed in chocolate.

Edith told Pilar, "The doughnuts'll make 'em feel better."

Pilar told Edith, "I made sure all three of 'em got mostly milk in their coffee."

Edith said, "And I made sure they had plenty of crayons and construction paper, all three of 'em."

Naum started to tell the kids about Adam and Eve and the Garden of Eden.

Rubin told Naum, "You know they were naked?"

Naum sat back. He said, "They were?"

Edith and Pilar almost spat out their tea.

Jessica said, "Yeah. Just like dogs."

Naum said, "Is that right? Adam and Eve?"

The kids thought it was funny when Rubin said, "Later they got leaves." And held up his crayon rendition.

Naum said, "You ever hear about when God brought all the animals by for Adam and Eve to give them names?"

"No." Both kids seemed interested. Interested enough to stop coloring for a minute.

"When he brought the pigs," Naum said, "Adam said, 'Pork chops.'"

The kids laughed and said, "No . . ."

"When God brought the cow and said to Eve, 'Give it a name,' she said, 'Cheeseburger.'"

"No." The kids were laughing.

"When he brought the chicken . . ." Rubin said. Both kids yelled, "Nuggets!"

All three, dunking doughnuts and laughing.

Jessica said, "Why do the pigs make them that shape, Urata?"

Naum said, "Make what?"

"The pork chops."

"Oh," Naum said. "We'll ask Mommy later." He didn't have the heart to tell her the pork chops were the pigs.

Jessica said, "Okay."

Rubin said, "The animals were Adam's friends."

Naum said, "Eve's too."

"And they didn't eat their friends, Urata," Rubin said.

Naum said, "No. It's like Great Lent before Pascha, when we don't eat anything from an animal. You understand, right?"

Rubin said, "Right. We only eat tomato sandwiches."

"'Cause we don't eat our friends," Jessica repeated.

Then the little girl said, "And you know they could talk to them? Adam and Eve could talk with the animals, and they could understand each other."

When Naum said, "Really?"

Rubin said, "Absolutely."

Jessica was sad when she said, "Luan understood me. He came when I called him. He knew I loved him, and I know he loved me, even when I yelled at him." She had drawn a picture of herself hugging Luan.

Rubin said, "He loved us anyway. No matter what. And we knew it without people words."

Naum wanted to tell the kids that the desert Fathers say a dog is better than a human because they don't judge like people do. But right then, Naum. Why ruin maturity in time?

Rubin said, "Miss Raskova told us in Sunday school, when Jesus comes back a lion's gonna lay down with a lamb. So how's this gonna happen if there ain't no lions in heaven? So Luan must be in heaven, right?"

Naum looked around the church hall and considered where they were sitting. On one side of the table sat a maturity of relationships. On the other, maybe, maturity of thoughts. Naum had to be careful. He realized it was two against one, and he knew maturity of relationship trumped that of thoughts.

Two or three together sparked the Scripture to life. That had been his experience in the church.

Jesus invited a little child to stand among them. "Truly I tell you," He said, "unless you change and become like little children, you will never enter the kingdom of heaven."

Naum was beginning to see that a child may actually have a clearer vision of the Garden. The Kingdom of God belongs to such as these. When it came to being as communion . . .

Jessica and Rubin were telling stories one after another,

About pigeons and sparrows

And ladybugs and ants

Squirrels stealing pistachios and dogs treeing squirrels

Kittens chasing puppies and cats chasing mice

Kids catching grasshoppers after supper in the park

And jars filled with lightning bugs in the cemetery at night

Neighborhood parables so profound and full of symbols

Vestibular icons colored in crayon so rich and complex in their pictorial simplicity

Naum had to put up a hand and say, "Wait. Wait. You two are too fast."

Scriptural images they had spoken and scribbled in crayon came to life, held hands in a circle, and danced the Albanian *valle* around Naum's coffee cup, like a hologram Ferris wheel on the table in front of old Prifti Naum.

Everything that has breath praises the Lord.

Listening to the kids had Naum thinking. If being is life, and life is communion with God, who is truly Life, maybe animals have being with life because of their relation with the people who have communion with God.

Naum said to the kids, "You know the story of the ark."

They told Naum the whole thing, beginning to end. "*All* the animals," Jessica said. "God told Noah to bring all the animals in the ark."

"You know the church is called the ark?" Rubin said.

"Why?" Naum asked.

Rubin said, "Because it doesn't leak when there's too much rain."

"Yeah," Jessica said. "'Cause it floats."

The rigorist, Eddie Gjarper, sat down in Naum's head, wet his finger with his tongue, picked up doughnut crumbs one at a time with his fingertip, then swept the dancing hologram Ferris wheel from the table and whispered, "Go ahead, Urata, do your duty. Explain the human soul to children. The essence and the energy not dissolved with the body but lives after the separation; a spiritual essence, even though it's created . . . Explain the animal soul as a simple thing that dies together with the body."

Looking at Jessica and Rubin had Naum thinking, this could be a little too much too soon. Timing, Naum, timing. Maturity seasoned in time.

TWENTY YEARS PASSED like the sun passes across an empty window. Like a day fades from sunlight to evening. Fades slowly and forever from our lives. Or that's how it seemed when the gate creaked and they came holding hands.

Rubin said, "Father, we're so happy you're the one doing our wedding. You know us."

"You were kind when we were kids," Jessica said.

Rubin saw the paint set up and said, "You two want some help painting?"

Naum said, "No. You must have so much to do. Besides, gives us old guys something to do."

Kusheri liked that. He said, "Where ya going for the honeymoon?"

Jessica said, "You oughta know, Kusheri, the island."

"Two weeks in July?" Kusheri said.

Rubin said, "Yep. Same house we always rented. And the reception at the Island Grand."

Jessica opened her bag. She gave each of them an invitation.

Looking at the young couple, Naum considered how faithful they had been all these years. Rubin and Jessica rarely missed. Even when their parents slept in on a Sunday morning, Jessica and Rubin were there—singing in the choir, her, and him, serving in the altar, even when Johnny C, Rubin's father, died.

Something had kept these two close to God. Close to one another, participating in the life of Christ in His Church. Somehow they had come to a maturity of faith beyond concepts when it came to facing death.

Rubin said, "You know what it was, right, that kept us in the church? When Luan got hit by that guy in the pickup."

Naum said, "Kind of."

"Saint Peter and Paul day," Rubin said. "When you sat with us coloring and eating doughnuts."

"Partly what you said," Jessica said, "partly the way you said it. Kept us close to God. Even when Rubin's dad died. We know it ain't easy, Urata."

Naum said, "I just remember being with you two. But you actually remember what I said?"

"I do," Jessica said. "Something like, the devil was the first one to move away from God, and so his spirit died, and he tricked people trying to get their soul to die too and everything else with him, animals included . . .

"'Cause God gave the animals to people so they could learn to be kind to each other by being kind to animals. You told us, so the way we think about it when animals die . . . Remember you told us to make the cross when we saw an animal that got hit in the road? The way we think about and treat animals when they die is gonna put us either with the trickster and the way he thinks and regards this life, or with God."

Naum said, "I said that?"

She said, "You did."

Rubin said, "You know Jess has one of those eidetic memories. She keeps quoting you to people. But what sticks with me is when you said, 'You know how Jesus comes back, right, Rubin, you remember?'

"I started hopping in my seat, Urata, when you said, 'He comes back riding a horse.'"

Naum smiled.

"Yep. I don't know how you knew I loved horses. And then you said, 'And if there ain't no animals in heaven, where'd he get the horse?' That did it for me."

When the kids left, Kusheri opened his wedding invitation.

Reception to Follow: Island Grand at the Shore.

And there was Magic Carpet Nastradin

Summer-colored Kusheri

Flying up and away from the church
A kite without a string
Dancing the valle
On divergent currents
Free and lost aloft
Spinning like a dervish in his fustanella
Just a few nautical miles over the horizon from Atlantic City.

"Sometimes in the summer people forget about church."

The old priest Naum wasn't making excuses for folks when he and Kusheri Nastradin took a break in the shade on the side steps of our little Saint Alexander the Whirling Dervish Orthodox Church.

He just didn't want to forget, again:

Even the stork in the sky knows her appointed seasons. The turtledove, the swift, and the thrush keep their time of migration, but My people do not know the requirements of the LORD.

Evening Bells

NINE KIDS," FATHER HESHLER SAID. "One must have at least nine, Feldmaus, if you want one of them to end up staying in the Church. Exactly as we have done, Matushka Veronica and I."

They were sitting on a long padded piano bench. The gray-bearded kapellmeister, Father Herman Heshler, renowned composer of hymns and lecturer in liturgical music, loved an audience. Even if it was only an audience of one.

He sat with his cassock spread out, grandiose as a debutante on a divan, demonstrating the theory of proper cadence to a barely remedial seminarian called Feldmaus.

He often told his students, "To be Orthodox is to be a Slav. And to be a Slav you must be Orthodox."

His *halupki*-inspired girth occupied the middle two-thirds of the bench, and the smell of the still-fresh tomato stain in Father Heshler's beard and on his cassock caused Feldmaus on the precipice to think mouthwatering thoughts of the lunchtime offering in the seminary trapeza which his failing music grades had forced him to miss.

Neither student nor teacher was Slavic.

Feldmaus wanted to ask, "How many rice, beef, and pork halupki encased in cabbage, drizzled with thin spicy tomato sauce, must one eat to gain admittance to the kingdom of the Slavs?" But he didn't. He had a lisp and he knew it.

The seminarian, Clement Feldmaus, was squeezing his skinny buttocks sidesaddle astride the bench so as not to slip from the narrow portion of the bench to which he'd been exiled.

He was doubly sorry he'd missed the final class on znamenny chant. The melismatic style eluded young Feldmaus, and the strange stolp notation, the *kryuki,* gave the nearsighted seminarian a headache.

Plus, he was hungry.

Heshler the choirmaster was constantly pivoting to breathe in his face. "We must astonish the ear and penetrate the heart," Heshler told Feldmaus.

Between the constant breath and the crescendos with Heshler shouting "Fortissimo!" to disguise his sporadic cannonades of flatulence, Feldmaus had removed his glasses and polished them so often Heshler told him, "A job polishing glass, are you considering, if you fail here at seminary, or perhaps selling insurance? It seems to interest you more than our sacred music."

Heshler did not appreciate the familiarity, the insolence of this newly cassocked seminarian. He considered it highly inappropriate, impertinent even, when the student he referred to in class as *the* Feldmaus had asked, "Do you have life insurance, Father Professor?"

Feldmaus—being married himself but with only two children, and being of a practical mind, having worked in civil service—wondered if priests provided for their families in some way or if the Church did, should something unexpected happen to the husband, that is, the priest.

After all, Marina, his wife, and their children, Michelle and Lucian, meant the world to Feldmaus. He had given up a lucrative career with a future, good benefits, vacation days, and a pension, as well as a home they had worked years to afford.

He'd sold his car, bought a used four-wheel-drive Suzuki, said goodbye to his family and Marina's family, and bundled kitchen, kids, and everything in their closets off to Saint Wenceslaus monastery-seminary in the remote wooded mountains of the Northeast.

Poor Marina cried every day. She missed her colleagues at the metropolitan university hospital, where she had administered a busy surgical practice. She missed modern conveniences, shopping at a real supermarket. She missed strolling through the mall. She missed screens on the windows.

And having to kill a hundred flies every day and then again at night before putting the children to bed—noisy, supersized juicy black flies that someone said were sent by the old sorceress Baba Yaga. Flies that seemed to multiply in winter when they should all have been dead. It was making her think she was losing her mind in a Krylov fairy tale.

Most of all, she admitted, she missed her mother and her sisters. Often Marina was alone.

Feldmaus worked the overnight shift as a security guard to provide for his family. Sagerman's was a large warehouse/retail operation. They sold everything from groceries to automotive parts, from clothing to eyeglasses. There was a dentist to fix your teeth and an accountant to fix your taxes. Oddly enough, no one seemed to mind that they were both the same nearsighted woman.

Feldmaus and an old Ukrainian priest, Father Nestor—a retired priest who carried a Polish-made Gward .38 Special—alternated making the hour-long overnight rounds, walking the darkened aisles of Sagerman's, stopping to munch an apple from the produce section and turning a key in each of the equidistant security lockboxes located throughout the elongated retail plant and shelf-lined warehouses of the big-box store.

The retired Ukrainian priest sometimes dozed while Feldmaus made the rounds, especially after a snoot or two. He often surprised Feldmaus on his return to the guard booth with "Halt, who goes there?" pointing the Polish pistol.

Feldmaus, ducking behind tire stacks, would say, "Father. Batyushka. Please. It's me, Feldmaus, the seminarian. Don't shoot."

Batyushka joked, "You bring the vodka?"

Feldmaus knew better than to answer with words.

Many a morning Feldmaus barely made it home. "Stay here," Father Nestor would tell him. "Don't be crazy. That mountain road is so slippery tonight, you can't even *lay* down on it."

Fishtailing sideways. Sliding in and out of ditches. Skating over the mountain. Snow plowed to both sides of the road as high as the windowsills of his battered four-wheel drive. When he finally made it home, Feldmaus would go to the monastery church, kiss the doors, and on his knees thank God in the cold, snowy dark.

In the woods by the monastery church Feldmaus saw deer, skunk, squirrels, raccoons, birds, and two black bears, and in the middle a hooded silhouette, the old monk Father Vasily, standing in the dim yellow running lights of the four-wheel drive.

"I'll save you, Father."

The animals turned slowly and one by one disappeared into the woods.

The old man is senile, Feldmaus thought, or confused. He's locked himself out of the monastery and can't get back in.

Reassuring Father Vasily everything was okay, Feldmaus led the silent monk back to his cell. Not realizing till many years later the thing he had witnessed and what an idiot he had been. How there, in the scented woods and hilly fields, the highest holiness and the most mundane seemed to grow up together side by side.

MATUSHKA VERONICA HESHLER, the kapellmeister's wife, gathered the seminarian wives every week at her home. Mostly they talked.

"Seminary prepares your husbands, somewhat," she would say. "But who prepares you, the matushki?"

Stories. She told stories from her years in the parishes. "Things the people will never tell *him*, they will tell you."

"Why?" Carol wanted to know. Carol Ospensky, peasant-dress hippie-Orthodox. Floor-duster skirts hand-stitched from pin-wale corduroy trousers. Sandals cobbled from pottery-shard souvenirs scavenged from the caves of the Dead Sea Scrolls. Embroidered Cossack blouses stained with scented-oil sweat. Home-knit woolen vests that smelled like a wet flock in a muddy field. Lambs bleated when she went by. Hair pulled back and babushka-wrapped so tightly in a scarf knotted at her chin, looking at her gave Matty Veronica Heshler a headache, a toothache, an earache, and the mumps, all at the same time.

"Why? Why will they tell us and not him?" Carol asked again.

Matushka said, "Propriety, girls! Because . . . because of some twisted sense of ecclesial propriety, which, as it turns out, is neither ecclesial nor proper.

"The same morbid notion that keeps us from walking on a grave or telling our mother-in-law how we really feel about her stew or her grandchild's piano playing. Same thing that keeps us from being honest with our husband the priest about his weekly homily. Bloviating that could anesthetize an elephant. My own reverend husband at the top of the list. We even hide our doubts about God from God. What? God is up there scratching His head?"

Sometimes she just laughed with her girls, Veronica did. Drank tea or a little vodka. Talked about girl stuff and had fun. All in all, Veronica was a good mother. And like some mothers, she had a favorite too. A favorite among the seminarian wives.

"Marina, look." And she showed little tricks to the wife of *the* Feldmaus she didn't share with the rest. "This, Marina, is what makes for a really good prosphora."

Baking the holy bread was an art. Not everyone was good at it. But Matushka Veronica Heshler was known for hers and for the excellent vestments she made by hand.

Marina Feldmaus may have missed the mall, her career, screens in her windows, and her mother and sisters most of all, but she didn't miss what many others overlooked.

Matushka Veronica Heshler, walking alone along the market road singing the prayers of the Liturgy when she thought no one could hear. Pleading with God for each person by name. Saying the prayer of the heart, and *Out of the depths have I cried to Thee . . .* Holding on by a thread and appealing to the One Who Hears, telling the trees, "I still love the Theotokos."

There was something in Matushka Veronica Heshler
The same something
That silhouetted the tops of the barren trees
At twilight in the monastery woods.
That thing that swayed
The tower bells at windless dawn
And caused still dreaming
Marina Feldmaus to rise
And go barefoot to the graveyard
Where glistening clouds
That descended during the night
Shrouded the graven headstones
Like winding sheets of white linen.
And mystical forms gathered
In the fields to intone
A wordless ison
Like otherworldly monks
Hovering just above
The silvery surface of the monastery lake.
There was something in Matushka Veronica Heshler
Some natural tonality
For sustaining life
That went beyond
The pumping regularity
Of her heart

A quality of God-given
Longing for the icon
Of our original being
Singing like a choir
In the depths of the matushka

A longing Marina Feldmaus would only come to know after many years of walking down the lonely graveyard lane.

Things deep within that transcend the damaged and the mundane. Things that somehow survive the sin of human being beguiled by the malice of the snake. Things woven into the fabric of a woman's being that persevere in calling out to Christ and holding onto Him as her sure and only hope. Even when she and others in the family failed.

Things that kept her looking for the lost coin, for a way to keep the promises of His grace hidden in her secret heart, where even her own sin could not reach to corrode.

"You will many times be the choir. Singing the responses alone for your husband. For weekday liturgies. Funerals. Baptisms."

Truth be told, and many there were who thought it, but only a few would say what Marina Feldmaus whispered to the other girls, "Father Herman teaches the musical theory of prayer. Matushka Veronica sings it."

"Girls."

They'd sit sewing in a circle.

Inner cassocks
Greek and Russian style
Riassa, the voluminous wide-sleeved garment worn over the inner cassock
Every liturgical vestment

Deacon

Bishop

Priest

And the miters the woman made?

The patriarch himself would have wrestled the emperor of Byzantium in the middle of the agora to wear such a crown

Chalice covers

Communion cloths

Altar dressing and aers

"What the soul is in the body, the priest's wife is in the parish," she would tell her protégées. "You are the little mamas. They will go into the parish house and borrow your tablecloths from your hallway closet for altar covers. Iron up spilled candle wax from the church rugs with your iron.

"But learn to sew these vestments, and you will have your secret stash. Never tell your husband exactly how much money you've squirreled away. Your exit strategy and your escape money. Once you've had enough, just knowing you have it and a secret life insurance policy or two on him will keep you sane. Always have a way. A good matushka always has a way."

And when they were alone, she would look up at the icon and whisper to Marina Feldmaus, "A way to keep hope in Him."

Half the seminarian wives believed her. Half had heard the rumors and thought she was a drunk.

The crystal stemware mini-goblets decorated with the Romanov double-headed eagle only held a small amount of vodka, a truly miniscule amount.

"But I can hardly stand up after the tenth one." Carol Ospensky took off her wire-rimmed glasses and rubbed her eyes. "And

I can never think of anything clever to say when it's my turn to offer the salutation."

"You always say the same thing," Anastasia said. "*Na zdorovye.* Health. And after the tenth time nobody's listening anyway."

Carol Ospensky looked at Anastasia. All the girls couldn't help but look at Anastasia. If ever there were a girl custom made for the wife of a priest, it was Anastasia Lisette Danovich, the deacon's wife.

Anastasia with the angelic face and the serious green eyes. Anastasia with a voice from the other side. Lustrous dark hair parted in the middle and braided halfway down her back, thick as the bell pull in the cupola tower. Gracefully slender. Petite. Delicate and ethereal as the ancient wood churches from the Russian north.

Diakonia Anastasia Danovich embodied the effortless soul of prototypical ecclesial feminine perfection. If ever an icon of a matushka typos was written, no one doubted it would look like Anastasia.

She was the perfect balance and complement to her husband, the protodeacon. The fat, burly, white-haired protodeacon with the percussive timpani intonation.

He loved it when they were alone and she gave in to the part of her nature that was Basque and loved to dance. But after seven years of marriage, he'd managed to coax no more than one nesting secret from his mysterious matryoshka doll with the Fabergé face.

Carol Ospensky stood and held herself up on the table. She raised her glass in salute. "Ten is too many."

"And she does double that. Twenty shots easy. And it doesn't faze her," Anastasia whispered. "I hear her at night, chastising the children and yelling curses at their dogs, our Matushka Veronica."

Anastasia was very observant of everything but especially when it came to drink. It was said her husband, Protodeacon Vladimir Ivan Danovich, had a hut deep in the woods built entirely from vodka bottles of a certain brand and geometric shape. "I keep track," she confided to Carol Ospensky. "When the deacon comes home wanting me to dance," Anastasia said, "he knows damn well he's not sleeping in the house. Go to your secret place, I tell him, your dacha made of vodka."

And if her robust deacon dared to criticize anyone in her presence, Anastasia was many times overheard telling the boisterous brick-wall protodeacon, "A man like you should throw stones?"

Carol saw her chance to confirm the rumors about the vodka-bottle hut. She wanted to ask Anastasia if it was true her husband also smoked, but Matushka Veronica wobbled to her feet and started at the girls again.

"You know how many parishes are subsidized by matushka money? Yes and no. They do not pay the priest enough for the family to live on. Benefits, insurance, a second car? Hardly. Not unless *you* are working outside the home. *And* they think nothing of it . . . if after working a full day at a full-time job, eating nothing, keeping the fast for the evening service, for *you* to rush to church with the kids and sing the responses, through the whole of Great Lent."

Marina Feldmaus was listening and feeling a little guilty. But not overly so. Was it lack of faith? For some inner reason she had secretly sent in the fee to maintain her certification as a practice administrator.

"And your kids? Under the microscope. And you too," Veronica said. "Even if you and your yellow dress go two towns over for wrestling."

Whatever that meant? Carol Ospensky was certain she didn't know.

Around many a Sunday dinner table in the seminary parish community, Jimmy the Spitter and Matushka Veronica Heshler and her yellow dress had come to usurp Father Herman's sermon as the topic of post-liturgy gossip.

"And pirating things from your cupboard, dishes, serving trays, silverware, napkins, and cups. Buy extra, girls."

Veronica could feel herself winding down. Twenty vodka shots, even minis, was a lot. At this point a standing dismissal was better than having them carry her to the couch, like the last time.

She told them, "Well, till next week, then, my girls? I'm gonna go have a little lie-down now." She kissed each of her *daughters* with tears in her eyes, telling them, "Remember, girls, a good matushka always has a way."

It was surprising, then, when late that evening Veronica came knocking at the Feldmaus door. "I want the keys to your four-wheel thingie," she demanded.

THE FELDMAUS FAMILY lived at the end of the graveyard in a three-story structure that *dilapidated* itself would have declined the adjectival prerogative to describe.

When the ecclesiarch, Father Tymon, met them their first day, he said, "Married student housing is sparse. You, however, are lucky. *Vecherniya Kolaka*, Evening Bells, is a house that is half-and-half, and it's available. See, I will walk you to the end of graveyard lane. From your house you will every day at Vespers clearly hear the evening bells."

Feldmaus and family followed Tymon down a winding dirt track under a canopy of trees to a gully that in rainy season became a surrounding moat, where sunfish dived for tadpoles and beavers built dams.

There, in the dim depression of the graveyard gully, sat the romantic Evening Bells. "Half in this world," Tymon had said, "half in the world to come. Every monk for a hundred years," he told them, "looking out at you over the crosses and headstones, such neighbors, praying for you."

Marina Feldmaus could see why it was called half-and-half.

The roof was half-and-half. Half on. Half off.

The porch was half standing and half leaning.

Half the windows were glass and the others covered in weather-worn plywood.

One side of the house was a faded white, and the other was government-issue green.

One side was clapboard shingle. The other? Stick-on brick veneer.

Every other door and window had a mismatched shutter.

The front entrance steps featured weathered treads and risers, minus balustrades or handrails. Only the ghosts of saw-cut stringers rose up on either side as a reminder that there had once been an actual set of steps ascending to the side door, itself half glass, half fly-poked screen.

So many gophers, possums, and field mice ended up in Evening Bells, in the closets and under the counters, birds and bats scurrying back and forth up in the ceiling . . .

Every night alive with the noise of unidentified critters scratching under the beds and flies buzzing around their heads to such a lively degree that Marina Feldmaus took it seriously when her four-year-old, Lucian, told her there was a rabbit under the kitchen sink. She was in a tizzy. She blockaded the cabinet with boxes, and when Feldmaus got home, she insisted, "You get that rabbit, dead or alive, out from under the counter or there will be no supper served."

He took off his cassock, armed himself with a broom, and prepared for the fray. Feldmaus cautiously cracked the cabinet door, peeked in, and immediately slammed it shut. "Look," he told her.

She said, "I am *not* looking at any dead rabbit, no."

"Don't be squeamish," he told her.

"No," she said.

Feldmaus said, "Okay, then, Marina, it's either take a peek or I'm leaving it there for you to deal with."

There, stuffed in under the cabinet, was four-year-old Lucian's Bugs Bunny doll.

They had to laugh. What else could they do?

"At least it wasn't a real rabbit," Feldmaus said. He knew Marina was thinking of the time their daughter Michelle had walked out of the Evening Bells bathroom with a snake she thought was a toy. "Look, Mommy," the eight-year-old said. "A big worm."

NOW CLEMENT FELDMAUS SAT AT SUPPER with his mouth full of peas from their garden.

Matushka Veronica Heshler was banging on their door and demanding the keys to their Suzuki. The very vehicle he needed to traverse the icy mountain to do his overnight security job at Sagerman's Super Store.

He looked at his wife. Marina scolded him for the second time for chewing with his mouth open, which made the children laugh, which made Feldmaus sneeze and snort his peas.

Lucian and Michelle burst out laughing uncontrollably and started shouting, "It's in his beard! It's in his beard!"

"Enough." Marina took them all in hand.

Marina showed Matushka Veronica to the table and said, "It's like having three children."

Matushka Veronica Heshler, wife of the seminary kapellmeister, was not deterred by such antics. "Now. Please." And extended her hand for the keys. "I'm due at the arena."

It wasn't hard for Marina to see. Veronica was in a state of ten. A decade decanted. Decimated by ten tiny vodka goblets. Maybe times ten, but ten at least.

Marina said to her mentor, "Sit for minute and I'll see if I can find the keys. Let me take your bag."

Her bag was like the canvas bag Feldmaus carried on his bike as a paperboy. Matushka Veronica refused to give it up.

Feldmaus was astonished when Matushka Veronica pulled her chair next to him and asked, "Do you like Jimmy the Spitter?"

Her tight yellow dress was so short and so low cut, Feldmaus, who was extricating pea mush from his beard and nostrils, said, "I never knew nine kids later a woman could be so . . ." Inhaling her perfume, he paused and asked, "Does your husband have life insurance?"

Matushka noticed the skinny seminarian was staring. Actually, she didn't mind. Her husband, Herman Heshler, seemed to have lost interest after child number eight.

She said, "What did my husband tell you, Clement?"

In fact, Father Herman Heshler had told freshman Feldmaus, "I do not," indignant at the effrontery of this lunkhead seminarian with the bushy beard. "Insurance!"

Apparently Feldmaus was thicker than Heshler thought. He had the cheek to ask, "Well then, what happens to them, Father, if something happens to you?"

"That's their problem, sir," the older man said. "Not being here to worry about it, *should* something happen, I don't and I won't care one way or the other. They'll just have to fend for themselves, now, won't they?"

"You're not serious, Father?" Feldmaus was sure the music teacher must be joking.

"Feldmaus," Heshler said, "if you were as intent on learning your znamenny chant as on quizzing me about things that are really none of your business . . ." He stopped for a moment to regain his composure, took a breath, and said, "Yes, Feldmaus. That's my firm policy. I will have nothing to do with scams or schemes like insurance. Not of any kind. It's just one more sign of lack of faith, not believing God is able to provide."

Feldmaus was more inclined to subscribe to the Moslem dictum, *Trust Allah but tether the camels*. But at this point, Feldmaus was convinced Matushka Veronica had no need or desire to be enlightened by him concerning tethering, camels, Muslims, or the views of her musical halupki-eating husband.

When she asked what her husband, Father Heshler, had said about life insurance, Feldmaus had a feeling she already knew that she and the nine kids were pretty much on their own.

Feldmaus told Matushka, "I had a canvas bag just like that when I used to deliver the *Evening Bulletin*."

Marina was coming back from the front room. She'd settled the kids in front of the TV for Daffy Duck and Bugs Bunny. She poured coffee and wondered what was going on.

Veronica removed the cross-body canvas bag and dumped a pile of postal packages wrapped in brown paper.

Feldmaus had a bad feeling, like the time he was sitting outside the bishop's office. Sagerman's had offered him some much-needed overtime, and he needed a blessing for additional time away from the campus. He had the kids with him. Lucian had gotten away from his older sister, Michelle, and broken an old and treasured pysanky egg from the bishop's display in the waiting room.

Feldmaus stood in the doorway, picking up bits of colorful eggshell fragments, waiting to apologize, and considering the wisdom of repeating seminarian gossip about a certain professor's midnight visits to the single men's dorms, when he overheard the bishop on the phone telling the seminary dean: "More complaints." The bishop was shouting. "Father Dean, he's in the dormitory half the night. Ostensibly doing bed checks. But the students are alleging inappropriate touching again. He's back at this again, now? This is the third year in a row."

Feldmaus took a step back. Overhearing was embarrassing. He took the kids to move away, but the bishop looked up and motioned for him to stay put.

"I gave him a prescription," the bishop said. "Go ahead, watch your favorite film. I insisted. I am his confessor. Watch it. Make a list of all the participants, actors, producers, camera people, the whole thing. First names only. Make a copy and bring it to me. I will put it on the altar. You watch that favorite film of yours every night."

The bishop was lost in his retelling. "For forty nights. No skipping. And then after each watching, each time, go to your icon corner. Light the candles, Father, and pray, pray for those people in that film and for yourself, your wife, and your nine children. For God's sake, Father. I told him, *pornos*, evil, dirty, *grapstitos*, writing. This is not something for you."

The bishop went on loudly talking to the dean over the telephone. "A father of nine? Our composer of sacred hymns? Not something for you to be bound by. I told him, you are in the devil's net. You are dragging your wife and family into that net with you, and your students, and every time you watch these boy-films it fuels your destructive appetites and contributes to the abuse and enslavement of the children and adults trapped in that soul-destroying business. It is not good. You will watch that film, and each time after you watch you will pray for those people in that film, and I will pray for you and for them and for your poor wife and children.

"Every day. For forty days. And we will begin to introduce the antidote, the opposing virtue, and a little at a time and by God's mercy, perhaps you will recover from this disease and begin to see these people you are devouring as human beings, as your fellow creatures, as the work of God's hands, as people for whom God has sent His Son, instead of objects of delectation for your perverse appetites."

FELDMAUS HAD A BAD FEELING.

There spread on his dinner table were magazines he was embarrassed for his wife to see, let alone the sadness that seemed to crush Matushka Veronica as she tore open brown paper wrapper after brown paper wrapper, let alone the despair that crippled Feldmaus in his chair.

Marina looked at Feldmaus.

The cartoons were loud in the background so the children wouldn't hear. Daffy Duck was Feldmaus's favorite. A clergy duck, all black with a white collar. Feldmaus used to joke, "If I'm ordained, all I'll need are big orange work boots."

Looking at the magazines, he wanted to say, "Suffering succotash." There were times when his own lisp amused him, like Daffy, just to say something stupid, so he did. He said, "Suffering succotash."

Neither Matushka nor Marina was amused.

Then he said to Marina, "I'll take her to the arena on my way to work."

Feldmaus turned to Matushka. He said, "Yep, Jimmy the Spitter. The wrestler in the tight yellow Speedo. I know who ya mean. Over at the arena tonight, right?"

Marina Feldmaus asked, "Where are your kids, Matushka?"

Veronica Heshler said, "Anastasia the deacon's wife has the

kids. I wouldn't trust that Carol Ospensky in her peasant getup. She's a lunkhead, just like you, Feldmaus. How you lucked out and got a girl like Marina is beyond me."

"I can drop you on the way," Feldmaus said. "But how ya gonna get back?"

"You," she said.

Feldmaus looked at his wife, Marina. She was more than looking at the woman in the tight yellow dress.

Feldmaus said to Matushka, "Not this little black duck."

Matushka Veronica liked that. She smiled and said, "Don't worry, Daffy, you get me there. I'll get home." She looked at Marina and said, "A good matushka . . ."

BEFORE GOING TO THE HOUSE the next morning, Feldmaus stopped to kiss the doors of the monastery church. He was lucky to have made it. The overnight snow on the mountain road had been plowed to either side and was higher than the windows on his old four-wheel drive.

Evening Bells—"half in this world," the monk Tymon had said, "half in the world to come. Every monk for a hundred years," he told them, "looking out at you over the crosses and headstones, such neighbors, praying for you."

Feldmaus walked onto the porch of Evening Bells and kicked the snow off his boots. It seemed to his sleepy overnight eyes, especially on these snowy mornings, that gray daylight took longer to reach down into the dim depression of the graveyard gully.

Inside the sleeping house, in the quiet morning light, he saw Matushka Veronica, lying on the sofa in her yellow dress, exactly as his wife Marina had left her the night before, after sending him off to work alone. A good matushka always has a way. Veronica Heshler, kissed and covered and smiling in her sleep.

The Crèche

THERE WAS A WIRE. An almost imperceptible thread. A filament, you might say. Lithe as a spider's web and fishing-line strong. Almost colorless. True and certain as the narrow overhead avenues traversed by gravity-defying high-wire walkers who appear to float on air.

Nicky Zeo had seen the wire in a choir-loft balcony in Saint Veronica's, a nineteenth-century church in our neighborhood. The cable slanted down from the loft, and as his eye followed, it almost vanished. Disappeared into what the clean-shaven Monsignor Maurice called a crèche.

Nicky Zeo was an electrician. He had to admit, being there on the morning of Christmas Eve, repairing the light fixtures in the choir loft and seeing this crèche, this almost-life-sized Nativity scene, was probably what inspired him to surprise his wife. Truly inspired Nicky Zeo to gather Edna and the kids, little Nicky and Sammy, and shuffle them off to our little Saint Alexander the Whirling Dervish Orthodox Church for what some American Orthodox Christians called midnight Mass.

"Nicky, really? *You*? Going to midnight Mass?" Nicky's brother Louie couldn't believe it.

Nicky was still thinking about the setup with the crèche when Louie said, "Ya know they got one a those over ta the Holy Communion Protestant too. They got theirs lit up outside on the lawn behind the wrought-iron fence. Fulla life-sized plastic people, like manikins. Joseph and all the animals, but the animals they got're real live animals, like a donkey and stuff, from the pettin' zoo.

"Drag Mary outta the garage on 'er caster wheels, set 'er up, let 'er do 'er thing once a year, and then put 'er away till the next go-round. Lucky Jewish girl happened ta be in the right place at the right time is all, what one a Pastor Cal's guys says. Prob'ly takin' my kids ta see that. Live animals? Kids love that stuff. Got the little vending machine ya put a nickel in and get animal grub."

"Yeah, but Louie," Nicky said, "you shoulda seen it. The people over at Saint Veronica's had this little wire, right? And it goes all the way from way up in the choir loft, down, down, down," and Nicky Zeo made the slant in the air in front of Louie. "Like the long-sided hypotenuse in a right triangle . . . And on this wire, somebody up there cinches the baby Jesus with a zipline hook, and then just five seconds before midnight, bang! There he goes, sliding right down that invisible wire, and damn if he doesn't land like a perfect slider right in the catcher's mitt, smack in the middle of this Nativity scene the Monsignor told me was a *cretch* . . . Right there at midnight Mass, surrounded by the donkeys and the shepherds and the Holy Mother, the baby Jesus ziplining right smack into the middle of the little straw-filled manger. And ya know what they got waitin' for 'im?"

Louie said, "No. What?"

"A birthday cake," Nicky said.

"No shit? An edible one?"

"Yup, candles and everything, and they sing 'happy birthday baby Jesus' to 'im, right there in church."

Louie was amazed. He said to Nicky, "We gonna get one a them? That why ya going to our church?"

"If we're not, we oughta," Nicky said. "Less maintenance than a pettin' zoo. But, nah, I don't think Father Naum'd go for it."

"We did, I'd go," Louie said. "Pettin' zoo or no."

CHRISTMAS EVE, Edna was there singing her heart out on the *kliros*, the section reserved for the choir, and when Sammy and little Nicky got restless, instead of giving them a thump, like his father used to give him for yawning in church, Nicky Zeo took the boys out into the vestibule, the narthex, where it was cool and they could run around and air out a little.

Stairs from the vestibule led up to the church hall. Nicky knew the hall was filled with good food. Food they hadn't tasted since the beginning of the Nativity fast, back in mid-November. Meats. Dairy. Cakes. Coffee with cream. The community kept the fast together, and they'd break it together.

Everyone brought a basket of celebratory delicacies to share. People went table to table, sampling the dishes each family was known to make best. In the old country they had a saying, *Bardhe me lugen ne brez*—"I've come with my spoon in my belt." Nobody had to translate that saying after a fast.

It was dark at the top of the stairs for a reason. No one was supposed to be up there during the Liturgy. Still, Nicky figured the boys would have plenty of room up there to run around, more than in the narthex. But on the other hand, Edna would kill him. Then again, what harm would it do? Couple a kids. Let 'em sample a few cookies, a piece of cake. A small piece?

The rules of the pre-communion fast weren't so stringent for younger kids, and they'd been receiving since they were baptized as infants. Moses didn't leave the kids in Egypt, did he, or Noah not let 'em on the ark? And Lord Jesus did say, *Suffer the little children . . .*

Besides, Sammy and little Nicky did pretty good not eating or drinking. Practicing a little restraint early in life. Building up your spiritual muscle. Learning to delay satisfaction. Getting in the ring and punching it out with your appetites ain't gonna kill ya . . . is it? And boys especially gotta learn to channel all that energy. I mean, they gotta deal with girls, right? What Nicky Zeo thought.

Not only that, his boys seemed to like getting in line with the other kids. Well, maybe not little Nicky so much. He was getting to the age where he didn't wanna be called *little* Nicky.

But Sammy, the younger boy, just learning to walk and talk, he even looked forward to receiving, folding his little arms over his chest, "like angel wings," his mother taught him. "Open wide. Big mouth. Wide. Good boy," Mommy would say when she led him forward to receive.

His eyes got big as his mouth every time Father Naum put the Holy Communion in his mouth.

Well, yeah, maybe better stay down in the vestibule, Nicky thought. The people in church were sure to hear them through the ceiling, running and jumping over their heads, shaking the dust off the chandeliers, start thinking he was a bad father. And Edna *would* kill him.

Besides, the stairs were pretty steep, and there were a lot of them. Smoothed old wood. Rounded edges and slippery from all the years and all the feet that had gone up and down.

Nicky Zeo was one of the men who was enlisted on nights like this to carry hundred-and-five-year-old Olga up to the hall in a stiff-backed chair. Couldn't take any chances letting her walk. Anything happened, Teddy the Horse, her son, would not be happy.

Edna too. She'd kill him twice if one of the boys went tumbling and slid down those sliding board stairs.

Nah. Better to stay put. Let 'em run around down here in the vestibule.

BACK IN THE DAY, when Nicky was a teen, Daphnia was the most beautiful woman in the parish. The ladies said that of all the brides who'd ever come down the aisle and been crowned in the parish, the most elegant and refined was Daphnia Durres. She married a shipyard worker named George George and became Daphnia George.

There were a lot of those in those days. Costa Costa. Vasil Vasily. Steve Stefanie. Michael Michaels. They were sons of—the son of George. The son of Vasil. Son of Michael, like that.

Old Mrs. Durres, Daphnia's mother, was a widow for more than forty years. No one had ever seen old Nunna Duress in anything other than black. Even up to the day of her daughter's wedding. Black shoes. Black head covering. Black glasses. Black sweater and gloves. Even her *bastun*, her cane, the one she used to poke us with, was black.

So you can imagine the shock when Nunna Durres got out of the limo at Daphnia's wedding fresh from Besa's Beauty Salon. Smiling like Queen Teuta in her new silver-rimmed glasses, wearing a dress the color of cantaloupe and honeydew, with a watermelon-red pillbox hat dotted with black seeds in a happy summer pattern.

So proud, Nunna Durres. Fine white gloves. A new walnut gold-knobbed cane gripped in her right hand. Her never-before-seen handbag. Fat and shiny as an overripe papaya. The mother of the bride. Escorted by the groomsman in her avocado shoes like royalty up the aisle-runner and seated front left pew in front of the icon of the Virgin. You could hear her smiling all the way down to the river.

Not long after the wedding, Cramp's Shipyard down at the end of Broad Street got a new floating crane, and one day it went down with all hands on deck.

Daphnia's husband, George George, who had come to like a little raki in his lunch thermos, homemade liquor fermented from grapes, mulberries, plums, or whatever George Leka couldn't huckster that week—Raki-George George was never found.

Daphnia collected the life insurance, and Father Naum made the memorial prayers, and life for Daphnia the beautiful bride was never quite the same. She hated black, but her mother was still alive, so what else could she do? Remarriage was not a common thing in those days.

Nine years a widow, people said Daphnia was still young and attractive, and too young, they all said, especially the girls in the Teuta Ladies' Baking Society, "Too young to go around the neighborhood like an old nunna with her head covered all in black," Carol said, "and those old-lady shoes."

Then George George resurfaced in Atlantic City, with an American woman named Teresa Del Vecchio, who owned a bar on the Boardwalk. The news reached Daphnia the day before Christmas Eve.

Any gossip at Besa's Beauty Salon that had been corked under the shampoo bowls with the bottle of hidden raki suddenly got popped and poured all around. The whole neighborhood knew, no more black for Daphnia. No more holding back.

Old Nunna Durres still had a substantial cache of her dead husband's homemade raki stashed under the kitchen sink, so aged and strong it could've peeled the linoleum off of Nunna's kitchen floor.

And Daphnia had a crimson crinoline of spinning satin mesh that flared so beautifully when she spun that any whirling dervish worth his fustanella would have traded the balls off his *opingari* slippers.

In the vestibule, Nicky Zeo was thinking about the invisible choir-loft wire he'd seen earlier in the day when Daphnia appeared in the darkness at the top of the stairs, like a halo of Christmas lights.

Little Nicky and Sammy looked up and saw her too.

The silent apparition at the top of the stairs caused the boys to stop chasing each other in circles. The two-ring little-boy circus in the vestibule spun to a stop, lacquered in their tracks by the miraculous appearance of what Little Nicky described to his speechless brother Sammy as "Santa Claus's wife in a ball of light."

Five seconds before midnight, elegant Daphnia lowered herself and took a seat on the satin-smooth edge of the very top stair.

She wiggled into place, and bang, off she shoved, like a magnetically levitated monorail on a boisterous cushion of *fasule*-fueled propellant, sliding down the risers, legs splayed, arms aloft, with a smile smoother than Ramona's *kurabia* butter cookies.

Popped to her feet at the bottom, gave Nicky Zeo the shrewd eye, rearranged her crinoline, and breathed in his ear, "Your brother Louie told me about the crèche, Nicky, and about baby Jesus on the zipline at midnight," and then she vanished into the candlelit church, where Father Naum was calling the faithful to Communion.

The boys looked at their father. The word *amazed*, not yet a part of toddler Sammy's vocabulary, was shining like wonder on his little boy face.

He looked up at Nicky Zeo with glee in his eyes, dancing the two-step in his new Christmas shoes, saying over and over, "Why, Pop, why? Why, Pop, why?"

All three of Edna's boys laughed. Tears ran down their cheeks. Laughed so loud Edna came out from the choir and quieted them down with the kind of look boys learn when they're little and don't forget when they're old.

From the cool dark vestibule, Nicky Zeo watched Daphnia sit down in the front.

Everyone heard her ask, "Where's the crèche, Father? Where's the cake?" She told Father Naum she'd like to sit in the manger and rock-a-bye baby Jesus.

When Father told Daphnia they didn't have a crèche, Nicky

Zeo was sure there'd be a scene. He said to the boys, "There's cookies upstairs, boys."

Little Sammy looked in at Father Naum, standing in the Royal Doors, holding the chalice. The little boy opened his mouth and folded his arms across his chest like the wings of an angel, the way our kids lined up, prepared to receive Holy Communion. The way Edna taught her sons.

Nicky Zeo finally got it, the thing Naum was always saying about Liturgy and participation in a real Bible event. He didn't want to be reduced to a paralyzed spectator watching some diorama imitation of life, even if the animals were real.

He saw Carol and Ramona and the Teuta Ladies comforting Daphnia. Kissing her tears, arms around the girl in the crinoline, sitting her between them. Ramona holding her hand, Daphnia's head on Carol's shoulder.

There wasn't gonna be a scene or any scenery. That kind of thing just wasn't us. No live reenactment. We didn't need a crèche or a cake or a plastic figurine sliding down a wire.

What we had was something different. The Liturgy was a living portal, not a pixelated screen of virtual reality that hid from our view what was really true. No stage decoration. We weren't props in a play.

In the Eucharist of Christ Jesus, we were offered the possibility of uniting the created with the Creator. Offered communion in a unique event that exists in eternity. The love of God became a Person, inviting us to participate and be saved from death by Communion with the One who truly *is* Life. The Eternal Being came into time, uniting time with eternity.

Nicky said, "Okay, boys. Mommy's right. Christ is Born! Communion first. Cookies *after*."

And when both boys shouted, "Yay!" Edna gave 'em the look, and all three of her boys said, "Sorry, Mom. Glorify Him."

Evil Creeps

When Hani Medhat's wife, Azura, died, he threw all the theology books on the floor. It all meant so much that it now meant nothing. With her gone, every ancient and thickened scar in his heart began to ache.

Kusheri Nastradin told Naum the priest that from his second-story window over the El, he saw old Professor Hani walking the Tunnel after midnight, talking to himself.

Long-forgotten stains ground by careless habit into the fabric of Hani Medhat's baptismal garment began to weep as he wandered the night, grinding his teeth at the many times he had been curt or condescending and taken his Azura for granted.

Two-Beer Eddie said he saw Hani walking down Third Street and stopping on the pavement in front of Shooky's Tap Room. "Just standin' outside staring at who knows what. Lookin' like he wanted ta go in . . . Then after an hour, dude just walks on. No coat either. Holding his hat in his hand in this freezing cold."

Sins of the past that Hani had incubated in laziness and dismissed as not worth the bother now opened their eyes, stretched and yawned, came to life, and did a jig on his grief. They mocked his former indolence, joined hands, and danced around him as he sat shroud-faced in the sickly shadows of remembrance and regret.

Father Naum went to see him. He knocked. He knocked again.

Professor Hani pulled back the pale panel of sheer curtains on the door, looked Naum in the face, and mouthed to the old priest, "Go away." Felt bad, turned back, and mouthed, "Maybe later."

Like a hoarder whose nation and currency have suddenly gone extinct, good Professor Medhat, Chair of Philosophy and Religion, sat naked in front of his flaming library fireplace, feeding the inferno, rummaging through interstacked hills and muddled mounds of monographs, essays, syllogistic axioms, reams of Bible passages too impressive for a professor to address as anything less than pithy pericopes. Quotes he once found so salient now decorated the floor like deflated dirigibles.

When Madeline, Carol, and Ramona brought food from the Teuta Ladies Baking Society, he put on his socks, opened the door, said "Thank you." Took the tray, left the door wide open, turned his naked backside to the women, and padded inside, like a man suspended in a waking daylight dream.

When Carol saw the darkened bottoms of his white socks, she said to the girls, "Ran outta clean clothes, probably."

Esoterica produced for manuals of theology, PDFs read only by grad student transcriptionists who entered them online, all fed to the teeth of the shredder, spun to Hani Medhat's carpet as he scattered years of research like confetti in the air.

Professor Hani Medhat, wrenching his arm each time he swept another row of books from the shelf, shouting like a willful epileptic, "Concepts. Concepts. I despise you useless goddamn foreigners . . . You fatherless unchanted bastards. What do you have to do with people who actually live together, get up every morning and go to work, make babies, go on pilgrimages, take vacations, sit vigil in hospitals all night by deathbeds, people who have to make bastard-hard decisions?"

If his late wife Azura could have seen his library now, his "desert of theology," she called it . . . Kept locked up in such pristine order all those years . . .

Professor of Bioethics Azura Hurren-Burrat-Medhat would have found her husband's current tantrum of havoc an outrageously comic and ironic feast.

"This is delicious," she would have said. "Let me, let me, let me help you." And Azura Medhat would have danced in circles as she poured more propellant on the pathetic bier of the body she'd once labeled as "Medhat's sacred cow. Hani's inner sacred harem. His true love, his longed-for imaginary mistress."

Texts uprooted from a thousand obscure sources now lay stretched out on the floor in front of the fireplace like a line of desiccated corpses waiting for cremation.

The life syllabus of Professor Hani Medhat, exposed, dry as salt-cured jerky in the arid reality of irrefutable loneliness, anger, confusion, and despair. Hani took off his socks and threw them in too.

Kicking piles toward the fire with bare feet, he stubbed his toe and began hopping around the room, laughing at himself, kicking and cursing over and over, "Mute mother *******'s, mute mother . . ."

Later, at Betty's Coffee Shop, a worn-looking Hani told Kusheri Nastradin, "Life is coming apart."

If Nastradin hadn't known better, he would have thought the professor was drunk.

"The ark of bulrushes I hoped to float and waterproof with a line of candles every Sunday, a line of faith Queen Azura said was stupid, sad, and lacking. A line of faith she said needed filling in with the secular utilitarian ideas she called her royal jelly . . .

"Well, the whole damn thing just came apart at her death and oozed royal jelly like a leaky beeswax sarcophagus. It failed me, Nastradin. It all failed me. Broke down at the first sign of a storm. Deflated my sails. Drained all my hope. Left my soul to sink, hollow as an empty honeycomb."

Nastradin took Hani's hands across the table to stop him from shaking. The demitasse cups of dark brown Turkish brew puddled the space between them.

Hani said, "Now the God-damned wind of evil nothingness creeps and howls like a sandstorm through the cracks of my being and sweeps to hell any prayer I have of what once passed for faith. Now let go of me, Nastradin, you idiot."

He pulled back so violently he tipped over in his chair.

What could be done?

Nastradin said, "What can be done has been done, but the good of it is yet to be remembered."

Visitors came to Hani Medhat. After Azura's funeral, for weeks after the funeral, visitors called and came. Some invited him to breakfast. Some brought food. Most thought to say something of comfort. Some even came close. But what do you say to comfort a man who's said it all himself?

Hani knew it. Walking toward the church, waving his arms in the frigid air . . . "After all these years of teaching, Hani," he said to himself, "with any luck, perhaps you haven't succeeded in failing to inculcate in your students this disease of words that fizzle and fail when you need hope the most . . ."

Arguing aloud with himself . . . Steam billowing from his nostrils . . . "Words that fail to indicate some way to hold on, fail to point to a way that leads beyond the pain, beyond feeling betrayed . . ."

Stopping midstep and poking a light pole in the belly to emphasize his point . . . "Fail to offer some antidote to uncertainty, to offer something solid, something as solid as you, mister pole of wood, to wonder on in hope . . ."

A crazy Hani kicked the wire trash basket chained to the pole and spun on his heel to shout at a passing car. "Some *thing* that makes you know and say, yes, yes, it is true, it's all true. There is something more."

Manny, who owned the corner candy store, was out front sweeping snow-dust from the pavement when Hani came by. He said, "Morning, Prof."

Hani told him, "Go to hell. I'm busy."

Some grieving men lose all reason.

A moment of clarity came when he saw poor Manny staring. He could tell the man was worried. He said, "I'm sorry, Manny. I was arguing with myself and spoke out loud to a pole."

They both knew it wasn't true, completely.

"No worries," Manny said, his customary cigar fixed unlit in the corner of his mouth. "I get it. I can't say anything anymore without biting my tongue . . . Talkin' too much and not sayin' enough."

Hani knew.

He had become the slave of words to such an extent that once pronounced and printed they formed the boundary of a rigid master who punished crossing the border by choking the chain and shortening the leash.

But Hani couldn't help himself. He was possessed.

Another block down the street, he stopped to talk to his reflection in the Schmidt's Bakery window. He took the nub of a pencil from behind his ear and a spiral wire-bound notepad from his pocket. Scribbling notes and all the time talking to the window full of cake.

"By Babel didactics," he said, flipping pages and wetting the pencil tip on his tongue, "I isolated myself from life as being and from being as communion."

He tore out a page, crumpled it, and tossed it in the air. "By repetition and insistent repetition I thought to inoculate myself from any admission of doubt . . ."

Another page, and he couldn't scribble fast enough. "And to fend off or at least minimize suffering in some bizarre exchange with the god of linguistic signifiers."

Almost tearing all the pages from the wire-bound pad. "But instead I ended up immune to the reciprocal existence that willingly accepts the seed of suffering and opens the way to the other through a convergence of opposites, life found in . . ."

Hani caught himself up short, closed the pad, and said, "There you go again, Herr Professor Medhat."

Enough, Hani.

The time for words is over.

Pad in pocket, please.

Pencil behind ear. Thank you, sir.

Something must be done.

Early that evening, as he sat in the dark, clicking the remote with a vengeance, something in a part of him that was impervious to logic or words stood up and blocked out the reality-screening infomercials.

Something in him said, "Get up, Hani." It called him with a voice that sounded like his mother in the morning, "Get up, boy. Get up."

Everyone has a different season and time.

He wiped the tears. Splashed his face. Hani combed his hair and his beard. Tied his shoes. Amazed again after so long doing it without thinking. Seeing his fingers think all for themselves. Same delight as the first time he'd ever laced his shoestrings together.

He straightened his professor bowtie, put the keys in his corduroy jacket, left the TV on, on purpose, and stepped out onto the iced marble front steps. Newly widowed Hani Medhat locked the door, held the iron rail, and trod carefully three steps down to the slick salted pavement.

Down at Shooky's Tap Room, Lefty said to old man Shook, "Is it better for the man to go first or the woman?"

Old man Shook, he'd seen a lot of death back home in Pirmasens, the German town not far from the French border. He said, "Lefty, my friend, when he goes first, at least she keeps the house in order. The kids still come to visit on Sunday. The blinds are opened every morning. She does the sheets. Him? He's lucky if he shaves. There's no cooking. He grows a beard like a bum, not something you'd trim in your barbershop. In fact, from his shoes to his head, you could tell by looking, his eyes give him away. He sits at home with the blinds closed and cries. And a visit to your barber shop? Not likely, Left, unless the kids go and nag him because it's some special occasion like a birthday or Christmas. And at the end of the visit, even though they won't say it, they're glad he's gone. And at home? He admits to himself in the shadows that he behaved worse than a sullen brat and it's better for him not to be around the living."

Lefty said, "Yeah, that seems to be the theme."

Chicky and Two-Beer Eddie were playing two-man shuffleboard, and an unbelieving Chicky asked for a do-over when Professor Hani Medhat walked in and Chicky overshot his slide.

Eddie said, "Yeah, but you do got the hammer."

"Don't matter," Chicky said. "Hammer or no, going last is going last, but you saw yourself—" He paused to wave at Hani. "How ya doing, Prof?" Turned back to Eddie and said, "This is not an everyday occurrence, when the professor comes walking into Shooky's."

The professor? In Shooky's?

Shooky's old brick building, with two wide marble steps and a wider angled landing, sitting catty-corner on Third Street somewhere between Oxford and Orianna, would've doffed its hat, polished down the granite bartop, Murphy-oiled every wooden walnut shelf and cabinet, rewashed all the glasses, shined up every tap handle, buffed the mirror, wiped the blackboard behind the bar, filled the bowl with pretzels, loaded fresh hard-boiled pickled eggs into the big glass jar of brine, swept the floor, and sat swiveling on one of its own chrome stools, even if the professor hadn't come in by the ladies' side entrance.

Hani said to Shooky, "Whiskey, neat." The old Hani wanted to give a definition, "Water of life . . . whiskey means . . ." But the new Hani stuffed an egg in his mouth.

Old man Shook didn't ask, "You got a particular maker you like?" Instead he placed a shot glass on the bar, poured an ounce and a half of Old Overholt, told the professor, "Good enough for Ulysses S. Grant." Poured one for himself and said, "An honor to have you in my establishment, Professor. *Prost*!"

Hani Medhat was glad there was no jukebox or TV. *The acquisition of small, plain words—simple ways of saying things,* he reminded himself. *That's why I came here. That's what I want to hear. That's the syllabus I intend to study.* He wanted conversation, but damn if he knew how to get it going.

When he caught himself wondering if there was a book or an online course in small talk, he purposely skinned his own shin with the back of his heel, and that took care of that.

"You okay?" Old man Shook was surprised by the wince on Hani's face.

"Not used to the old rye before supper, is all." Hani was surprised. There it was. That easy. The parley-starter that was gonna make him Fishtown's number one everyday conversationalist on the topic of *how ya doin'?*

He said to Shook, "So speaking of supper . . ."

Old man Shook, round as a wheel of Bavarian Bergkäse cheese, was known in the neighborhood as the only man capable of giving Hofbrauhaus a run for its money, and at half the price, too. The big man told him, "I cooked the wurst in the kraut, and the potato dumplings are so tender your mouth will forget it has teeth."

Hani downed the whiskey and said, "And a beer?" He'd read about boilermakers. In Philly they called the drink a City Wide Special—a shot of whiskey followed by a beer chaser.

"Ja," Shook told him. "And a beer. George Esslinger was a personal friend." He pulled the tap with the Esslinger Pirate emblem and said, "Professor, you gonna drink a barrel full. And I got strudel from Schmidt the baker when you're ready for dessert."

Hani thought, *now we're getting somewhere.* True, there was something deeper he wanted to get at, and it might take a while. No matter. Tonight there was whiskey, time, kraut, wurst, beer, tender dumplings, and strudel for dessert?

What words could spoil that?

Serious? Yes, the subject he wanted to get at was serious. You could say that, but it could all steep in kraut juice while he ate, and then a boilermaker, a shot and a beer. Few a' those probably wouldn't hurt. So he said to Shook, "How 'bout another? And a round for the house."

It was right about that time Hani said to the boys playing shuffleboard, "Why don't you join me for some supper? My treat."

They moved from the bar to a cozy booth in the back. Lefty squeezed in next to Hani across from Chicky and Two-Beer Eddie.

Lefty said, "Prof . . . we got one condition: supper's on us."

But Hani wouldn't hear of it. Turns out Hani could drink too. Lefty and the boys could hardly keep up, but they did their best.

When it got around to coffee and strudel, old man Shook

pulled a cane chair perpendicular to the boys in the booth while his wife, Liselotte, took the bar.

Hani looked at Liselotte over the table and said, "What if, God forbid, *your* wife got sick, so sick that she couldn't stand the pain and didn't want to live?"

They all knew what he was saying. They all knew why the man was hurting.

Shook said, "God forbid."

"Doesn't she have the right to die with dignity? Why all this suffering?" Hani said.

Old Overholt rye had Hani by the brain, twisting the anguish out of his limbic system like Hercules wringing out a rag. And the old pirate brewer Esslinger had limbered up the professor's tongue with ale so cold and pale, he had no doubt he could have sung the Latin alphabet backwards standing on one foot touching his nose with his eyes closed.

Down the hatch went the acquisition of small, plain words—simple ways of saying things, all the reasons he had come to Shooky's, the short syllabus of simplicity he'd intended to study.

"Ordinary conversation is maybe not so easy, Mister Hani Medhat," he confided to the amber veneer at the bottom of his glass.

Hani tilted back the empty shot glass, thinking, now we're getting somewhere, leading ordinary men to that something deeper. And before he knew it, he was tripping over his own tongue, raising his glass and telling old Shook, "Another, barkeep! And another round for the house."

Brave Hani Medhat, letting his mind trick his mouth into agreeing when he finally said out loud that maybe he could understand it when his wife had told him, "I don't want to live like this. This is not living."

Lefty said, "I thought the same thing, seeing my mother suffer . . ." Then he stopped himself. Lefty was one of our boys who made it home from the war. "Mom musta read my mind that night . . . Me thinking, maybe it's just better to end the misery. Thinking that about my mom. But it was me I was thinking about. Trying to get out of it. Selfish. My own mom. She waved her finger, slow, told me, '*Mos e marr dhuratën time* . . . Don't take my gift.'"

Chicky wanted to ask what that meant, but he knew. It was the same with his mom. He knew the old-timers had this view of life as something like climbing a ladder.

Chicky said, "My mom told me, 'I got to go from where I am to where I want to be, with your father, with Krishti and the Mother. Maybe it gonna hurt for a short time to climb up, I know, but I don't let them take my ladder. Don't let them take my ladder, Jacob. My angel is helping me.' Mom kept saying that over and over, 'Don't you let them take my ladder, Jacob.'"

Eddie asked, "Who's Jacob?"

Chicky said, "I don't know."

The whiskey projector was rolling a memory reel on the inside of his eyes that only Old Man Shook could see.

"The Americans bombed our town. It blew the pot of soup sitting on the kitchen table right out the window. We had to duck in ditches, we, little kids, on the way to school. We could see the stars on their wings when they strafed the road with machine-gun fire. They knew we were kids, the Americans!

"And what the Nazis came and did to our Jewish neighbors . . .

A phony dodge. Some of the Gestapo's best agents, a man and a woman who were Jews, coming to our door asking us to hide a little Jewish girl they had with them. Turning in not only other Jews, but anyone who offered to hide the little girl. So take a chance, or . . . what? Nobody does all the good all the time."

Shook pushed his strudel to one side. "About choices, I don't know, Professor. But about people? What I see, there are only two kinds. The decent and the others. So what if you escape on your own? That's living? That's not a phony?

"I'm sorry, Professor. I don't usually drink. I said too much." Shook was wiping tears from his face. "Look at me, I wanna control others, tell them live, don't live? I even demand an account from God because *I* want to control the universe, and I can't even control *myself* . . . All these years, I still feel I shoulda done *something*—I was just a boy. Even if I suffered. They were suffering too. I think there is only one suffering, Professor, and we all share it."

Two-Beer Eddie said, "I got a goal for myself. Got it freezing my ass off in the forest during the war. Heaven is my goal. Evil creeps. You go ahead and try and stop it. Not me, man. I did my dirt, and trying to deal with it only made it worse."

Lefty said, "You hear about the woman in her twenties, bought a kit online and offed herself causa she'd been sexually abused when she was five? Had that PTSD thing going on. Anorexic. Flashbacks. Always depressed. Poor kid. Doctors gave her the intensive psych-therapy thing. Ended up telling her she was incurable . . . Said she was mentally competent. No mood disorder or anything like that affecting her thinking, but she was never gonna get better . . . They agreed, told her go ahead, end your life."

Hani lifted his head and said, "I have a colleague—well, my own wife, actually—who calls it rational suicide. Says it's hedonistic and utilitarian, good for individuals and for society."

"'Dat some crazy shit." Chicky regretted it as soon as he said it.

"And it makes you do crazy things," Hani said. "My Azura, she says the right to life is essentially tied to a being's capacity to hold preferences, which in turn is essentially tied to a being's capacity to feel pain and pleasure. That fetuses and even newborns are neither rational nor self-aware and can therefore hold no preferences."

Old man Shook said, "Heard it before."

Hani said, "And as a result, she argued, the preference of a mother to have an abortion or kill her newborn automatically takes precedence. The newborn infant lacks the essential characteristics of personhood, rationality, autonomy, and self-consciousness, and therefore killing a newborn baby is never equivalent to killing a person—that is, a being who wants to go on living. I asked her, 'But that doesn't include suicide, does it?'"

Does it ever go quiet in a bar?

The sound of the chalk on the blackboard.

"Is that tomorrow's menu, Liselotte?" Old man Shook blinking his eyes, looking at the board, thinking she was writing:

We will follow our own plans and will every one act according to the stubbornness of his evil heart . . .

He blinked again. No. It was the menu.

Green-eyed Liselotte had no desire to participate in the perpetually unresolvable problem of individual personal opinion.

Spend enough time behind a bar, and you find out quick. Every expert with a glass in his hand is dying to convert all the other bar-leaners to his particular cast-iron cavalcade of concepts. She figured consensus must be a drink they offered at some other establishment. She rang the last call and told Shook, "Time, my honey."

Lefty said, "I think I gotta get going if I wanna go on living."

He took Two-Beer Eddie by one elbow, and Chicky got him up by the other.

Chicky said, "Yeah, ya gotta know when it's time."

He bent to look Eddie in the face and said, "We shoulda stuck ta shuffleboard."

Hani Medhat wasn't ready for them to leave. He said, "But when you're faced with that situation—when a person says they don't want to go on living—and you have these ideas about personhood in your head, like royal jelly from the queen . . . You can understand, boys, can't you, how . . . ?"

Eddie was slurring his words when he said, "Depends, Prof . . . on which icons you got in your corner."

Nobody knows why Naum was in the church when Hani came banging. Way after midnight, but when the old priest looked out and saw Hani Medhat standing in the snow, no hat and his coat on backwards, standing on his toes kissing the cross on the gate, Naum opened the door.

Garden of Souls

SOMETHING WAS HAPPENING.

I'm not exactly sure what, but it was something. I stood down by the garage and watched.

Probably five women. Probably none of them under seventy-five. I did hear one of their names. Mariam. The others kind of looking to her. Mariam this. Mariam, where? When is ____ going to get here?

There were four men. If any of them were younger than eighty, I'd be surprised. Little guys, three of them. One man still big for his age. Holding up the one having trouble staying on his feet. Kept saying in English, "You forget your cane?"

The other one, stretchy shirt straining to cover his belly like he liked his beer a little too much, he was saying, "I'm no' using that damn walker."

Usually I can recognize a language. Working all these years in the burial ground, I come across lots of different kinds of folks from a lot of different places. This lingo, though?

That day I showed up just getting light. Had to be early. There was lots of trimming and cleaning and mowing needed doing around the headstones. Taking care of my people. Forty or fifty thousand interred in my care, and my crew was a man down. So me being the boss, I gotta pick up the slack. First on the scene. Last to leave.

But maintenance aside, people—whether they're living or otherwise—people always gotta come first. Whatever thing you might be dealing with at home or on the job gets to be insignificant real quick when you see the limos emptying out and the hearses pulling in. People probably dealing with the most broken day of their life.

Knowing that pain to be true from years of leaning on my shovel and waiting and watching is how I got my rule, "Today, you can yell at me many times as you want."

I wanted to go help. The lady's talking a mile a minute. Setting up card tables. Wrestling with those pole-skinny hollow legs. White cloth table covers. Never get them table legs to stand even on that graveside grass. Five buzzing bees. Man, I hope I got that kind of energy when I get to a certain age. If I do.

The men had bags. One with wine. One with bottles of some clear liquor I found out later was called *mastika*. One of the women said something to the big man. He held up a sleeve of plastic mini cups from his bag and got that same smile from her that my mom used to use. Boys never forget it. That *You better be glad you didn't forget* smile.

By the time that priest from our neighborhood walked up the hill to the grave, there wasn't a free space on the tables. Trays? I never seen so many silver trays at a grave.

Crammed. Breads. Cheeses. Olives. Muffins. Filo pastry. Bet you there were five different kinds at least. They had bottles of juice. Fruits. Bananas. Berries. A case of water too. Took two of them to carry it. Cakes and pies. A feast in a field. And me not having time for breakfast or even a coffee.

The priest got kissed and hugged all around. When he saw the one man holding up the other one, he said something to the big man and headed down the hill toward where I was standing, in the doorway of the garage.

His skull cap had embroidery that was so colorful and foreign, it was like I'd seen it all my life in a dream. Especially the needlework cross in the middle on the front. The man could've hid a fair-sized pony in the sleeves of his robe.

Always friendly to me, he was, every time he saw me in the burial ground or around the way. He said, "How's it going, Luther?"

I said, "We're still one man down on the crew. Got that shovel with your name on it, Padre."

"Maybe twenty years ago, Mister Lou."

I knew why he came to the garage. "You want me to carry it up?"

He said the same thing he always said: "Nope. You work hard enough as it is."

"Well, then," I said, "you know where it is." And looked in at the back of the garage by my desk, in the shadows.

He came out fireman-carrying that oversized three-wheeled office chair, upside down with the armrests on his shoulders. It was embarrassing, really, how stained that thing was once you saw it in the daylight.

Next thing I knew, the old man with the belly who couldn't stand so good was sitting on the hill in my ratty stained chair, and the big guy who'd been holding him looked a hundred pounds lighter, and there I was standing with my hat in my hand, staring at the tables.

It wasn't the first time I told the priest "No. No, thank you," three times in a row and then ended up saying, "Oh, okay. I'll come up. But just for a minute." And I figured it wouldn't be the last time the old fox'd rope me in.

Truthfully, I didn't mind. I didn't know exactly what they were doing, but every time I went up there, I knew something more than meets the eye was going on.

It was a thing between me and him when he used to ask me, "Mister Luther, how many times a day can you have your heart broken working here doing what you do?"

Every time I'd say the same thing: "Many as you want."

The priest went around the circle and asked the people, "Tell me about Josif. I can't believe he's been gone a year. Anybody dream of him?"

The woman I took to be the widow went first. "He doesn't talk to me," Mariam translated. "He smiles at me." The widow said in her language, "But he only talks to that damn parrot that outlives him. He say . . . *Chichi! Chichi Chichi.*"

"I dreamed of Uncle," Mariam said. "At first I ignored it. But when it happened three nights in a row, I just went out and bought him slippers." She motioned to her husband and said, "For my Risto."

"Let me get this straight," the priest said. "Josif, your husband Risto's brother, came in a dream and told you to buy Risto slippers?"

Mariam said, "Yes. Three times, Father. What does it mean?"

Risto said, "He always knew I had cold feet."

A pottery bowl in the center of the table wore a painted floral lace so sweet around the rim you could almost smell the flowers. Mariam handed the priest a beeswax candle. He looked at the bowl and said, "Who made the boiled wheat?"

She said, "I did."

"How do you call it?" the priest said. "In Macedonian."

"*Esianisa*," Mariam said.

It looked like porridge to me. The priest put the candle in the center of the wheat. Mariam lit the candle.

There was something about the way the man went into the battered black bag he carried. Everybody watched. There was another world in there. The men took a direct interest. Me too. The women, except for Mariam, sort of watched sideways. Several times a woman called Dora—I could tell she was asking if he needed help—and when the priest came to a red jar with a fat candle inside, he said to her, "Dora, would you light this for me, please?"

He unfurled a fancy stole around his neck, down to the hem of his robes. Pictures of Jesus and saints on the table. A Bible. A cross. A small lidded cup on a stand. I found out why the inside was black when he put a stick match to a round of charcoal, started blowing on it till it sparked, and then placed the charcoal in the cup.

Told us, "Put out your hand."

Placed a pebble in our palms. "Frankincense," he said. "What they brought to Jesus. Put it on the charcoal. Watch! Don't burn your fingers."

Risto said, "*Temjan*." I knew it meant incense.

The priest said, "Our prayers, rising up to God." He was singing to himself, "Let my prayer arise in Thy sight as incense."

They prayed for Josif, a year gone. They didn't know I knew. *A garden causes what is sown in it to spring up* . . . Many an overnight by myself, but never alone among the graves.

The priest Naum named every one of us and asked God to keep us by His grace. I told him the first time we met, "James Michael Daniel Martin Luther Gill . . . my full name." And damn if he didn't remember when he came around to me.

Had that lacy blue bowl in his palm, scattering wheat around the grave . . . "Verily, verily, I say unto you, except a grain of wheat fall into the earth and die, it abideth by itself alone; but if it die, it beareth much fruit."

Then they sang a hymn so sad about God's memory, I don't believe there was a voice across the garden of graves who went that day without weeping.

We ate so much after the Lord's Prayer. A feast in a field on a hillside by a grave. The big man had a thermos of coffee. I was at a banquet in God's garden of souls, a headstone marking the name and location of each seed, and all His people as far as I could see came alive with us that sunny morning on the hill. God's memory really is eternal.

"So good," I said.

The priest said it was "love made edible."

I wasn't exactly sure what, but something was happening.

Mariam said to me, "This is church, Mister Luther. You should come and see."

That day, just getting light. Had to be early. The priest got up. He told me, "Mister Luther, I said to myself, I got a day off. I told my wife, Greta, make coffee. Nothing to do for nobody but me. Gonna spend the day in my underwear. And man, Luther, I needed a day off. I *was* gonna skip 'em this morning. Was gonna skip morning prayers. But morning prayers have a way of making the rest of the day . . .

"So when I got to praying for God's people . . . and I got to their names and looked at the clock . . ."

I don't think firemen get out to the fire quick as he got his pants on and out the door to the burial ground that day.

When he was getting ready to leave the burial ground, he said to me, "How many times you think me and you're gonna keep carrying that chair up and down to the garage?"

I told him, "Padre, many as you want."

Fourteen and Pretty

AN HOUR BEFORE SUNSET
The sand under the kid
Had turned
A muddy pink rouge
Fourteen and pretty
Lay knotted like a sock
Summertime crowds
Passed overhead
The casino light show
Leached down through
The splintered wood decking
And gave a pallor
So strange
To the scene
Playing out under the boards
When Naum finally found her
Nothing ever hit him so hard
Not even in the perpetual shadows
Under the Tunnel
On Kensington Avenue

JESSICA AND RUBIN were getting married, and the reception was at the Island Grand, on our favorite barrier island down the Jersey Shore. Half the neighborhood and all of us from Saint Alexander the Whirling Dervish Orthodox Church made the drive.

Couple of kids from Fishtown, Brian and Cullen, were out on the island's main drag, looking for help. They spotted Zaza and Naum turning the key in Naum's lemon-yellow two-door beater, getting ready to head home.

Cullen recognized the '66 Impala right away. He said to Naum, "You from Fishtown, right? I know you from under the Tunnel."

Naum said, "I remember. I just can't remember your name."

"Cullen, and look, man, one a' our girls is in trouble."

Cullen told Naum he ran away right before Christmas. "Came down here with some friends, and all of us been living at the Underwood ever since."

"You think I might see that girl?" Naum said. "What's her name?"

Cullen said, "I don't know. I don't know her real name. Everybody just call her D. She been out here long time, Preach. Working. You dig?"

Naum knew what that meant.

Cullen said, "Do-goods come around. Give us food, sandwiches and stuff . . . Try and get us to come in. Hoodies and mittens. Backpacks . . . But you gonna come and see this girl or what?"

Father Zaza said, "I wonder if I know her?"

Cullen looked at Zaza's sandals and said, "D is all I know."

Cullen's friend Brian hadn't said a word.

Cullen and Brian were in the back of Naum's Impala. "The Underwood. Down near Roosevelt Place."

When they got out, Brian said to Naum, "Her name is Dora."

It was hard to say who was more naïve—Zaza and Naum, wondering how a pretty little kid her age had managed to survive all this time without her parents, or Dora for thinking the midnight friends she'd met at the bus station and on the Boardwalk were really her friends.

The Underwood Motel, what the kids called the cardboard shanty-town labyrinth they'd dug out under the boards.

Nestlings prematurely flown—kids from anywhere, Southern California to right around the corner, for whatever reason, seemed to radar in on this sandy beachfront landing strip, where they did their best to care for one another.

By the time Zaza and Naum crawled under the boards, dusk was coming on, and the carnival glitz overhead was swinging like a lit-up gondola stopped at the top of a Ferris wheel.

The sky over the North Atlantic faded. The sand and the sea lost their shine. Something about seeing it from under there made the whole down-the-Shore thing go grim.

End-of-day grit. Naum and Zaza crawling on their knees, sand fleas in their beards, their nostrils, breathing it in.

Naum stopped. He handed his keys to Zaza. He said, "Go back, Father, see how close you can pull the car."

Walking to the car, Zaza asked Cullen, "What you guys do for money down here? How you survive, if you don't mind my asking?"

"We stretch out a sheet on the beach under the railing down near the last casino. People throw some coin or trash or nothing." Cullen shrugged. "Stopping up on the Boardwalk with their mouth open. Leaning on the rail gaping. Saying stupid stuff about the giant lobster battling King Neptune and the other stuff we mold in the sand."

Cullen looked at Zaza. The barefoot priest in sandals. Big beard. Wearing a cassock. Everybody said the biggest suckers on the street were priests. He wondered how long Zaza would survive out here. He said, "We do our best. Smarten up the new ones. . . . But the monsters still get 'em."

The constant stream
Of runaways and throwaways
Irresistibly easy pickings
For the hustler dealing pimps
Trolling the stations
Buses and trains
Traffickers
Back-lot cheap motel
Serial soul killers
Monsters with names like
Mister AC
Candyman
Hard-Hand John
Evil Evelyn
Swooping in wherever
Hustling boys and girls

Zaza backed the Impala up the dead-end beach block as close as he could and ducked under the pilings.

Later, he told Naum, "Truthfully, when I first saw her, Urata, I thought maybe . . . But when you called her name and she managed to turn her head, and I saw those blue eyes open."

At the same time he asked if he could, Naum slid his arms under her body and scooped her up. Slender and tall. Kid didn't weigh a thing. Not a goddamn thing.

"Don't leave my bag. I need my bag," was all she kept saying.

"'I got it, sugar . . . I got it . . ." Naum kept telling her.

Torn-up and wet, swinging on Naum's arm like an empty nest . . . Up and out from under . . . kicking sand as he went . . . carrying Dora and her backpack.

Dora's parka and most of the few things she'd brought from home had been lost, pawned, or stolen. Her backpack had that gnarled sea-gray look from being constantly in the damp and the grit.

In the hospital, she didn't take her eyes off Naum. Made him hold her hand. "You're from home," she kept saying. "You're from home."

Zaza and the boys were outside. Naum knew they didn't want to be there. He didn't blame them.

He handed Zaza thirty dollars and said, "Get something to eat. In the meantime, Father," he said to Zaza, "call home. Try and find some family contact. The doctor's been asking me like I should know, and Dora ain't saying."

Naum knew nine reasons he ought to go, and only one why he couldn't let go of Dora's hand and leave the kid alone on the exam room table.

When the doctor asked him to leave, Dora said no

He held her hand

Not a whimper from the kid
Not a sound
But tears
Tears like a baby's
Big and wet
Silent
Soft
Ran and ran and slid from the corner of her eyes
Soaked the white-blue pad thing under her head
The kind of sterile pad they put
On a styrofoam tray
At the supermarket under baby veal
The doctor turned down the lights
She said she'd be back.

Dora asked Naum, "You gonna go too?"

Naum brushed back her hair, kissed her forehead, spoke to her; tried to be like an uncle, like a *good* dad, said, "What's wrong, sweetie? What's making you so sick?"

She told Naum, "My name is Theodora."

What disfigured love grows daddy's baby girl into some stranger's prey out in the streets?

All Naum could do was squeeze her hand.

She said to Naum, "I want my bag."

He raised it from beneath the exam table. Held it up where she could see it.

She said, "Get my baby out of the bag."

No breath came to Naum.

In or out.

"My baby," Theodora whispered.

Naum didn't want to go into that bag.

Time washed over Naum and the girl on the table like waves coming into shore.

There it was. Out of a wrinkled brown-paper bag. A glass iced-tea bottle.

Dora told Naum, "Hold it up to the light."

He couldn't . . . but he did.

"Do you see him?" Dora said, like she was displaying pictures of a newborn. "Maybe we could come back to the neighborhood with you."

Forty years of Last Judgment Sunday sermons came up in his throat and got stuck.

A line from the *Didache* he'd been always too quick to quote: *Let not thy word be false nor empty but fulfilled in action.*

Talk dissolves in time. Time, Naum. Put up or shut up.

Any word out of his mouth that didn't include *I did it to the least of your beloved* would be nothing more than ecclesial ego writing a check the priest didn't have the theological grit to cash.

Theodora looked at Naum.

Naum from the church, hungry, naked, sick, and imprisoned by a situation that had him out of options and asking, *How do you come to be here?* And finding he had nothing to say . . . no wedding garment . . .

Tangerine-colored liquid
Floated there
A miniature
Perfectly formed
Newborn
Same curved silhouette

Like an infant curled up asleep
Eight, maybe nine, ten weeks with child
The kid'd miscarried
Fished him from the Boardwalk public toilet bowl
Put his little self in a bottle
Put the bottle in the paper bag
Baby
Bottle
Backpack
Boardwalk
Bag

"Minors across state lines." The doctor and the social workers said they couldn't release the child to Naum even if he could demonstrate he had the means to care for her properly.

"Maybe if the parents came with documentation and signed a release."

"We wanted her with us," Naum said later. "But we didn't have a suitable place. Thought maybe we'd reunite her with her parents, if we could find them."

Turns out, even after Zaza did find her family, it wasn't that simple.

Three days on clean hospital sheets, her bed was empty, and where was Theodora?

No one knew.

But Theodora knew the drill.

Old enough to take the abuse and too young to do anything about it but run. The kid knew the system better than half the social workers in the system.

Dora told Naum, "A minor goes to the state system if she

won't go home, home with the father who did it to her and who knowingly permitted her brothers . . . Well, if no one else knows it, Father, I do, and now you do too."

Naum learned more from Dora about how things work than he did from any training, expert, academic study stats, or law enforcement report.

He told Zaza, "And I ain't downplaying those things. They have their place. And the people who do it have a tough job."

Naum went to the house on East Berks Street, Dora's house. Him and Father Zaza and Captain Donna, who grew up in the parish—our resident Philly SWAT unit leader, went and spent time with the father, saw the brothers . . .

When they left, Captain Donna said, "And I've no doubt they would've—And *it* would've continued, just saying . . . If that girl'd been forced to go back there. I'da run away too." She looked at the two priests and said, "Nothing the church can do, Fathers?"

Naum closed his eyes. He said, "No."

Later that year, Naum was sitting on the church steps. He looked up and said, "Dora?"

Before he could stand, she brushed back his hair, kissed him on the forehead, and said, "It's me, Father. Theodora. It's me."

Icon in the Fire

THE BEDLAM BEGAN in the middle of the sermon, when one of the big shots from Fishtown Savings and Loan stood from his seat and went to the red runner in the center aisle.

"We're orphans," he shouted. "Ya threw three hundred of us out. Where we gonna go now, *Father*?"

Igor Yevgeny Kornelyuk, the babka-shaped man with the brush-cut flattop, the bowtie, and the Buddy Holly glasses, dropped to his knees, raised his hands to heaven, and started five hundred men, women, and children doing the heebie-jeebie shivers right there under the gold dome of Saint Josaphat Cathedral.

Pavel Grigorievich Chesnokov, the choir director—around the neighborhood we call him Singing Chessy 'cause he's always walking around singing—before Chessy retired, he served thirty-five years on Ladder 60 at the firehouse over on Belgrade Street. He said all that commotion got people panicking like a five-alarmer.

Mothers herding their kids into the Ladies or out the door, if they could beat the crowd to get there. Grown men hiding under pews . . .

The altar boys loving it, stuffing mouthfuls of antidoron,

raining handfuls of incense into the crowd, dancing in circles like spinning gold-robed pysanky-dreidls and draining the single-swallow cups of leftover wine like it was Frank's Black Cherry Wishniak soda.

Only Pafjessi Doku sat still, weeping like an icon in the fire.

Old Father Ilarion Kopko—our Naum knew him—was up there behind the pulpit, ducking flaming candle-arrows, pleading, "Stop this," dodging incoming, "immediately!" Giving orders like he still had some say-so.

Singing Chessy, the fireman-choir director, said the hurly-burly went on for eternity, "and then some."

Even the cops from the 26th were ashamed for the priest in the fancy vestments. Neighborhood officers who knew us all, embarrassed for the melee-rumpled congregation sweating through their Sunday best.

Sergeant Sikorski—we knew him from Saint Veronica's Catholic Church—he said, "Can ya imagine havin' ta use your billy club ta truncheon a bunch a' middle-aged punch-drunk palookas brawlin' through the precincts of such a holy-looking place?"

The saints on the iconostasis covered their eyes.

The whole thing played out again Friday morning the following week, in front of Superior Court Judge Winfield Todd Booker. The judge, a serious fire-and-damnation Presbyterian, was not amused.

When these clowns started acting out again in his courtroom, Throw-the-Book-at-'Em Booker stood up in his robes, ripped off his glasses, bounced them off the bench, grabbed his gavel, and unleashed the bailiffs. "Get 'em, boys."

Adjudicating ecclesial mayhem was awkward enough when

litigants acted like Christians before the tribunal. But here was Father Ilarion, inciting the courtroom chaos: "They're lying. They're lying."

Newly mown crew-cut Igor Yevgeny Kornelyuk the banker snatched off his Buddy Holly glasses, heaved them at his accusers, and had his supporters on their toes, pointing to the priest's contingent. "You and yours are the children of *the father of lies.*"

Stephen Gazinski, Goliath of a guy, was some kinda rocket science professor down at Polytechnic College of Pennsylvania offa Penn Square down there on Market—remember him, guy with the big head, had long hair even back then, always wore the same shirt and tie you could never see with that long black monk beard, married Ollie Dudnik, always wore dark glasses, remember . . . ? He was on Kornelyuk the crew-cut banker's team. He tells the judge, "The priest went on a tirade, worse than a tornado. The man hasn't the finesse to be a priest. It was unseemly, Judge, in the sanctuary? Pointing at poor Korny, blaming him for getting political in the church. We're the majority, the people from our town in the old country, not these *salyany*" (country bumpkins).

Before Judge Booker could pull it together, a conflagration of mean-faced debates spontaneously combusted in various parts of the court, like sparks on the Fourth, and the next thing we knew, elbows were elbowing, ribs were cracking, balled fists were flailing, shoulders were being thrown, and all the wind getting knocked out of the combatants was shaking the courtroom chandeliers.

Judge Booker cleared the court. One hundred and fifty pushing, shoving, squabbling co-religionists duly rounded up and shepherded out the door to the sidewalk by Philly's finest and reminded in Fishtown terms by Sergeant Sikorsky.

"The cells in the cellar are mere feet away, and being how it's Friday, I promise yas on my grandmother's headstone over in Palmer Burial Ground—once the doors are closed, I'll be damned if I'll be able to find the keys before late Monday morning."

PAFJESSI DOKU—it was hard to tell her age, not young enough to wear red or old enough to wear black—both parents gone now, alone in the world as long as we could remember. She was what people in those days used to call *slow*.

Naum came to unlock the doors to our little Saint Alexander the Whirling Dervish Orthodox Church early Saturday morning so he could do some cleaning, and there was Pafjessi, getting off the bus.

She asked the blessing of the priest in the worn black cassock. He put aside the broom and the bucket and made the prayer.

"Can I come in and light a candle, Father?" she said.

Naum gave her the key and said, "Open the door for us, Jessi."

He remembered her icon. He'd been with Father Ilarion during the season of home blessings. Now she took the small paper icon of the Mother and Child from her purse and put it on the analogion next to the icon of Saint Alexander. She lit her candle and put it in the sandbox on stilts, made the cross, kissed both icons, and whispered her prayer.

Only Pafjessi Doku had remained still during the melee, weeping like an icon in the fire.

Naum knew she was crying. "Why did they fight?" he asked.

"Politics," she said.

Flags. Language. Culture. Borders. Lines on a map. Costumes and cuisine . . .

Naum had died, twenty minutes, more—no heartbeat, no breathing. He used to say, "Before I was alive and waiting to die. Now it's the opposite." He said, "Those things weren't there on the other side of the iconostasis. They have no place in the eschaton."

Naum said to Pafjessi, "Politics have little potential to save our souls, but great potential to . . ."

If she was *slow* . . . why didn't he have to finish the thought?

The woman who prayed alone in her apartment five times a day with her paper icon was upset in her soul with the vision of the zealots. Pafjessi couldn't explain it, but something deep in her knew their actions took the Holy Name in vain.

Pafjessi had perception unspoiled by the wisdom of this world. She could tell when people took their eyes off the icon. Naum had seen it.

When people thought they could capture the fire of the Holy Spirit for their own purposes and make the Church a vessel in which they boiled their brethren . . . he had seen Pafjessi run away and hide.

Maybe reading wasn't so easy for her, but Naum and Father Ilarion had witnessed her, one word at a time, praying through the Psalms, never missing a day.

Now they stood together in the narthex looking at her paper icon. Pafjessi Doku said to Naum, "The priests don't like my icon."

Naum said, "But she likes *you*, doesn't she?"

She smiled. "They always try to give me another one."

Naum knew their thinking. He was pretty sure he understood. Western religious paintings were not icons. The perspective was not ours. The naturalistic depiction captured something, but it wasn't the something beyond. It evoked emotion, perhaps, but not presence.

And yet, somehow, the Mother depicted in Pafjessi's icon had a sweetness, a sad sweetness, but a sweetness still. And the Child, well, what kind of person would see a child and not smile because God hadn't given up on us?

"I pray all the time," Jessi said.

Naum said, "I hope you remember me."

She said, "I do. Ever since you came to my house with Father Ilarion for the blessing. You saw where I pray. You saw the place up in the corner where my icon stays in front of the electric bulb that in eight years—" she held up fingers— "has never gone out."

Naum wanted to tell Pafjessi about Tolstoy's story of the three hermits who prayed in their own way on an isolated island till the bishop came and corrected them, but when the bishop saw them walking across the water toward his boat . . . well.

Naum said, "I know God hears your prayer, Pafjessi, no doubt."

That made her smile.

Back in her pocketbook, the three-by-five icon. Out to the bus stop. Smiled and waved out the window as Naum stood watching and worrying.

He tried to remind her before she left. He wondered, did she hear? He could never tell through her smiling.

"I hope you're not still walking over your kitchen table and standing on the stove to get to the cabinets."

A little sheepish, Pafjessi. "Sometimes I forget."

He was terrified during that visit with Ilarion. The gas stove burner, blue flame, and the bottom of her skirt . . . How it didn't catch? Both men stood and reached for her.

She said, "I'm okay."

Later, Father Ilarion went to see Pafjessi's sister, Llamba, and told her. Llamba said she'd take care of it.

PAVEL GRIGORIEVICH CHESNOKOV, the choir director—singing Chessy, we called him. Before he retired, Chessy served thirty-five years on Ladder 60 at the firehouse over on Belgrade Street. Now his son, Lieutenant Paul Chesnokov, was on the scene at Pafjessi's apartment building.

New Year's Day, cold and windy. Temperatures in the thirties. They even almost cut the Mummers short. People leaving the parade early. Taking the kids and heading home for ham and cabbage. Put their feet up on the radiator. Tell the kids, "We'll watch the rest of the Mummers on TV." Take a week for the little guy's feet to get warm again.

Getting dark just after five that time of year. Late afternoon shadowing black corners around every skyscraper in the city.

Fire department personnel getting ready for the six o'clock shift change, and the damn street-corner alarm boxes start going like City Hall was on fire and Billy Penn's statue was dancing in the flames.

Old Chessy was banging on Naum's door. The two of 'em, running a block, walking a block, joining the crowd pushed in behind the barrier across the street.

Hoses and hook-and-ladders everywhere. Sirens. Red lights spinning in the wind. The heat from across the street did nothing to stop the shivering. It made it worse. People huddled close for more than shelter. Orange was the only color on every face.

Chessy's son walked over. "Pop," he said, "I need Father to come with me."

"Can I come, son?" Chessy said to Pauly.

The lieutenant said, "Pop, you know you can't."

Pafjessi's neighbor, eighty-one-year-old Anna Andrews, she'd been a widow more than fifty years, sitting in the open ambulance doors, wrapped in a fire department blanket, crying. Naum had only ever seen her in black.

Pauly said, "What's she saying?"

Nunna Anna Andrews explained to Naum in Albanian.

He told the lieutenant, "In her bureau drawer, her life savings, five thousand dollars, it's all she has."

Pauly said to Naum, "She's in the first-floor rear. There's no danger of collapse, at least not right now. Mostly just water damage back there. You wanna come with me, I'd appreciate it. I want a witness."

The apartment was dripping black water. The bureau drawer was wet but untouched by the fire. Pauly opened the top drawer. Only clothing.

The middle drawer. Same.

The bottom drawer. "*Shikoni.*" Look, Naum said. "That's way more than five thousand."

Bakery-string bundles wrapped in wax paper marked with black marker. A thousand dollars in each. Fifty bundles, maybe more.

Outside again, Naum was spitting cinders, charcoal bits, and splinters. The smoke was reaching the civilians across the street.

More firefighters were arriving. Command radios were squawking about the entire top floor of the building becoming fully involved and the fire spreading rapidly downwards.

The building was beyond saving, and the concern shifted to curtailing the spread of the fire in this densely populated, densely developed area.

The police started to move the crowd. Two EMTs came out of a blackened doorway with a sheet-covered stretcher.

Everyone was thinking it was time to go. Naum waited.

Chessy tried to get him to go. A fuel-oil depot and feed-and-grain warehouse between the railroad tracks and American Street were that close.

Lieutenant Chesnokov took his father and Naum, an elbow of each old man and said, "Time."

Naum was turning to watch the men with the stretcher. Was it her?

Pauly Chesnokov looked back at the stretcher. When he had his father and Naum halfway down the block, he lifted the oxygen mask and took the icon from his breast pocket. He said, "Everything . . ."

The young Chesnokov's face was covered in soot except for the place where the mask had been. "Everything except this . . . Nothing survived, Father. I'm sorry."

Pafjessi's icon was untouched.

Not singed. Not a corner curled. Not soaked through with water. Nothing.

THE COURT CASE WAS NEVER RESOLVED.

A new bishop was consecrated for the splinter group with the hand of a bishop who had died a year before. They dug him up to do it.

A new priest was ordained by the new bishop. A new congregation was formed.

Judge Booker observed, "Division prevailed."

Igor Yevgeny Kornelyuk, the babka-shaped man with the Buddy Holly glasses and the brush-cut flattop, one of the big shots at Fishtown Savings and Loan, stood from his seat in the new church, went to the red runner in the center aisle, dropped to his knees, raised his hands like a praying saint, and started the bedlam of flag-waving and cheering, saying, "We're orphans no more."

Stephen Gazinski, Goliath of a guy, some kinda rocket science professor down at Polytechnic College of Pennsylvania offa Penn Square down there on Market—remember him, with the big head, had long hair even back then, always wore the same shirt and tie you could never see with that long black monk beard, married Ollie Dudnik, always wore dark glasses, remember . . . ?

After the Gospel reading: *That all of them may be one, as You, Father, are in Me, and I am in You. May they also be in Us, so that the world may believe that You sent Me . . .*

At coffee hour, the professor told the new priest, "You work for us now. We're the majority in this church, people from our town in the old country, speak our dialect, not those salyany with that old fraud Ilarion with no finesse over at Josaphat's."

NAUM PUT PAFJESSI'S PAPER ICON on the altar at Saint Alexander's for the forty days of Great Lent. On the Sunday after Pascha, when it began to weep, he took it to Saint Josaphat's and gave it to Father Ilarion.

Pafjessi's paper icon, the icon in the fire, wept for a year.

The Purse

What happened was, this lady left her handbag on the ledge inside the Tunnel Carwash bay where you get change for your bills from the change machine. All quarters.

Butch? He'd been working there since he got out. Did his ten and change for what he did to that fifteen-year-old with the broomstick. On a young girl? Damn. Sick dude, Butch.

One time his girlfriend, Lorraine, brought him his birthday cake to the carwash, and we was all around, ya know, singing Happy Birthday.

Butch's got this real lightish blond-red hair like redheads get causa they don't right away go gray. Had a mop of it, too, and the alcohol-flush whiskey cheeks to go with it.

Mumbled when he talked. Talked to himself a lot, walking around through the carwash tunnel and the bays, like he was prison-muscling his way through the gen-pop yard, trying to bluster his way with his mouth outta havin' ta throw down.

Must not 'a' worked too good, him side-steppin' throw-down fights with his mumbling bluster, 'cause from what I could see, his yap had as many tooth vacancies as it had occupancies. We used to call him Every Other 'cause he only had a gum nub every other space. The man spat a lot. Ya had to take a step back when Butchie talked at ya.

So we finish singing Happy Birthday, and we're trying not to laugh 'cause he'da kicked our asses, but Every Other blowing out the birthday candles—and there was fifty of 'em—made a sound like a cat passing gas.

Butch puts out his pan-gasket hand, fingers thicker than a radiator hose, only his girl Lorraine has any idea what he's mumbling, and she hands over her car keys.

She's standing there stupefied with the rest of us, hands on her hips. "Butchie!"

And damn if he don't pop the trunk and sit the whole cake, candles and all, in the lug-nut spare tire circle.

She's telling him, "Butchie. That's for everyone. Share."

He goes, "I ain't got no knife, and I ain't breaking off nothing till tanight after 'paghetti."

Next morning he comes holding up his T-shirt, rubbing his belly, and smelling up the outdoors like a pink hog.

Butch smelled like lockup anyway. If ya ain't never been in, even just to visit, ya wouldn't know. But just try imagining breathing in years of fifteen guys living day and night in a cell built for four.

Night sweats? Panic attacks? Butchie had 'em.

Neighbors called the police. Butch out raising sleepwalk hell in his underpants, barefoot on the ice, swinging a broomstick bat at something he was fighting in the air between his ears.

Once he saw me sitting on the curb by the bay, carving my thing. Ya' know? Here, look. Two-by-two square piece a wood I found in the dumpster, 'bout as thick as two fingers. Carved it in my off time.

Cross in the middle. IC XC in the upper corners. NI KA in the lower corners.

Or he'd catch me reading, like *Beginning to Pray* or *Way of the Pilgrim*. Never said a word, Butch. Butchie couldn't read.

Or he'd yell from the front, "What the f***'s that? Knock it off." Me echoing the Trisagion in Albanian down the carwash tunnel.

I tried to keep the God thing a secret. No dice. I mean, I'm just a civilian works graveyard at the putty factory. My Judy said I couldn't keep a secret unless I didn't know it.

When he figured out what the whole thing was, he wanted to talk God, but only so he could blame God for all the shit he'd messed up in his life.

Everybody else at the carwash, like Vlad, or Mousie, or that hardcore Maria, either just got out or was out on bail or on probation or waiting arraignment or dipping and diving trying not to go back in. Detectives and warrant squads dropping in unannounced, and the crew ducking in the dirty-towel room, hiding.

Butch may have given me a hard time, telling me I scrubbed whitewalls like a faggot, but I think it was causa the God things he saw me doing.

And because of the God thing, I was the only one this caveman trusted to sift with him through the vacuum-cleaner muck, picking out pennies and nickels, and sometimes dimes and even quarters, when we did the filters and washed out the slime at the bottom.

Us sitting up to our elbows in industrial-vacuum crud, him dividing the spoils. "One for you. Three for me."

I didn't care if the piles weren't even-Steven . . . Bought me and Billy John Marco a beer here and there at Shooky's, and anyways, old man Shook said he could use the change. Said one time he even found a Buffalo nickel and an Indian head.

I didn't ask what that was. I don't like decapitated animals.

So what I like about the priest Naum is, he didn't interrupt when I was confessing. Hardly blinked. You woulda thought you was the only person on the planet, the way he was looking, like a praying mantis paying attention to an aphid he's about to eat.

Focused? Naum was jailhouse-focused, like what the professor told me was some kind of scattering-invariant mode of indestructible light wave traveling through material like it ain't even there.

Believe that? Prof said it was true. He also said some people doubt about God being able to see to it the Virgin had a baby without . . .

Well, I myself ain't got any doubt about there being things beyond the walls of the carwash or the putty factory or the prison.

So what happened was, this lady in a damn nice two-seater Lexus SC430, black with a red leather interior, Pebble Beach Limited model, with the hardtop drop-top down, leaves her handbag on the ledge by the carwash bay where you get change for your bills from the change-machine. Quarters is all it gives so youse can use the big do-it-yourself Metro Vac N Blo . . .

And you guessed it. Handbag ain't there no more. But she don't miss it right then.

Lady comes back an hour later, says to us standing there

watching her bent over by the vacs, “Excuse me, I left my purse there by the change machine.”

Butch didn’t even mumble, and nobody else in the lineup answered either. Just looked at her like none of us spoke American.

The whole crew of pirates scoping her tight white four-hundred-dollar black lettered Givenchy-Paris no-bra T-shirt. Maria too.

Lady is upset. She says, “Look, I don’t care about the cash. The credit cards. I don’t care. I have pictures of my kids, my driver’s license, personal stuff . . . a letter from my mom, who just died.”

I could smell prison-breath Butch breathing through his teeth. Nobody even had to look. None of us.

Say something. Go ahead, God-boy. I dare ya, say something.

Butchie knew I saw him dump her pillaged purse in the dumpster.

So, I ask Naum, "What am I supposed to do? What would you do?"

Up till then, Naum was one big ear. He had his right hand up touching his lips, like he was contemplating giving his pointer finger a nice long kiss. Took his finger away and pointed it at his temple and shrugged his shoulders, like, damn if I know what I’d do in a situation like that.

I mean, Naum knows working at the putty factory ain’t cutting it, and me and Judy need the extra pennies and the tips, and it all adds up, is why I’m working the extra carwash job anyway.

The lady’s yoga pants got us nailed there, watching her walking back to her SC430, and before Mousie repeats his lewd comment loud enough for her to hear, I yell, “Yo, lady.”

Soon as the words come outta my mouth, Butch and everybody and everything around me do the scattering-invariant mode of indestructible light wave traveling through a diorama peephole.

I'm like, oh shit, what am I doing?

She's standing legs shoulder-width, like a high-noon showdown shadow in the middle of that street our mothers used to tell us about . . .

Don't lie and always do the right thing . . .

A street called straight.

Gotta be some way, I'm thinking, between just letting her take her loss for being so stupid and getting myself broomsticked by Butch and Co.

"Lady," I said. "Prob'ly, prob'ly not, but sometimes lost shit ends up in that dumpster over there. They come before daylight. Before we open. None a' us got nothing ta do with that cause at that time there ain't none of us here."

Everybody knows I been pulling graveyard at the putty factory. I seen 'em, towards daylight, when I was getting off. Coming to empty the carwash rusted green dumpster.

Like phosphorescent shadow puppets
Moving in morning spray
Needle fine drizzle mist
Swirling in and out of the headlights
Ghostly auras around the men
Hydrophilic membranes
Swallowed and exhaled
As the mechanical wench
Shimmering in the steaming darkness
Hoists the dumpster

On whining

Well-greased cables

But the morning drizzle was long gone, and I was standing there evaporating in the heat with Butchie and the boys at my back, wishing I was one of those garbage men responsible only for myself and simple things like garbage and predawn clatter.

Hardcore Maria came and stood right by me.

But the priest Naum told us about the one who was responsible for the purse. And this guy Judas didn't care about other people. Not even about Lord Jesus. Only about himself. He woulda kept the whole birthday cake too. 'Cause the man was a thief. He was the keeper of the purse, and he used to steal from it.

So that's what I did, Father. That's my confession.

I know Naum wanted to ask about the lady and about the carwash crew and Butchie and Maria.

But all he did was put the stole on my head.

"God it was who forgave David through Nathan the Prophet . . . May that same God forgive you all things . . ."

He prayed that and the rest of the prayer and removed the stole.

I kissed the stole. I kissed his hand.

We bowed to each other. He said, "Forgive me, brother."

I said, "God forgive us both."

Then he said, "Coffee at Betty's, got time?"

I said, "Yep." Causa I saw he had jelly doughnuts from Schmidt's.

Then he said to me, "Ya quitting the carwash?"

I said, "Already did."

Missing Pop

I am longing
For something that no longer is
Nor shall ever be again

IT WAS ONE OF THE SADDEST THINGS Naum had ever seen.

Alexi, the son, grown and just beginning to show that silver-gray frosting twisted into every third strand of his thick dark hair. Coming to the deacon's door. Tentative. Sticking his head in. "Father, can I stand in the altar today? I'm missing Pop."

Lisa and her husband, Steve, both COs up at CFC Prison. The no-nonsense correctional officer. The young woman too pretty to be wearing that old nunna scarf.

The smiling man with the close white beard. Tattooed biceps straining the Tuskegee Airmen T-shirt he wore in remembrance of his father. Her tapping the verse on her iPad. Schooling him in the proper tone. Bossing him around. Steve loving her correcting him again.

People understood why Liturgy never started *precisely* on time.

Naum waved Alexi in and saw the son of a priest who never came when his father was alive. Saw the boy step into the longing of the man whose hair was turning gray. Step into the hope that maybe his longing might abate for a minute. His regret maybe somehow be healed.

Time and liturgy. What they had to do with each other, Naum couldn't say. To him they were one another inside out. Two sides of the same epitrachelion.

Time purposely creates
What appear to be empty places
In the folds of Christ's priestly vestment
In order to translate otherwise
Ordinary optic-nerve impulses
Into otherworldly impressions
That render absence a presence
In the familiar spaces of the church
Where our loved ones once stood
And somehow, for us, always will

But then again, what did Naum know about time? He didn't keep a watch on the altar. The man never owned a watch.

He'd seen clocks in some altars. He'd seen some priests take off their shoes and put on special slippers before serving. Others took off their wedding rings.

Orthros was coming to a close. Steve and Lisa were at the psalti stand alternating verses from the Doxology. Naum asked Alexi for the censer.

Father Negovani's son, Alexi, had some idea of the closeness. The liturgical proximity of persons that transcends space and time. "He's here. I know it. I just can't figure how."

It made Naum sad to see someone living with a hole in his net. Looking through the space and knowing they missed it.

Missed the tactile icon
The presence of the other
The other we couldn't wait to escape
Their touch. Their voice. The way they smelled
Just beyond the reach of our time-bound senses
Knowing our desire to be on our own was an existential trap.

Naum had heard of something called quantum entanglement: particles so profoundly related that even if they became separated across vast distances of space and time, if one was stimulated by a mysterious force, the other could feel the movement of life, even without the two interacting in direct physical contact.

Sometimes a connection can be reestablished even if one end of the loop gets severed . . . as long as both ends of the desire remain alive, receptive and longing, breathing for the other.

The only *Breath* Naum knew was liturgical. The priest praying in Naum was pretty sure there was a way.

After Liturgy he told Alexi Negovani, "Go talk with Nicky Zeo, Two-Beer Eddie, some of the older guys. Go see Teddy the Horse over at the Auto Heaven. They knew your Pop . . . They knew where he hung out, on what corner. Who he visited. Where he ate. Knew him as a kid. Knew what kind of priest your father was. Visit those guys. And don't forget Mrs. Elias. She taught your father when he was a kid in Sunday school. Taught all of us. When you get back, we'll talk about what happened to you today at Liturgy. Okay?"

Alexi said, "Maybe you're right. Maybe it'll give it a frame. Make it so I can understand, if I go talk with those guys."

Naum said, "Good icons are bound without a border."

SHOOKY'S TAP ROOM didn't seem to have a border. Same sawdust floor and neon signs in the window, *Schmidt's Beer on Tap, Esslinger* with the pirate logo, and *Yuengling, America's Oldest Brewery* . . . Shooky's smelled like shuffleboard and beer.

Nicky Zeo was at a table in the back. Had the blue-and-white checkerboard tablecloth rolled half back and was writing numbers on the wooden tabletop with the stub of a yellow pencil.

When Alexi sat, Nicky said, "Jeet?"

Alexi said, "No, jew?"

Fishtown parlance: Have you eaten? No, have you?

Old man Shook came over with a potpie, told Alexi it was duck confit, wiped his big hands on his apron and said, "I got another one ready, Alexi."

"If Nicky don't mind. That and a Rolling Rock."

Nicky said, "Be my guest, kid. Duck was one a your father's favorites."

Shook said, "I got Schmidt's, Ortliebs, Yuengling, and Esslinger."

"Take a Schmidt's," Alexi said.

Shook said, "*Sehr gut.*"

"Your father," Nicky said. He went in his wallet and took out a creased stack of Kodak Brownie sepia-tone pictures. "Your father won that little Brownie playing checkers. City-wide champ. There he is holding it. I think it was Sharky took the shot with the same kinda Brownie he got at the PX down at Fort Gordon in Georgia, I'm pretty sure. Augusta, I think."

Alexi ran his fingers over the snapshots. He felt liquid

time running backward through the desiccated veins of the brown-and-whites.

There he was, sitting on the steps on the corner with the boys. Look at them. Boys. Just boys. His father. Nicky Zeo. Two-Beer Eddie. Chicky. Lefty. Teddy the Horse. How in the hell?

But there it was. And there Alexi was, sitting with all the men he knew growing up. Till filo crust duck on the porcelain-white plate steamed up his eyes.

Before Alexi left, Nicky said to him, "I got something for ya, kid," and took a small book from his pocket. "This was your father's. They asked us our religion when we were sworn in. We told 'em we're Orthodox, and the chaplain gave us this little red paperback prayer book the night before we deployed. Your dad was the only one came back with his. The rest of us lost ours. Some from the neighborhood never made it back.

"And that time he got mad at the church, your father," Nicky said, "and walked out. You remember hearing about that, when they wouldn't give your mother communion 'cause she wasn't Orthodox? He threw this book at me, and for some reason I kept it." Nicky opened the cover. "Got his name inside."

Alexi said, "I didn't know he got mad at the church."

Nicky said, "Well, he did. And it was your green-eyed mother who straightened him out. She said, 'The priest is right. I shouldn't receive communion. You got one marriage. One table ya eat at. Ya don't go jumping table ta table or bed ta bed . . .' But she said it better'n me, Alexi."

Alexi couldn't think about Mom. Missing Pop was one thing, but missing her? Something else entirely.

Nicky Zeo said, "You know he used ta beat the hell out of all of us, your father? Best boxer in the neighborhood. Still and all. We knew he was gonna be a priest."

"C'MON IN, KID." Alexi followed Teddy the Horse up the steps into the blue-and-white mobile trailer on blocks they used for an office over at Auto Heaven, on the Avenue under the Tunnel.

"Take a load off." Teddy motioned to a sofa the color of eggplant. He said, "Nicky called. Said you might be stopping by. Missing Pop, eh?"

Alexi said, "Yeah. Certain times a year."

"You know your father helped build our parish, right?"

"I didn't," Alexi said. "Well, I mean I had some idea. I was just a kid."

"Well, he did. Him and your mom. Ya wanna talk about sacrifice? And Pop died of a broken heart when they forced him to leave. Vasil Vasily and some of them old-timers, meaner'n cat pee. He pleaded with the church board, your pop did, to let him stay and serve the people, even as an assistant to the guy they were replacing him with. Pop told 'em, 'For no pay I'll serve, like we did in the beginning.'"

Alexi said, "In the beginning?"

"You didn't know they never paid him for the first few years?"

"No."

"Well, they didn't. Almost nine. And from what I heard, they could've. But they let him work, keep his old job. You know Pop'd been a butcher, like a meat cutter. Doing all kindsa shifts at the slaughterhouse. Come Wednesdays, him and your Mom'd go and clean that church, top to bottom, and still serve all the services . . ."

"I can still see him in that bloody apron," Teddy said. "Mind if I smoke?" He lit up a Camel, reached behind, slid open a window, and blew smoke that blew right back in. He said, "But they were intent on replacing your pop with a younger priest. Single guy. American. Spoke English without an accent."

Alexi Negovani couldn't believe what he was hearing.

Teddy said, "Emelia, your mom, before she died, told me they promised your pop retirement money. 'Hey, don't worry about nothing. Nothing's too good for our priest . . .' What they told him. And nothing's what he got. Nothing.

"Apparently, for years they took money from his salary," Teddy said. "Supposedly they were setting it aside, month at a time, they told him. That's how they justified reducing his shabby salary. Truthfully, Alexi," Teddy said, "I don't know how youse made it."

It was coming back to Alexi. The bloody apron. All of it. The reason he'd left the church. The reason he and Mom quit attending. The thing he couldn't put into words that made him finally tell Pop, "I don't know if you and your imaginary friend, the one you call God, are anything more than a mental illness . . . These people? The way they talk to you and treat you and Mom?"

Teddy the Horse stubbed out the cigarette. He said, "Your mom told me if it wasn't for the kindness of Barenbaum, the Jewish grocer down here under the Tunnel, allowing them to have stuff on the book, there were times when they would've had nothing to eat but the things she canned that your father grew in his summer garden. Remember that, out back? Do you know they made him and her pay rent to live in that parish apartment over the garage? Told him, 'Somebody's gotta pay the mortgage.' Believe that? 'Hell,' Vasil Vasily used to say it right in front of

Pop, 'he only works one day a week on a Sunday for an hour. Let him do something to earn his bread.'"

Their priest. The one who baptized, married, communed, and buried them. Took care of their parents. Their children. The man who came when they were sick. Who persisted in trying to be an icon of God's love . . .

Teddy said, "The new guy they replaced your father with was single. Like the Catholics. 'Save a bundle,' the church board said. 'No deadweight family to drag along.' They like it he didn't have no beard too.

"You remember your father and mother at the retirement thing that Sunday after liturgy? You were just a little kid, standing there between 'em, holding both their hands. Remember? 'Surprise!' Everybody yelled when youse came in the hall. Your father didn't even know it was coming. Didn't know it was his last Sunday. The cake. Your parents thinking it was just another Sunday coffee hour. Your mom started to cry when they asked him for the keys. She told me your pop said, 'I'll have no reason to live away from God's altar.'

"What did they care? And ya know what, Alexi? You remember the guy they got, the replacement priest, clean-shaved no-accent guy, Father Harbam? They gave *him* your father's retirement money, the money they'd been putting aside, as a signing incentive causa the guy insisted on more money."

Alexi Negovani. Missing Pop.

Teddy was on a roll. "And ya know what? Three months after being forced out . . . Well, you know, Pop got sick whiles youse were packing up the apartment. Mom begged them to let yas stay so he could be in his own bed in the place he was used to. They refused. And you know, he died in that rented dump on American Street by the tracks near the Black Bridge.

"Vasily and the boys on the board, know what they said? Said, 'Good thing we fired his ass. Could you see if he would've died in the altar?'"

Teddy said, "Your mom never forgave 'em. You know she gave Father Naum your pop's vestments, right? Her and your pop always loved Naum."

"He wore them at Liturgy when I was there," Alexi said.

"And you know what happened after, right?" Teddy said. "Father Whatshisname turned out to have a predilection for altar boys . . . Had to leave town . . . Yeah, Vasil Vasily's son, one a' the altar boys he got . . . What I heard. Why Vasily's boy ended up hustling downtown at the Merry-Go-Round's what somebody said. The poor kid . . . Yep, 'From the butcher block to the altar block,' how they used to make fun of your father. . . But he refused to give in and give 'em tit for tat . . ."

Alexi wished he'd never come to Auto Heaven. He said, "Thanks, Uncle Ted."

"Know what impressed me most about your old man? I told him once he oughta fight back, like we did in the war. Fight fire with fire. He told me, 'I'm following the one who said, *Be completely humble and gentle; be patient with one another, love, because love covers over a multitude of sins. Love each other as I have loved you.*' And then your pop told me in Albanian—you still understand a little, dontcha? '*Besim, shprese, dhe dashuri*—faith, hope, and love. But the greatest of these, Theodri—' that's what your Pop used to call me. He told me, 'the greatest thing is love.'"

Alexi said, "You remember all that, huh?"

Teddy smiled, went in his desk drawer, pulled out a cassette and popped it in. "Got the deck and the speakers outta a '74 Plymouth Satellite."

After they listened he handed Alexi the cassette. "Ya like it? Here. You can have it. I recorded this talk your father gave. Got copies made. You heard it starts with him and your mom singing church songs and an opening prayer. Listen to it in my car on Sunday mornings when I smoke too many Camels and don't feel right going to church."

Hearing the voices of his parents left Alexi in water deeper than sad. He wondered where he was gonna find a vintage tape player. One that could handle a brittle old cassette without devouring the tape. Without being inwardly devoured by his own heartsickness at not having sung with them while he could. By the sound of his father and mother, by the two made one in prayer, singing "God grant Thy servant, Alexi, many years."

MAGDALENA ELIAS.

He often heard his father talk about Nunna Elias, the teacher who taught him to love the Liturgy and made him love the Scripture so much he wanted to eat the pages of the Bible.

Magdalena, the wife of Samuel Elias. The woman with the beautiful green eyes who taught church school. Magdalena, who wore long dresses, her head always covered. But gold earrings. She couldn't resist.

Magdalena baked prosphora, the meshe, holy bread so good, the boys serving in the altar, Alexi's father included when he was an altar boy, couldn't wait till after Holy Communion.

Alexi and his father's teacher, Magdalena, drinking tea on the enclosed front porch of the Elias house. Magdalena, back and forth to the kitchen, baking *byrek*, the spinach feta filo pie others call spanakopita.

Late morning sun curled the peeling paint and warmed the enclosed porch through panes of wavy old glass. Magdalena called him from her kitchen. The lamentation in her voice told him what her words would never say. "Come, Alexi. Can't you smell the byrek?"

What widow wouldn't appreciate someone to eat her cooking? If she still had the heart to cook. The joy is in the sharing of the feast. Sharing it with that *one* . . .

But what person sitting at her table, even as pleasant as Alexi Negovani was, his conversation, the memories he caused to rise like the yeast in her holy bread . . .

What person could fill the seat left empty by her Samuel?

"Absence has its own presence," she told Alexi. "Real presence that presses in on me."

At the door, she put a bag in his hand, a brown paper bag stuffed with byrek wrapped in wax paper, and told him, "It was your father's favorite, sauerkraut byrek or, in your mother's village, they called it *lakror*." She said, "I know you said you ate with Nicky Zeo, but save it for later so you'll remember your father when you eat it, and remember mother, and me, too, Alexi."

The seal of her lips stayed on his cheek.

And Alexi Negovani
Kissed by his father's teacher
Found it hard to speak
Because he could feel the love in her kiss

Sweeter than layered butter in filo dough
A mother's ancestral kiss
Reaching every branching dendrite
Down far in the reaches of his being
Every cell of Alexi Negovani
Stood upright like a paper bag
Full of love made edible
He kissed her hand
The only place left to look
Was back with the priest
So Alexi went.

THE SON WALKED THE NEIGHBORHOOD, looking for traces of his father. Past Hollander's Drug Store, catty-corner from Spic N Span Cleaners.

Pop wasn't there.

Down past Schmidt's Bakery. He could smell the George Washington spice cake cut in squares. Trays of doughnuts, every kind, in the window. A cup of coffee and a fresh, soft jelly doughnut powdered with confectioners' sugar dying to be dunked.

Pop loved nothing better.

Looking through the rusted cyclone fence at the auto scrapyard, waving, yelling Alexi's name, Little Harry and Getzy, greasy as the piles of corroded junkers they were hauling.

Flattened dreams Pop used to drive.

There may have been a reason Alexi could never look directly at Donahue's Funeral Parlor or walk on that side of the street. Instead, he'd cross and take the path that led him through the wrought-iron gates of Palmer Burial Ground, past the section with the roughcut Orthodox altar. The lane that brought him out the other side along the same canopy of trees where he and Pop held hands and walked singing back and forth to school.

If he could, Alexi would have made himself stop and remember, but he was afraid to remember what they sang, and afraid to consider what might happen if he failed to recall their song.

Saint Veronica's Catholic Church, with the rectory and the convent and the K through 8 school. Pop always said those folks knew how to build a way to serve their people.

Alexi waved to Rabbi Aaron and his wife, Maureen, at Emanu-El, the synagogue across the street from our parish.

Pop used to take him to the center Rabbi built. The beautiful center with the indoor basketball court and the gym. Rabbi tried to teach Alexi Krav Maga, the Jewish martial art thing.

Alexi and Pop spent hours talking about what they saw at the Holocaust Museum. And when Doctor Baks was on his yearly two-week vacation, there was always Rabbi's free medical clinic next door to the daycare run by the synagogue.

Pastor Cal's Holy Communion Protestant Church had a turret with a blinking blue neon sign on top, flashing out *Jesus Saves.*

Pop loved that sign but told his friend Cal it just wouldn't fit with our Orthodox dome.

There was no hiding in the neighborhood. The city might be anonymous, but around the way, from the synagogue to the church, the doctor's to the drugstore, from the baker's to the butcher's, just wasn't no place to keep a secret.

Everybody knew Alexi was missing Pop.

At the Horn and Hardart Automat Cafeteria, where every

window-portal coin-operated pie dispenser was full and freshly stocked . . .

There was no priest. Not at any table. Not occupying any empty chair.

In the fruit and produce stalls of the Reading Terminal Market, all along the marble countertops of the sandwich shops and the spinning stools of the seafood purveyors.

No luck.

The observatory deck atop City Hall at Billy Penn's feet.

Priestless.

The one place his father had been consistently every Sunday for all those years was the one place Alexi never sought him.

Why?

The priest had managed to remain faithful in one place. The place of his calling, "God help me," he used to say.

Why hadn't the son looked for him there while he could?

Father and son, both ravaged in their gentle sensitivity to the fragility of life. Innocent sinners guilty of a not unreasonable expectation of love and life. Living with sorrowful inner contradictions of being as life and human life as but a figure and a symbol of death . . .

Child and man, no longer satisfied with baby answers, but at the same time refusing to let go of hope.

"And damn if they should let go," Naum said. "Why let go of a childlike remembrance of things hoped for, of a primordial memory, of a liturgical longing for the Garden, where things were as they ought to be."

Alexi remembered his childhood friend Jamie, struggling

for faith and saying, "*You* try not losing *your* grip in this neighborhood."

It seemed to Alexi there were two things for certain.

One. He existed, at least he was pretty sure he did, and was somehow able to stand outside himself and be aware of his existence.

And two, because he could stand outside himself and be aware

He could consider if his existence had a meaning, a purpose

And if his life did have a meaning and a purpose

Then there had to be something greater than he, the thing that caused him to exist

Had to be the Cause that had no cause

That thing that just *was*

That *thing* had to exist for Alexi to have purpose.

And Alexi Negovani figured the Cause planted the purpose and the meaning for him and his existence in other people who existed, and vice versa.

Alexi walked along, thinking about what it was in him that made him practically run to the church to be anointed, the time the doctor told him he better be tested.

Fear? Yeah, but something else, too. Thinking, no, knowing, even if I die, there *is* something more.

It was dawning on Alexi Negovani the Sunday he walked back to our little Saint Alexander the Whirling Dervish Orthodox Church in Fishtown.

"Some message in code is happening where the priest stands every Liturgy."

Alexi Negovani walked alone.

What stopped me?

What was in my way?

Or *who*, should I ask?

I wanted my time. I wanted people to leave me alone, and I ended up alone with time that kept leaving and left *me* alone.

He could hear the voice of his father's teacher saying, "God is a mysterious delay that is always perfect in time."

The son, grown now. Showing that silver-gray frosting twisting into every third strand of his thick dark hair. Tentative. At the deacon's door, saying, "Just missin' ya, Pop. Can I come in and stand with you in the altar?"

Because
Pop
I am longing
For something
That no longer is
Nor shall ever be again
For men and places
For time
That has passed away
Like the sun passes
Across an empty window
Like a day fades
From sunlight
To evening
Fades slowly and forever
From our lives
For green trees
Against shaded red brick walks
Along houses in rows with marble steps

And iron rails
Where children live
Where people are
In small worlds
Worlds where I am known

The priest waved Alexi in through the open deacon's door.

The Nun

APOSTOLNIK

Why they still called her Apostolnik?

Some knew. Some forgot. Some never knew.

Some of the women in the monastery hadn't been in the struggle long enough to know it wouldn't hurt not to know.

More than forty years in the monastery, Mother Apostolnik said, "Lots of things forgotten in life which maybe should be remembered, and the other way around, too."

If you saw her at her age—maybe she was near fifty when her husband died and she came to the monastery for the first time as a visitor—if you had a certain eye, a farmer's eye, you wouldn't be out in a field alone if you said when you saw Mother, you saw a girl, an American girl.

Tall? Not Mother. Short? Not that either. Who could tell anything under all that black?

Happy? Most days. That you could tell in her eyes. Straight on at you. Bright green. Like an Amish tree of life looking out from a weathered clapboard barn. That weather-vane rooster high on top, calling out to the morning light that follows the night. The light the darkness can never comprehend.

She preferred to be alone.

One of the novices asked, "You're trying to avoid being disturbed or hurt by others?"

Apostolnik said, "The other-way-around thing."

If she spoke to you, she spoke to you alone. Even if all the others were flying by like bees in motion, it was just you and Mother.

The abbess, Mother Myraphora, a former Presbyterian pastor PhD, had long ago assigned Mother Nikki, that's what they called Apostolnik, assigned her to tending the goats and cleaning the kitchen.

Mother Nikki never said, "And the bathrooms too."

Mother Myraphora and the Mother Abbess before her knew why Apostolnik kept that certain ascesis, the discipline that informed her name, and they knew the reason she had asked to be permitted to persevere in what seemed a self-effacing discipline (which some might have looked on as prideful, but it wasn't), and the old nun had the blessing of the abbess to continue wearing the novice veil called *apostolnik*.

When Mother Myraphora walked in the kitchen one winter morning and saw Mother Nikki up to her elbows in white liquid, she said, "What is that smell?"

Apostolnik said, "You like it, Mother, don't you?"

Who knew goat-milk products would become a source of income for the community?

Soaps and lotions. Yogurt and nut bars. Kefir, butter, and beer. Apostolnik had chanced upon recipes that were unique and unexpectedly popular with monastery visitors and country neighbors for miles around.

"I never ask the record-keeper about profit." Apostolnik didn't care. "She tells me there's enough for the basics and to give to the poor."

Then she said to the kitchen novice, "My dear, would you spread me all over with some yogurt a piece of bread?"

Mother Myraphora the Abbess drew the line at the goat beer. "The local regulators said we could drink all we want, but no selling it."

When Nancy asked Mother Nikki, "What does it mean, *Apostolnik*?"

Mother Nikki told the first-time visitor, "Nancy, my dear, see my head covering? When a woman becomes a novice . . . You know what that is, *Liebchen*?"

"Like a beginner, someone checking it out, learning?" Nancy said.

"Vell, jah," Mother said. "That's it. It's like your probation period, you get to check out what it's like at the monastery, and the folks at the monastery get to know you."

Nancy said, "I think that's why I came, just for the weekend."

"You staying in the *dawdi haus*, the guest house?"

Nancy said, "Yes. Me and three other women."

Mother Nikki said, "Kinda different living in community if you're not used to it."

Nancy said, "I'm the oldest of twelve. Two and three of us to a bed. My poor mother."

Apostolnik said, "God love 'er."

Mother Nikki listened. Nancy named all the kids, her siblings, all grown now, and she still called them *the kids* . . . and she listed all their birth dates.

Mother sat there smiling. "Nancy, you're gonna fit in fine, if you decide . . . Anyhow, the Greeks call this veil an *epimandylion*. Here, at our monastery, we call it an apostolnik. See? This thing."

Mother pulled on the black veil. "It's a cloth veil is all. A little more than a scarf, really. You see, right? Covers my head, my neck, my shoulders. Sometimes, when I'm not working up a sweat, I wear it with a *skufia*." Mother unfolded a soft black brimless cap out of her pocket and handed it to Nancy.

Nancy ran the circle of it around her fingers and traced the red cross embroidered on the front. She held it over her head and looked at Mother, gesturing with the cap, like, should I, Sister?

Mother said, "Gotta save somethin' for the wedding night, Nancy, don't we?"

Nancy understood what that meant and handed it back.

Maybe with someone else, her gesture, making as if she was putting on the hat—no disrespect to the uniform—would have made Nancy feel awkward, like she was somehow inappropriate or out of line. But she didn't feel that way with Mother Nikki, with the way the old nun let her know it wasn't time, without building herself up or putting Nancy down.

Mother Nikki didn't ask about Nancy's prayer life, or if she fasted, or what she'd read. She said, "Nancy, you're really something. You didn't come here to learn, did you? You came to experience."

"Got me on the first try, Sister." And for the first time since she arrived, Nancy began to breathe.

The tonsured nun took it seriously. Apostolnik was many years a tonsured nun. Of course she knew tonsured nuns were addressed as Mother, not Sister. How was Nancy to know?

But timing—"knowing," Mother always said, "when and how to place the seed."

Nancy wanted to ask her something more. She noticed Mother's wedding ring, thin old gold, and she felt her own life-worn ring without touching it, sentient, alive around her finger, and Nancy knew both their husbands were still wearing theirs.

Can a widow tell a widow when a widow sees a widow?

It took Nancy by surprise when Mother Nikki said, "You're worried about your marriage—in heaven, if you become a nun, will you still be married, right?"

Nancy was tired of answers. She wanted to be surprised.

Mother spoke quietly, with a certain *Gelassenheit*, a calm serenity yielding to the will of God, like the Hannah she'd been, the Pennsylvania Dutch farmer's wife. Wasn't it her? Wasn't it her Meyer lemon cake recipe, with the goat milk buttercream frosting, that kept Mother Myraphora and the account books, and the visitors and country neighbors for miles around, happy and waiting for the end of Lent?

She said, "Nancy, you've been married. You already know. It's inside you. In marriage, we live, we trust, and we experience the transmission of life, in and with our husband, not in theory but every day, in life.

"Real, sweaty, sleeves-rolled-up life, everyday organic love. Okay, imperfect love, maybe, but love nonetheless. It's like a monastery of two, isn't it?"

Nancy could see the everyday Mother.

Mother Nikki said, "Marriage, Liebchen? I think it's a liturgy. I think it's like the living, moving water we used to have running through the farm. We get a bath, married people. Don't we? Our humanity is cleaned up and restored. Man, woman, and child. An icon of the Trinity. Like the way we were in the Garden—that must have been a beautiful farm, before the snake whispered."

Nancy said, "I do read. And I pray, every day. And I believe. I believe about Jesus Christ, the Bridegroom, and the Church being His Bride. I heard the priest say something like that. That marriage is an ongoing eucharistic event, the bridegroom and the bride. Just stuck with me, the way the priest said it.

"And Sister, I want so much to believe our marriage is like that . . . beyond time."

Mother Nikki said, "For sure and certain."

The semantron started. Mother said, "Banging that board with the mallet. I love to do that." It was time for the midday meal.

Nancy said, "Can we talk instead?"

Mother Nikki said, "Not me." And patted her middle, smiled, and said, "Sure. I'll get us something to go."

Out back by the goats, Mother said, "Nancy, you start, eat. You don't mind, I'm just gonna say it plain."

Nancy said, "The plainer the better."

"I'm the child who committed the unforgivable," Mother said. "And I've come to die here, begging." She stopped for a moment and then said, almost to herself, "There must be more.

"We believed, me and him, my David. Then, after school, I got smart. Said there was no God. I made fun of everyone and everything about the *Haus Kirche*, about his faith. I can't even think about it now. It makes me crawl. The things I allowed my thoughts to walk with.

"And then when he died and I found his journal . . . *That's not her, Lord. You knew her when. You know her now. You know the true her. Please, Lord. Please.*

"And I closed up. The house. The farm. Sold it all. Gave it to the shelter up there in the city. Came here. Just gonna be for a weekend, because I didn't know what else to do, and he'd written in his journal he was becoming Orthodox. I didn't know what that was. All I knew was, he was looking into it, he said in the journal, for both of us.

"So selfish me withdrew to be alone and goes and discovers her true self. It was like childbirth. Like being pregnant. Nancy, I can't explain it. I don't know why I think it, I just do. Real life doesn't happen, can't happen, when you're alone.

"Nancy, I clean the bathrooms and when I look down, look in . . . I see it . . . clarity, a defining clarity. . . there, in that . . . spot.

"It's like a world of wonder, cleaning the toilets." Mother Nikki, calm, serious, serene. "Takes the mask off the rest . . .

"And what He let Himself in for when He came here? My goodness, Nancy. Putting Himself in our hands, knowing the end, what we would do, still do, to Him. I guess I see the end there, what it would be without Him.

"And then, knowing what we'd do, left to our own devices. What we did. And prob'ly will do again? He came anyway. And that's what it is. That's the thing we do, when we come to the monastery. Begging to experience not what *we do*, Nancy, *not* doing something that makes it about me and evicts Him and ruins everything in life, but instead coming here to experience who *He is*, what *He does* . . . Struggling to do what He did, what He's still *doing,* and finding out we can't do what He did, what

He did because that's who He *is*, finding out who we really are and who we're called to be."

A goat came to the fence. Nancy swore he was talking. "Sounds like he's drinking his own beer," Nancy said.

"Yeah, they like beer. We give it them when they're under the weather. That's Eli. He's telling me to get back to the question at hand. So, will we still be with the one we love, married, in heaven?"

Mother reminded Nancy of the story from the Gospel about the woman marrying the seven brothers. She knew the story was a dodge used by the Sadducees. They rejected the notion of resurrection because resurrection wasn't out-and-out mentioned in the Torah.

These guys were out-and-out intent on embarrassing Lord Jesus. The kind of jokers who couldn't care less about the woman or marriage or anyone but themselves.

Mother told Nancy, "They probably neglected the poor and lived like a bunch of fat cats, because far as they were concerned, this world was it." There was no accountability in the next world, because there was no next world.

"Can you picture that?" Mother said. "They got the very icon, the reality of the resurrection, standing right there in their face, in the person of Lord Jesus, telling them they're missing the point. God is the God of the living. Abraham and Moses and the patriarchs are alive in Him, so there must be life after death.

"I'll bet you two goats and a shoofly pie these Sadducees are the same bunch Master Jesus was telling about the rich man who goes to hell and that poor beggar Lazarus at the gate. And I'll bet they didn't get that either."

Mother said, "Nancy, the intimacy we had in our marriages is the measure of the union we'll know in heaven, times ten."

Mother Nikki started talking to the goat, Eli.

"Whaddaya, think, you old goat, after thirty years of marriage, we're just gonna walk up to each other in heaven, me and my David, and shake hands? 'Well, how have you been, sir?' 'Fine, thank you, Muttie. And how are you?' Doesn't make sense, does it?"

Eli knew when he was being called by name. He leaned in for Mother to scratch his back.

Mother told Eli the goat, "Now, about those who remarry . . . ? Don't know about that."

There was quiet during the evening meal in the trapeza. They were eating things from the monastery garden. Some visitors brought bluefish caught at the Jersey Shore. Nancy was surprised they served beer.

In the middle of the table was a large wooden bowl filled with crispy kettle-fried potato chips. Nancy let her pile sit. The first crunch was way too loud. Nobody looked at her, but she couldn't bring herself to do it again.

A novice from Philadelphia was reading while they ate. She had a raspy voice. Her name was Philoxenia.

Nancy knew the reading was from Genesis, about Adam and Eve. *And God blessed them, and God said to them, 'Be fruitful and multiply, and fill the earth and subdue it. Therefore a man leaves his father and his mother and cleaves to his wife, and they become one flesh.*

It made Nancy think of their wedding crowns. Harry and her.

The priest, when he removed their crowns, said, "Receive their crowns into Thy kingdom, preserving them spotless, blameless, and without reproach, unto ages of ages."

The next week, when they came to church, the priest held their crowns and prayed, "Preserve their union indissoluble, that they may evermore give thanks unto Thine all-holy name, of the Father and of the Son and of the Holy Spirit: now and ever, and unto ages of ages. Amen."

They were in a frame, the indissoluble crowns, their crowns, over their bed.

Sometimes in the night she swore the crowns came alive and she could reach out and touch him across the space. And sometimes in the morning Nancy had experienced her answer.

Driving home she was pretty sure she understood why Mother Nikki asked a blessing to remain Apostolnik.

Mother told her, "What part of the sacrament of marriage we're able to preserve here, by His grace, will be preserved and completed there, in Him. Remember, the one who has been faithful over little . . ."

Nancy knew what the Master said. *He who is faithful in a very little thing is faithful also in much.*

"I'm the child who committed the unforgivable," Mother Nikki said. "And I've come to die here, begging." She stopped for a moment and then said, almost to herself, "There must be more, Nancy. I have to hope . . . There must be more.

"I have to hope that everything about our marriage and my behavior in it, everything that was strictly earthly in me, in my faith or lack of it, will pass away, and only love, our love, perfected in Him, will remain."

Made Nancy smile. A little less nervous going through the Blue Mountain Tunnel on the way home. She hated tunnels.

Actually laughed a little, Nancy, remembering Mother Nikki telling her, "Nancy, Liebchen, think you could call me Hannah once in a while, if you come back?" Had that Amish farmer's tree-of-life green-eyed happiness when she looked at Nancy. "*Vas sagst du*? Call me Hannah, just when we're alone, me, you, and the goats?"

The Day Will Come

I GUESS WE ALWAYS KNEW the day would come.

I knew how much it hurt him when he said, "I'm so sorry, sugar, that I can't walk you home."

In our neighborhood a guy didn't let a girl walk home alone. Just wasn't done.

I remember the first time I saw him. It was at church. The Liturgy was ending. I went with my mother to venerate the cross and receive God's blessing by the priest.

He was with his mother too. Not too many guys did that.

The thing I liked about him was the way he smiled at my younger brother and sister, the twins. We were in line in front of him waiting to receive the nafora. The twins, maybe three or four at the time, kept turning around and laughing.

He had long hair then and a lot of it. He was making funny faces and playing with the kids.

My mother turned and scolded him, "Not in church." She was stern. And in our language, too.

I liked it that, even if he didn't know the words, he understood what she was saying, and he respected my mother. But he must have understood. He called her Nunna and apologized in our language.

I took the twins in hand. Father Naum told the twins, "Watch." And he kissed the blessing cross. Then he said, "Now you." And Naum made a big smooching sound as my little brother, Winnie, kissed the cross. "And you." And he made the sound again when my little sister, Samantha, kissed it. They loved it.

Naum used to say, "When I was a boy, our teacher, Isabelle, used to tell us we must love our church. And it starts when we're young. So the priest has to find some way to engender in our young people a deep love for Jesus Christ and do everything he can to instill in God's people a true love for His Church."

Naum the priest thanked my mother for bringing the kids. He told the twins, "Put out both hands." Their chubby little hands. He filled each one's cupped hands with the nafora.

The polite boy behind me with the long hair said, "Doesn't get any better."

I think we were the same age.

Our mothers were by the coffee urn in the hall, watching us at our separate tables. They were whispering to each other. Then his mother came to him and said, "Go to Mrs. Llamba and ask her if you can bring her a couple of kurabia cookies."

He said, "Okay, mom."

She told him, "And don't forget, three times."

His mother, Evdokia, knew my mother would say "No, thank you" the first two times. I don't know why the old ones did that, but they did. Good hospitality among the Albanians said you must ask three times even if they refuse the first two.

"You sure?" the boy with the long hair said.

My mother said, "I'm sure, but thank you."

The young man said, "Please, just one cookie, Nunna, so Ramona doesn't feel bad. She's the one made them today."

We all knew Ramona and Bernice made the best kurabia in the parish.

"Oh, okay," my mother said. "Maybe a small one. I don't want to hurt Bernice or Ramona."

My mother smiled and took two kurabia from the young man. She said, "You're Llamba and Theofan's son. What's your name?"

He said, "John."

My mother motioned to me. "Emilia."

I told the twins to stay put. I had them busy scribbling with crayons at the table. When I came to my mother she said, "Emilia, this nice boy is named John. He brought me a kurabia. Go ask his mother if she'll come and sit with us for coffee."

And before she could tell me, I said, "I know, Mama, three times."

We didn't live far from the church. None of us did, really. Maybe a short trolley ride for some, but most of us lived close enough to hear the bell. John asked my mother if he could walk me home.

"Sure," she said, and our two old nunnas walked half a block behind us, occasionally calling out, "Slow down and stay where we can see you so you don't get lost."

The twins were between us, all of us holding hands. Old man George going by on his huckster wagon had that mischief in his eyes only uncles have. He teased us in a way so pleasant and full of the opposite. "No holding hands."

John stuck out his tongue, and the twins did too.

I scolded them. "Don't do that, you two." I guess I'm like my mother.

John said, "Ah, Emmy."

"Don't ever call me that, ever."

He just looked.

I said, "I hate it."

He smiled. "Emilia—Emilia—Emilia." And each time he said my name, he kissed my hand. "So I won't forget," he said.

We lived on Hewson Street right off Tulip. That was the first time my John walked me to my door. And I'm pretty sure he would have kissed my lips right there in front of our tiny two-story brick row home if our mothers hadn't turned the corner and started waving and calling like they hadn't seen us just minutes before.

You should've seen the two of them on our wedding day.

Something about our mothers back then, when they got dressed up for happy things, reminds me of the colors in the stands at the Ninth Street Produce Market when the Amish farmers bring everything fresh and shining like field gems in the sun.

NOW WHEN I LIE IN BED just before drifting off, lulled by his breathing, trying to weave wisps of memory into a picture of our wedding day, it's almost like looking up into the sky and seeing a bird fly by. Like a faraway image from another time that passes too quickly. Like a dream dreamed by some other person from another time.

And then the nurse comes in.

It's the middle of the night. The monitors are beeping. Digital zigzag blue lines are dancing over my eyelids and across the LED display.

I'm not in my bed.

I sit up in the chair. I feel like a person shocked by a taser. My mouth is dry, and I can taste my own tongue. I say, "Thank you, nurse."

I wonder if she knows I'm thanking her for not turning up the lights too bright.

The way she says, "You're welcome, sweetie," I know she knows.

My eyes are slits. I never thought a person could cry so much their eyeballs would hurt. I always thought there had to come a time when there'd be no more tears. But I was wrong.

Just a few days ago, my boy tried to be brave when the priest came. Maybe because Maureen our daughter was there.

He sat up. He made the cross. He confessed right there in front of me and Maureen. He said to Naum, "We never had secrets."

Somehow the Trisagion Prayers and especially the Lord's Prayer went to a depth in me I didn't know was there and took on a meaning they never had before. They made me swallow any useless words my head might have tried to put on my tongue. I didn't know what to do with *Thy will be done* . . . I had to just let it be and leave it at that.

John told Naum, "You know we never missed a Sunday."

The priest moved the water cup, the newspapers and the pills, the graham-cracker packets, and the TV remote. He began setting up communion on the bedside table. He wiped the table with a disinfectant baby wipe and spread a red cloth.

Naum unpacked the communion kit his mother had given him

when he was ordained. We remembered Naum's mother. She'd been gone now more than thirty years.

The mini church in the middle of the red cloth. Eight inches high, four inches wide, and three inches deep. Plated in gold and topped with a Byzantine cross. A long gold chain was attached on either side of the golden box. The door opened in the front like a perfect miniature church building.

He took a small chalice from an interior recess and a spoon to scale from a special holder on the inside back of the door. Naum the priest removed a small lidded box from above the chalice recess. It contained the bread of Holy Communion. A small vial from another recess contained the wine. Another vial held anointing oil.

We stood either side of the bed and held the Bible open on John's head while Naum prayed.

Naum did not light a candle or the charcoal for the small hand censer. He told John, "I did that once."

John said, "Yeah, I heard about it. Set off the alarms, and the fire company came in their helmets, raincoats, boots, axes, and all, didn't they? I remember Joey Berati's family telling about that."

It was the first time in a long time I'd seen John smile.

Naum asked, "Shall I close the door?"

John looked out into the hospital hallway and said "No."

The hand cross was on one side of the little church. The Gospel book on the other. Naum opened the Priest's Prayer Book of Needs. He blessed the epitrachelion and placed it around his neck.

The one thing that was needed was placed in the chalice; warm water was added with the wine.

When she saw Naum in his cassock and beard, the nurse who had been so good to my John came in and asked if she could stay.

John looked at me . . . What? As if I would say no.

I said, "Sure, honey."

Naum went to the man in the other bed, introduced himself, and asked his name. Naum said, "Mind if we say a little prayer, Mister Gold? I promise we won't be long or loud."

Leonard Gold, the man there in the other bed, said, "I don't mind at all, Father. And say a prayer for me too, please. I need all the prayer I can get."

And the six of us brought together somehow, that day at that hour in that room, prayed.

John talked as Father was packing up. Father Naum listened.

John said, "Father, here's the best part of this short story. The Mother of God must've looked down on Fishtown one day, saw me at the putty factory, and said, 'Here's a decent guy with need of direction,' and sent Emilia to me. Never has there been a greater need fulfilled. She has guided me. Protected me from my own impulsive stupidity and given me all the love I required, our Maureen and then some. How could a guy like me ask for more, Urata? I'm blessed."

After the priest left, Maureen went home, and we held hands, like when we were kids. We were quiet for a while, and then in a sort of whisper he said, "Well, sugar, not long now and off I go, into a far better place."

When I told him, "John, don't talk like that."

He said, "Jesus said He goes ahead to get a place ready so we can be with Him. I'm just trying to take care of the gift He gave me, girl." Then he kissed my hand each time he said my name. "Emilia. Emilia. Emilia."

I don't know if it was the Holy Communion that initiated my John's . . . I don't know what to call it, his transition, or what the priest said, translation? The beginning of his leaving me. The beginning of his suffering.

At one point John was squeezing my hand so hard, telling me, "I didn't know a human body could feel so much pain."

But I do know I never left that room in those last hours. Not even to eat.

The nurses must have . . . I think about it now. I must have been driving them crazy. Running out in the hall every time one of the beepers went off. Brushing back his hair. Talking to him. Singing to him. Kissing him over and over again. Constantly straightening or trying to straighten the sheets. Cleaning him and changing the bedclothes myself. Propping up those damn pillows till I just didn't know where I was going to get the strength to move him one more time.

But nothing I could do could comfort my boy. There were times when he seemed angry or annoyed with me, even though I know it was the pain talking. Still somehow it hurt.

When John stopped eating, and they came in and told me his organs were shutting down, and his breathing got to a point where every breath sounded like it could be his last . . .

If he settled down for a bit when daylight was coming in the window, if his breathing evened out and his moaning leveled off, I guess that's when I fell asleep in the chair, drifting off, lulled by his breathing, trying to weave the wisps of memory into a picture of our wedding day.

It was almost as if I was floating up into the sky and looking down on a dream from another time, a dream dreamed by some other person.

And then the nurse came in.

It was the middle of the morning. The monitors had stopped beeping. Digital zigzag blue lines were bouncing reflections dancing over my John and across the LED display.

He was twisting himself like wringing out a rag. But not a sound. Like *he* was trying not to worry *me.* Struggling and kicking against something only he could see. Whispering, "Nunna. *A je ketu*?" Are you here?

It slowly came to me. I was not in my bed. I sat up in the chair like a person tasered by a cattle prod. My mouth was dry, and I could taste my tongue. I got close to my honey and I said his name, "John."

The nurse was standing very still. There was nothing more to be done. The way she said, "Stay with him," I knew she knew.

I guess we always knew the day would come.

He pulled me close. I put my ear to his lips. I knew how much it hurt him when he said, "I'm so sorry, my sugar, that I can't walk you home."

In our neighborhood a guy didn't let a girl walk home alone. Just wasn't done.

THEN WE WERE AT CHURCH. Together again. Me and my John.

I was shivering so bad that morning. Maureen, brokenhearted, close on one side trying to warm me. She said, "Mom, he was the best father." What more could a man want to hear?

The twins, Winnie and Samantha, all grown with families of their own, were on the other side.

The only thing I remember is when I gave my John our last kiss and how I couldn't stop brushing back his hair and touching his face and kissing his hands.

The priest was censing and someone was chanting the prayer.

When you see me lying speechless, breathless, lifeless before you . . .
Come and weep over me, brethren, friends, sisters, relatives, and cousins of mine . . .
For yesterday with you I was conversing, but the hour of death came upon me all of a sudden . . .
Come now, all my friends who have loved me and held me dear, and give me your last farewell kiss . . .

I guess we always knew the day would come. And I swear I could hear him saying, "I'm so sorry, sugar, that I can't walk you home."

And all I remember thinking is, I wanted to get in that box and go with him.

Two to a Pew

NAUM DECIDED IT WOULD DO HIM GOOD to visit Marion and Dean.

His cassock kept reminding him his pocket had something it wasn't used to carrying around. Five one-hundred-dollar bills.

Jack's American wife, Rita, got tired of Jack's old-world ways. She cleared out all Jack's junk, called the Salvation Army and Naum the priest. Blonde-haired Rita got herself a lawyer and told her slum-lord property-millionaire husband to pack his bags and hit the bricks. Spying on tenant girls through peepholes didn't fly in any world, old or new.

"I kept these back for you," she told Naum. A closet load of permanent press polyester golf pants custom-hemmed for her four-foot-eleven overweight husband. The whole neighborhood knew Jacob Yaqif, who called himself Jack Standing. And they knew the dude never got close enough to a golf course to tell a fairway green from a rough hazard tee.

Naum felt like he couldn't refuse the pants. He felt bad enough turning down Jacob's golf shoes. But even Rita could see the shoes were two sizes too big for Naum.

Dean Antonucci was a printer. Naum pictured himself

walking into Dean's shop, popping out the hundreds, and asking Dean, "Think we could print a couple a hundred of these?"

Tall, thin Dean. Blue printer's overalls. Mustache thick and dark. Had that year-round tan. The man loved a good joke. Would've told Naum he had a premonition Naum and the FBI were gonna be spending some quality time together, soon. Turns out Dean wasn't wrong.

Dean the printer said, "How about instead I just do your usual weekly bulletins?"

Marion Tiller worked in the Fishtown Savings and Loan across from Pastor Cal's Holy Communion Protestant Church. Naum figured she probably handled hundreds all day long.

Took him back to the time he had to supplement his parish stipend. Snuck out of the putty factory at lunch break and tried to get his paycheck cashed before the break bell rang. That's when he first met Marion. Naum standing in that long lunchtime line. The short blonde teller telling Naum when he finally got up to her window, kinda calm too, "I've just been robbed."

After an hour and a half locked in the bank with everyone else who was a potential witness and Naum telling the FBI lady, "I'm gonna lose my job on the loading dock," he finally got back and the boss said, "Where the hell you been?"

"The john."

"Eating at that Puerto Rican place again, ain'tcha? Don't deny it. I can smell the garlic."

Naum said, "Si. Mofongo."

"Well, you eat that mush, you deserve spending lunch in the can. Get back to work," the boss said. "And speak English." And that was that.

Reading Naum's weekly bulletin, Dean said, "Can I keep one?" Was how the printer decided he and Marion should take off one Sunday from their parish and check out our little Saint Alexander the Whirling Dervish Orthodox Church.

The Orthodox weekly bulletins printed at Dean's were filled with parish news, social happenings, fundraising events, birthdays, anniversaries, graduation news, items of ethnic interest—but the back page?

Weekly scripture readings, saints of the day, and short articles about how to live the life in Christ in modern America in an Orthodox manner. Naum knew Americans weren't gonna sit still for the history of the watch when they asked the time.

"Concise and enticing." The kind of answers Naum said we needed in our outreach toolbox.

Dean had been reading the back page, and Marion too. The printer produced a stack, a year's worth, and said to Naum, "Marion and I come . . . think we could talk with you after?"

He told Naum they read and reread the articles, and one in particular . . .

It was a quote from Metropolitan Anthony Bloom that talked about marriage. About how the inner essence of a relationship was what mattered, regardless of the external forms.

Sat that first time toward the back, Marion, Dean, and the twins, bulletin folded open to the marriage quote, one row from the icon of Saint Matrona the Blind of Moscow. No regular sat there, so it ended up being their spot.

Doesn't take long, does it, for a pew to take on the print of the person or family and make them its own? Even years after they're gone, folks still point and say, "Well, you know, over near where Llamba used to sit and pray."

Marion and Dean got adopted by that pew.
Positioned with a purpose
The pew made them feel
They'd come home
Introduced them
To a different vantage point
Permitted them
A new view
Presented in perfectly
Parceled portions
Of strange and familiar
Asymmetrical symbols
Whispering
What it means
To be called
Together to life
By the Being
Who inhabits eternity
Who unites
Time and eternity
Past and future
In His ever-present
Liturgical space and time
Perfectly positioned
That welcoming pew
Till trouble slid into the pew behind.
Turns out Marion had an ex named Cy.

Cy told Naum, "Yeah, my twins told me their mom was checking out the Orthodox . . . Ya wanna hear a funny coincidence . . ."

Cyrus Tiller. Neighborhood cob-head. Corn silk brown-tipped wild crop out the top. Man so annoying made you wanna husk his head.

Cy Tiller told Naum it was mostly her fault, Marion. "Yeah, she looks good. Beautiful girl, Marion. Inviting as a well-built fireplace and just as passive. Know what I mean? You don't have to guess who had to get the kindling and start the fire. Every time. Didn't matter to her either way. She told me early on she could take it or leave it. Whatever you want, she'd say. Left it all to me. I should've paid attention when I asked her about her fantasy and she said she didn't have any. After a while I got tired of being the only one interested in heating things up.

"Course I did what she said I did with the girl from the bakery. Miranda. I mean, you seen her, right? What man wouldn't? Besides, what Marion's doing now is going against the Bible. Ain't that say she's gotta wait, at least till the divorce comes through?"

Naum liked Cyrus Tiller. He didn't know why. He just did. He asked him, "I'm curious, Cyrus, where you getting this? About women and the Bible. This something you really think or something you heard somewhere?"

Growing up in the neighborhood and knowing the Tiller clan, Naum was pretty sure Cy Tiller never had a chance far as knowing God went. Cy probably knew the rules. With his father? No doubt about that. The man had a belt well known to his kids . . . and his wife. But relationship? The Tiller kids got sent to Sunday school at the end of a threat. Old man Tiller spent six days a week in the funnel pit at the putty factory and wanted to sleep on Sunday morning. His belt hanging at the bottom of the banister was a sign to the kids and Hilla, his wife, to get the hell out of the house.

Cyrus said, "I been watching YouTube videos on an app from Shadrach Jackson."

Naum knew Reverend Jackson. Everybody knew Shadrach Jackson from the local clergy breakfast.

Naum said, "Cy . . ." like, C'mon, man . . . They both knew the deal.

Some people pretended they didn't know YouTube Jackson was really Georgie Frascati, who sold Pontiacs during the week up at a dealer near Liberty Bell Racetrack. Said the Bible gave its blessing for him to have more than one wife at a time, and only the man could say when it was time for a divorce.

"Cyrus, you believe that?"

Cyrus couldn't look Naum in the eye. He said, "Okay. You got me. I just love her is all." And the man started to cry.

Naum didn't know what to say.

Cyrus said, "I messed up and I wanna try to get her back."

DEAN HAD NEVER MARRIED. His family knew they were dating. Their son was ten years younger than the blonde woman with the twin boys. His mother told him she was putting an extra yogurt in his lunch and said she hoped he had sense enough not to do anything foolish and wished he'd stop snacking between meals. "Just because things look good don't mean they're *good* for you. Just because they're in front of you doesn't mean you have to eat them."

Dean didn't like yogurt. He gave it to the kid who apprenticed in his shop. It made him feel good, mom thinking he was eating healthy.

Dean didn't do good with innuendo.

Marion knew what was what. She wasn't surprised when his family called in the lease on his shop and cut him off.

Dean Antonucci had an easy smile. Relaxed. He said, "Well, we'll find a way."

Naum asked Walter in the payroll office if he had any work. Walter told Naum, "Send him over."

Marion was a serious lady. "I'm of two minds with that, Dean. You, in the putty factory?" She knew it was a rough crowd. She couldn't picture Dean six days a week soaking up that dead-end dog-eat-dog. "But half a loaf of bread," she said, "I guess is better than no loaf."

That intense, Marion. During their year and a half as catechumens. It was Marion. All Marion and her job at the bank who bore the pressure of the monthly bills after Dean's family cut them off. Marion's overtime that paid the rent on the six-room house on Crease Street.

Day to day, no time for the fantasies of men who didn't pull their weight or pay their child support. Marion who read her boys Bible stories and made sure they were early for every service and seated together in Saint Matrona's pew.

They had a few months before being received into the Orthodox Church, and Marion told Naum, "Shrinking finances on Crease Street aren't making things any easier. But that aside . . ."

Marion had a list for Naum.

Communion

Bible

Baptism

Church authority

The Virgin Mary

Marriage

Annulment

Divorce

Marion wanted answers. Her drawer at the bank reconciled every night to the penny. Accounts had to balance.

RIBBONED WREATHS ON FRONT DOORS down Crease Street glittered with Christmas lights framing windows from the pavement-level cellar panes to the rooftop attic rounds. It made the two- and three-story row homes look like gift boxes wrapped in brick.

Outside, it was getting dark. Naum could smell snow in the air, and he could hear Marion's boys laughing when he stopped.

Dean opened the door he said, "Mar' . . . the priest is here."

"Boys, go in your room," Marion said. "You can play your video games till I call you."

Naum liked the toast and jelly. Dean said he baked the bread.

"I can tell," Naum said.

"Got the recipe from one of your church ladies," Dean said. "Mrs. Elias."

Naum said, "She taught me too."

Green tea, matcha? Even with honey . . . Naum asked for a glass of water.

It was close to two hours around the kitchen table before he finished writing notes on a napkin and left. They covered everything on Marion's list. Communion. The Bible. Baptism. Church authority. The Virgin Mary. Marriage. Annulment. Divorce.

Marion and Dean had one last question. "Marriage?"

Naum said, "We'll talk to the bishop. After chrismation. I'm sure there's a way."

Marion wanted to ask about Cyrus. Every Sunday, leaning over Saint Matrona's pew, messing with the twins.

Naum said, "I told him, if he's serious about being enrolled as a catechumen, we have a rule. Unless it's a family, it's two to a pew. Can't have one person taking up an entire row. I know he knew what I was doing. Cyrus ain't dumb. I spent a lot of time with the man. He's hurting too. I've known the Tillers a long time. I can't lie. I like Cy. Truthfully, they remind me of my own family. When I told him go see Father Zaza, he's better at dealing with what you're dealing with. Attend over at his church. Cy shrugged and said he got it. Said, 'No problem, Padre.'"

Marion said, "You think he'll go all the way out there? Cyrus?"

Naum said, "Somebody gave this to me. It's for you."

Five new one-hundred-dollar bills out of his cassock, on the coffee table.

Snow was coming down pretty good when they walked Naum to the door. His pocket full of nafora crumbs was asking him, "Now where're ya gonna get your bulletins printed?"

The Mouse

NONE OF THE FOUR BOYS was more than ten. They were chasing a baby mouse through Saint Alexander the Whirling Dervish Orthodox Church early Sunday before Liturgy.

Later, when Isaiah, Ezra, Julian, and Noah related the adventure to Father Naum and showed him the coffee can, the baby mouse had grown into a waddling capybara-sized rodent with a belly that dragged over the ambon and across the solea, whiskers scraping on the floor.

"Like a catfish," Ezra said, "with a shiny coat."

Julian was the youngest, maybe six. He said, "How's a thing so big fit in that can?"

Blond-haired Julian, the son of Michael, our choir director, was tempted and terrified, all at the same time, to tilt the container and see just how much of his imagination fit under the old coffee can.

Naum wondered how the boys would have felt about the canon forbidding dogs but permitting cats in the church.

The non-canonical mouse skittering around the circumference of the inverted coffee can had already lost their interest. They were on to other subjects, fighter planes, sailing ships . . . Are seahorses fish? Would you let a girl kiss you?

Isaiah and Ezra were the sons of our Protodeacon Dionysios. Both had dark hair and long eyelashes, like their mother.

Their father, straight, tall, by-the-book Deacon Dionysios, had a voice like a lion with hair and a beard to match.

His petite wife, Elizaveta, brought natural sea sponges to be soaked in water, wrung out, frozen, and then thinly sliced and ironed flat for use on the antimension. The boys agreed that sponges looked like brains.

"You guys know where sponges come from?" Father Naum asked the boys as they stood around the throne, what others call the altar.

"Yep," Ezra offered. "Bed, Bath, and Beyond."

"What is this?" Naum unfolded the cloth on the altar table.

Two large rectangles of cloth, one lying flat inside the other, the inner one a little smaller than the outer one. The large, lustrous outer cloth on the bottom was a rich, silky royal purple. "Boys, this is called an *eileton*. It means *wrapped* or *folded*."

The slightly smaller one sitting on top, within the larger royal purple rectangle, was made of creamy linen. Naum said, "This one is called the *antimension*. It means *instead of the table*."

Six-year-old Julian had to stand on a wooden stool to see. He looked at the smaller one, the creamy-colored inner cloth made of linen. He said, "It has a picture on it."

"Very good, Julian," Naum said. "Anything else?"

The little boy studied it for a moment, serious and careful, for a six-year-old. "Jesus is there. He's laying down. His mommy is holding him. His eyes are closed."

Then he stopped. We all knew Julian had lost his mom. He was there when she died.

In almost a whisper he finally said, "I don't know the other people."

Mother and child
Walking along
On a warm autumn afternoon
The first and most intimate of communities
Julian and Mommy
Chattering away the city blocks
Strolling
Happy talk
Giggling nonsense
Laughing out loud
Playing silly
Holding hands
Hold my hand, Mommy
Him
With his little-boy backpack
Full of little-boy treasures
Tonight's supper in her shopping bag
Almost home
The woman texting in her car
Oblivious to the curve
Mommy bent down
Kissing her squirming boy
Dabbing his face
Tucking away the handkerchief
She'd touched to her tongue

Her boy
Less than a step
Ahead
Alicia, his mother
Julian bent to examine a ladybug
Scraped raw
Forehead to feet
Dragged forward
Along the stone-embedded cement sidewalk
Enclosed in the protective shelter of her body above
Four
The boy was four at the time

How our choir director, Michael, stood and sang for her funeral in his gray cassock. His long hair and beard suddenly gone white.

And tears
Endless tears

Fell soft and silent as rain falling from the wide-eyed sky into the sprout-green grass of a springtime field, eyes never leaving his Alicia in her coffin.

Julian tucked in at the feet of his father like a baby penguin, hands lifted to his father's embrace.

Our parish community, the whole neighborhood, the entire sad-eyed city, all in mourning, "How?"

"Like a man with no choice but to walk on," was Michael's answer. "Me and my Julian, head down, together through a snow squall."

Julian on his stool in the altar every Sunday was a scandal to the rigorist accuser in Naum's head. Somebody told Naum,

"Those who seek scandal will be scandalized. Rigor will set in on the rigorist, and blasphemy will overtake the one who cries out blasphemy."

Naum would drape an old piece of vestment cloth around the little boy's shoulders, and Julian would stand on his stool at the side of the table and say he was learning to be a priest. His finger would beckon Naum to lean in close during the antiphons, and he would whisper with a smile, "Do you see my mother?" Both of them nodding through their tears.

Our parents in the Garden encompassed the entire communion of God's universe in their bodies. Children injured at a young age often retain the noetic senses we all knew in Paradise. Over time, these perceptive *organs of the Garden* atrophy, and the gift of loving communication fades. Our natural sensitivity to life as relationship coarsens, and we begin to see only the boundaries of our ego.

One Sunday his father, Michael, came apologizing to Naum. Julian had smeared a black beard on his face.

Julian whispered to Naum, "I had to lick a jelly bean. Priests have a beard and a mustache. But don't worry, Father, I can still receive. I only licked it. I didn't eat it."

Later in the Liturgy, just before the anaphora, Julian said, "She's smiling at me."

"She loves ya, kid," Naum said.

Julian said, "Daddy too."

Julian, who whispered a hundred questions and comments at each Liturgy, pointed to the antimension Naum was showing and said to the other boys, "There's a relic."

"What's a relic?" Naum said.

"Something from the saints," Julian said.

Naum was surprised Julian knew. "Where's the relic?"

"That lump—" Julian pointed to the antimension again— "in the middle."

"Do you know why it's sewn in there?" Naum asked.

"Something to remember how special they were. My father told me we can't let the devil even have a little bit of Mommy, not even dust from her shoes. It's all God's. That's why we keep my mommy's things, to remember her. You know he kisses her shoes? And I can smell her, and, and, and . . ."

When Julian got excited it all came out in a stutter, like he was remembering something he knew that none of us wanted to think about. Dealing with what he had to deal with. The kid was more of a realist than most of us at the parish.

He told Naum, "And that lump's a relic so we remember our saints and so they remember us."

My mommy remembers me, is one of the things he would repeatedly whisper to Naum during every Liturgy. He carried her handkerchief in his pocket, and at different times during the Liturgy—Naum never knew why or when—he'd take it out, close his eyes, and open it over his face.

"How do you know all this, Julian?"

Julian got that little-boy smile. He said to Naum, "You're silly."

When Julian saw Naum didn't know what to say, he said, "You know too much, Father."

Naum said, "Is that why my head hurts?"

Julian waved his hand, like *yes, silly*.

He got down off his stool, stood, hands lifted in appeal, with his shoulders in a shrug, and said, "I- I- I- I knew Larissa at school, but she knew me first. I gave her a flower and she tried to kiss me."

Julian the innocent. Julian missing teeth. Julian unaware of the irresistible effect added to his words by the unpretentious stutter and his little-kid lisp.

Sadness, a kind of weary resignation, a hopeful longing deep in the reflective mirror of Julian's "I'm sorry for *you*" blue eyes.

Julian scraped raw

Protected even now by his mother

Smiling and impervious

By reason of his *experience over explanation*

Immune to

Every kind and well-meaning adult attempt at explanation

Quotes of well-meaning biblical comforters

It's-part-of-life-God-has-a-plan evolutionists

And all the other well-intentioned offers of endless dead-end rationalizations big people offer like store-bought flowers severed from their root

All dying to avoid having to deal with

Julian looking out from unblinking eyes, eyes permanently injured before their time, saying, "It's okay, flowers are pretty like Larissa."

Maybe flowers are like a kiss . . .

Naum said, "Did you let Larissa kiss you?"

Julian said, "You're silly."

The priest looked at the boy.

In time Julian would forget everything he *didn't* know and become educated like the rest of us.

Greta, Naum's wife, said, "We are silly. Aren't we? We do know too much."

Priests and all those serving close to human suffering
Every marriage
Every conception
Every miscarriage
Every birth and baptism
Every nursing home visit or hospital call
Every terminal diagnosis
With every family
Alzheimer's
Birth defects
Mental illness
Cardiac or cancer
Every divorce
Addiction
Paralysis
Or death that reduces us to childlike helplessness
Resounds for the priest with the words of the Word.
These things I have spoken to you, so that in Me you may have peace. In the world you have tribulation, but take courage; I have overcome the world.

The priest Naum and the boy Julian looked at one another across the space of the altar. One of them was learning to be a priest.

After Liturgy, the boys debated around the coffee can, what to do with the shivering creature inside?

The consensus, as Naum overheard it . . . Life was God's. Only He could make it, and only He could take it.

"Some men killed Jesus," Noah said.

"We don't like that," Ezra said.

Out the door the noisy synod ran to set the beggar free.

Naum watched.

So what if they didn't know about sponge divers in Tarpon Springs with colorful boats called Saint Nicholas or Saint Panteleimon? They had no doubt about the goodness and the source of living things.

Naum always said, "Good parents inoculate, they don't isolate."

Naum collected wood and kindling all through the week and set it on fire right in front of us every Sunday.

"A small exposure, given by the parents to the child, of the world's negative icons—faithlessness, lust of power, pornography, economic injustice, racial inequity, religious hatred, judgment—a small exposure to these evils in controlled doses imparts the necessary antidote to the child. As long as we are careful to introduce the opposing eucharistic truth of being as communion in Christ, healthy, living icons—love of God and neighbor, wisdom, equity, justice, compassion, giving, sacrifice, good role models at home and here in our church.

"We can only protect our young ones from the toxins of the world for so long, from the truth that *Death has climbed in through our windows to cut down our children in the streets*. But if inoculated, first at home and then in church, with whole and healthy icons—icons that indicate the truth of eucharistic being in Jesus Christ . . ."

Each one of us sat there thinking Naum was looking straight at us.

"Icons of Christlike behavior, of relations . . . Olfactory icons, gustatory ones, auditory, tactile, vestibular, visual . . . Attitudinal icons concerning others, sexual health, icons of racial and economic equity, icons of loving response to difficult people and situations . . .

"If we can show them the world and creation as icons of the heavenly, the iconographic truth that all creation is God's and is meant to be cared for, shared, and offered in eucharistic love . . . then when confronted with the unthinkable—" Naum looked at Julian, Michael kissing the head of the child in his arms. "Then our young, having been inoculated with holy and healthy examples, will have living within their being the wherewithal, the antidote, to resist those things that lead to egocentric isolation, to dissolution, fragmentation, divided tribes, hopelessness, despair, and death."

Julian and the boys were sitting in the front row, holding onto the coffee can for dear life.

Naum was looking at them. He said, "And then our kids will have no doubt in the depths of their being that being itself is life, and life is communion, and communion is the living Icon and Presence of Christ Jesus, our Lord, God, and Savior."

Then Naum looked at the fathers and quoted, "Fathers, do not provoke your children to anger, but bring them up in the discipline and instruction of the Lord."

And to the mothers, Naum said, "The heart of the mother is the school of the child."

Then he quoted Julian, "My mommy remembers me . . ."

And that was all poor old Naum could say.

Three Red Lights

THE SUN DID MAKE AN ATTEMPT that morning when Naum was supposed to be downtown for a baptism. But it never did show its face. That time of year it rarely does. We go months with no blue skies.

The old priest saying his prayers on the landing in front of the doors of our Fishtown parish. The Sunday before, a guy they call Tiny the Russian Horse, visiting from Florida, got so mad at Little Harry from the junkyard for towing his car, he crushed Naum's church key in the palm of his hand. Naum had asked Tiny to lock up.

Now Naum was shiver-stepping foot to foot in front of the cold locked doors.

O compassionate and merciful God, who triest the heart . . .
Sanctify me wholly by Thine all-perfect, invisible might, and by Thy spiritual right hand, lest, while I proclaim liberty unto others and administer this rite with perfect faith in Thine unutterable love toward mankind, I myself may become the base slave of sin.

When he looked up, there facing him on the bottom step was a single crow, black eyes tacked on Naum. A second crow appeared, and before Naum could think what it meant, a third bird meandered out of the morning into middle position, shoulder to shoulder, wing to wing, like monks at a psalti stand.

Naum said, “Probably don’t mean nothing.”

Edgar Allan Poe’s house was all the way down at Seventh and Spring Garden. Probably nothing to that either. Still, it wasn’t a usual thing in the neighborhood, was it?

He shrugged it off. “Crows do what crows do.”

Naum tried to pray again. He looked up. All three birds black-eyed on Naum. All three eyelids on each bird open. Three beaks. No clicks. No caws. Not a subsong sound. Translucent black slicked-back feather-tucked wings. Six crows’ feet in a row.

If he’da hada soft pretzel or something he’da fed ’em.

When Naum finished praying, he said to the choir, “You guys can go now.”

Down the alley next to Donahue’s Funeral Parlor, the alley where they roll the caskets out to Palmer Burial Ground . . . crows walking.

Anything else that morning? Naum wasn’t sure. All he knew was, he was covering a baptism for Father Nigel. A baptism at our downtown sister church, Saint Christos the Gardener. Saint Christos was born in Permet, Albania, same town as Nicky Zeo’s father.

Naum rolling in his slow-moving ’66 lemon-yellow Chevy Impala beater. Nobody letting him move to the right lane. He overshot his exit off I-95 and ended up coming off the highway too far south. Traffic was the usual crunch once he got over to Sixteenth Street heading toward the church. Downtown Philly streets were not made for cars.

On icy gray mornings when the sky folds its arms and can't make up its mind whether it wants to snow or sleet, crowds of truth-or-dare pedestrians tilt their umbrellas, pull their scarves up over their noses, yank their beanies down over their ears, and play blindman's buff, sliding over the slippery colonial cobblestones, darting in the drizzle from between parked cars like ducks who don't care.

Naum didn't think much of it when the guy behind him in the black Escalade started laying on the horn. Blinking his high beams and revving his engine at every corner light. One of two things, Naum figured. Either *he* was driving slower, or this guy behind him and everybody else was speeding up. But in the bumper-to-bumper traffic, wasn't anybody going further or faster than two inches at a time. Unless their car sprouted wings.

In his rearview, Naum could see the man in the Escalade. Full head of silver hair. Suit and tie. Banging the steering wheel. Steaming up the windshield with curses out the moon roof. People on the pavement panicking.

After half an hour of inching along, Naum figured he was maybe three lights away from Saint Christos. With any luck, maybe he'd make a few and not get caught at every light. Cars were grinding gears and wearing out their brake lights. The column of vehicles took forever to reach a corner. Old ladies with canes were making better time under their umbrellas. It would have been faster to park and get out and walk. If you could find a place to park.

Each city block stretched four or five hundred feet, and sometimes the light at the corner up ahead cycled from green to yellow to red three or four times before Naum reached the intersection

. . . Arrived just missing the green and had to sit through another cycle of the same, yellow, red . . .

Sitting at red light number one in his rusty-bottom Impala, Naum was sizing up the food cart grilling sausages on the corner. It was like he could taste them on the air. Suburban train commuters were snaking out of the underground, lured by the aroma, queuing up for a breakfast sandwich on a toasted crusty roll. Naum was salivating sausage and peppers with extra onions.

Even if you could find a place to pull over, Naum . . . The fast before the baptism.

Between wiper swipes, the light cycled green.

Inching up on the Starbucks at Walnut Street at the next intersection, and he caught red light number two.

Something about coffee. Even if you don't like the taste. Nothing smells like coffee in the morning. A coffee'd be nice right now.

Naum used to have coffee right there at that same Starbucks with his friend Betim. Betim'd been gone a long time now. Naum remembered when he was invited to serve at Saint Christos for the funeral of his friend. Naum loved Betim. Betim Besmir.

He'd known Betim a long time. Often heard his confession. Strong, solid Betim. Man was a World War II hero. Got a medal and everything. Lost a baby son early in his marriage. His wife, Spresha, her name means *Hope*, had a different kind of hope after they lost that baby boy. Not easy. Chronic hurt flowing in every capillary and vein. An understandable melancholy. Spresha. Betim. Lots of people walking around with a wound only heaven can heal.

But the puzzle that puzzled Betim, the thing he confessed again and again, lived with, waking and sleeping, the ache that just wouldn't stop aching, was the Depression-era suicide of his father.

Lots of families lost their homes and were living in tin-and-cardboard shacks on the grounds of the city dump. The man told his teenage son, "Betim. I'm counting on you, son. Get the insurance. Tell them it was an accident. You saw the gun discharge while I was cleaning it. We're sacrificing, me and you, for the family, Betim. Take care of Mommy and the kids."

And at every confession, Betim would ask Naum, "Is my father in heaven? Do I have hope, Urata? I lied, I lied."

Betim.

Betim was on the floor by the bed. The nurses in the old folks' home told Naum, "He died saying some words in his language."

Naum began the Trisagion Prayers in Albanian. And when he reached the Lord's Prayer, the nurses recognized *Ati yne*, Our Father, and said, "Yeah, that was it."

At Betim's funeral, Father Nigel had asked Naum, "You wanna say a few words?"

Naum said, "Sure, Father."

Father Nigel told him, "But not in church. I'd rather you cover for me at the memorial meal, maybe say a few words there. I have business up under the Tunnel I have to get to. Besides, I don't go to memorial meals or graveyards, and I don't hear confession anymore either."

Naum didn't know that was an option. He told Father Nigel, "Okay."

Father Nigel had the kind of Halloween smile that made cats cringe. "'Sides . . ." he told Naum, "I asked Betim's tree-hugger sister, Kozmika—the one who goes to mediums, rubs the

Buddha's belly, the crystal-loving New Ager—I asked her to give the eulogy. I don't do eulogies either."

Kozmika and her artist husband, Pablo, looked to Naum as if they'd dropped unwashed through a wormhole out of that farmer's field at Woodstock. Wearing the same dungarees, sandals, and tie-dyed tees. Flying all the flags. Nothing about the 1960s in their appearance had drained except the color in their hair and the tattoo thickness in the collagen of their skin.

By the time Kozmika got to, "So I was bent over in my garden tending my wisteria when a flock of geese landed and a big one, probably *the* biggest one, wings flapping, toddled up behind me honking and bit me on the butt, and when I turned, I recognized him right away, my brother.

"I said, 'Betim, is that really you?' He flapped his wings and honked and honked, and when I went to give him a hug . . . Well, let's just say the cycle of the karmic wheel provides much fecundate to grow the garden of our becoming . . . Namaste . . ."

Father Nigel looked at Naum. He loved seeing old-school priests squirm.

Naum tried a small corrective at the memorial meal, but by that time . . .

The horn behind him started again. The black Escalade was a fiber-optic micron from being melded to Naum's back bumper.

And then it was hurry-up-and-wait onto the next block of slow-moving traffic. One maddening inch at a time. Naum wondered if he'd be on time and if there'd be anyone with a key to open the door at Saint Christos.

At Sansom Street, a provisions truck was unloading at the Happy Rooster and blocking part of the one-lane flow. The jelly donuts at Dunkin Donuts on the other corner were calling Naum by name, and across the perpendicular intersection, the clog of traffic was looking like the parking lot at a Phillies World Series home game on free bat night, but Naum somehow squeaked through the light with the Escalade riding his tail.

Naum and the Escalade made the light at Chestnut Street and got caught mid-block behind a trash truck and a diesel bus. A beggar came up to his window, but before Naum could crank down the rusty window gear, the beggar lost patience, gave Naum the gesture nobody likes getting, and trotted toward the black Escalade.

The man in the Escalade peppered out the moon roof with some kind of spray, and the beggar stumbled toward the curb.

Up ahead Naum could see a clutch of homeless folks shivering in the Sixteenth Street alcove of Liberty Place Mall.

Father Marku Spiro had been the long-time priest at Saint Christos before Father Nigel. Many folks found an icon in Father Spiro, found a way to believe again, were healed through Father's perseverance in Christ. Always kind to the poor. Well-loved by the faithful, a friend to everybody in the Saint Christos downtown neighborhood.

Man was a true servant. A good singer, too. Loved to play baseball, and three men from the parish baseball team had gone to seminary because of Father Spiro. If you had a calling, he could help you find it. And Mariam, his wife, made many a good match when it came to finding a priftereshe for her boys.

Saint Christos had three in a row after Father Spiro.

Father Anthony Bennett. Our Carol, always in a colorful wide-brim picture-frame hat, owner of The Village Thrift, had been hurt. She was embarrassed to come to church. Her online Mature Christian Singles Service match, Tony B, turned out to be Father Bennett.

Father Augustus Langtry.

Naum had gone on many early-morning quests after getting calls from Aunt Marie Noli, Saint Christos's old-time parish president. "It's three hours till Sunday Liturgy, Father Naum, and his wife says he ain't been home all night."

"Okay, Aunt Marie," Naum would say.

The crowd at the Misconduct Tavern on the Parkway knew Bennett and Langtry on a first-name basis.

The Very Reverend James Bill Wilberforce.

"I'm a mitered archpriest awarded the decorated pectoral cross and the right to celebrate the Liturgy with the Royal Doors open for the Lord's Prayer . . ."

Father J. B. was at Saint Christos just long enough to get the PIN to the Ladies Society's checking account. The bishop had decided to give Father Wilberforce another chance after similar financial questions at his previous parish.

J. B. Wilberforce told Naum, "I can't help myself. It's my one and only sin, when I see checkbooks lying around open and unused."

When Naum caught him switching a pregnant waitress's ten-dollar tip for a one, Wilberforce blamed Leonardo DiCaprio. "Exacerbated, my sickness, Naum. I see that movie, *Catch Me If You Can* . . . I see that handsome Leonardo DiCaprio, and it's relapse city. I jump in my little red Porsche and Sugar House Casino, here comes Slick Bill."

The man in the black suit from the Escalade was out of his car rapping on Naum's window. His face was practically hot-pressed on the glass. Tapping his big gold watch. "The nursing home called, Pops. Time for you to go home before they put out a silver alert."

Naum mouthed, "I'm sorry." He hadn't noticed when the traffic started forward. Naum was daydreaming on the fumes behind the diesel trash truck and the eco-friendly bio-fuel kneeling bus.

Traffic lurched along like a toddler pulling a wood-block train tied together with twine.

"Thank goodness," Naum said when they finally got close to the corner at Market Street and it looked like they might make the light, and then it cycled. Red light number three. Naum said, "Damn."

The congestion at the cross streets was gridlocked like Christmas. Naum sat far down the line, stuck in the middle of the parade, wondering how he ended up having to come downtown and do this baptism in the first place.

"It's my own fault. I agreed to serve as dean."

Outside Naum's window a man was hawking Phillies, Eagles, and Flyers pennants. The short man in the Ike jacket reminded Naum of his father. A wavy head of hair and a smile shining like sunlight through a pentagonal crystal prism rainbowing color onto the overhead flotilla of helium balloons tied to his cart.

The man was fishing change out of the green apron tied around his waist and handing it to the father of the little girl with the bead-braided dreads, holding her daddy's hand and looking up at her big blue balloon.

Naum *had* to call the bishop when the people complained. Father Nigel had introduced girl servers into the altar.

The bishop told Naum, "You're the dean. Investigate."

Father Nigel, who called himself a liturgical deconstructionist and did things like eliminating the proskomedia and the litany after the Gospel.

"They're fourteenth-century innovations, Naum. Get over it. They made you a dean? You? You're here to investigate me as dean? Big deal. Being dean and two-fifty'll get you a ride on the jitney. It's as meaningless as proskomedia."

Father Nigel, who told Naum, "I really can't say the liturgy is the center of my life. I preside because it gives me a wonderful occasion to be in a setting and culture, a liturgical event where I can preach performance-art theology and be in communion with the way of the *Universe* . . . Maybe here and there I can accept Orthodox eucharistic theology, but which one of us doesn't make the necessary adjustments when they imply the wrong thing? I'm inclusive, Naum . . . One human family. All people are created equal members of one human family. Have you visited the *better* seminary lately? It's a new world, Naum. No? Not you. You haven't, have you?"

Did the bishop look into this? Nope.

Father Nigel, who told the people, "Saturdays and Sundays, even during Great Lent, eat meat! Go ahead. You can. Saturdays and Sundays are not fasting days."

Father Nigel, the icon of the Virgin and Child with the rainbow halo on the altar . . . Naum truly didn't know.

But it was the long night under the Tunnel when Naum was out looking and found the girl he'd baptized all those years ago selling herself on the Avenue for ten dollars a pop.

He appealed to Elisa that night. "Please come back to church.

Please. You can help me serve the Clergy Brotherhood breakfast in the morning. Just this once. Please, Elisa. And we'll go from there."

At the breakfast, Father Nigel acted as if Elisa were a ghost.

The long-time juju man who haunted the Tunnel was pointed out to Naum with a scrambled-egg spatula by Elisa, the ghost wearing a serving apron in the upper church hall.

The knife of accusation against your brother, Naum, the devil's put it in your hand. Turn the blade on yourself. Self-reproach, humility, and obedience. Call out to Christ our God and call to mind the plank in your own eye.

"This girl?" the bishop said. "You expect me to take her word? Can you even say at this point she's Orthodox? Good God, Naum. The man is married. With children. You expect me to do what?"

When Naum didn't answer, the bishop said to himself, "Well at least it was a woman."

An F-sharp pro-blaster twin trumpet airsplitter cannonball electromechanical Escalade warning horn that coulda woke the folks in Palmer Burial Ground had nearly the opposite effect on Naum. Damn sure got him moving. The guy behind him relentlessly mad on his bad-boy Escalade blaster.

Up ahead, Naum saw an open curbside space just past JFK Boulevard as he approached the light at Ben Franklin Parkway.

The trash truck went left. The bus went right. Naum sped up and slid into the vacant space with the yellow lines that said *No Stopping Any Time,* and damn if that Escalade on his tail didn't slide right by, beat the light, and fly away, horn blaring all the way.

The lady cop in the raincoat told Naum, "Move it along, bud."

Half a block ahead, Naum watched the Escalade pull into the

tiny parking lot of Saint Christos. The burly SUV barely fit into the last available space. The man in the suit got out, slammed the door, and hurried into the church.

Naum took a minute to catch his breath.

It's his fault I'm here. Nigel. Father Nigel.

Holding a baby, a six-week-old baby, by the feet and dunking him repeatedly, like a maniac, face first into the font.

The parents couldn't catch their breath. The cell phone video posted on the internet. The baby at the hospital an hour later, aspirated water . . . practically dry drowning. Thank God the boy survived.

"Father Naum," the parents said, "you're the dean. Do *something*."

Naum left messages. He wrote. Evelyn and her husband Dimitri, the parents of the boy, didn't they give and give generously to the annual donations for the bishop's fund?

When the bishop finally returned from ecumenical conferences overseas, Naum told the parents, "He'll listen to you." Theirs was the call that did it.

Naum was so happy to cross Spring Garden Street. To escape downtown and the cobblestone streets not made for cars. Ben Franklin wooden-water-pipe streets so narrow and one-way, any healthy car with a full tank of gas would have to suck in its bumpers just to squeeze by and keep the pressure in its tires from hissing out the valves.

Streets where trolley bells ain't been heard since the Liberty Bell got cracked; slippery silvery tracks still running down the middle like split zippers that don't work no more. And whatever genius replaced all the trolleys with eco-friendly vegetable-oil kneeling buses that do just as good a job at clogging up traffic as the trolleys did. Except the trolleys were electric and didn't smell like sprout-eating goats in a bean field.

Naum couldn't wait to get back around the Way—back to the neighborhood. Back to the steps outside Saint Alexander the Dervish. Drop in over at Fufari's on Frankford Avenue and buy some soft pretzels in case those three praying crows showed up again.

Oh, and Naum never did mention, when the Escalade man introduced himself and kissed Naum's hand at the baptism, "Urata, I'm godfather, Greg."

Maybe he *didn't* recognize Naum.

Naum said, "Sorry I'm late, *koumbaro.* Couldn't find parking and ended up in a city Parking Authority garage."

"You need a couple a bucks?" godfather offered.

"Nah, but thanks. I'd just give it to one of the homeless out there. Besides, godfather, as luck would have it, Ligori, from our parish, works for the Parking Authority, was at the booth and gave me the clergy discount. That your black Escalade out there?"

Godfather said, "Yep."

Naum said, "I could tell."

The Jeep

Part I

Father Noni

MIGHTA BEEN LES AND DOREEN'S HAPPY TAP. Coulda been Fishtown Tavern or the Old Philadelphia. In the end it didn't matter.

Naum was a young man at the time and had finally made up his mind. If his father was gonna do what he said he was gonna do and go back to Albania, Naum was gonna sell the barbershop and do what he'd wanted to do since he'd been a kid, go to seminary.

He was nine or ten when he first told his father, "Pop, I wanna be a priest."

His father, Michael, snapped the razor strap and asked his wife, Izet, "Where did we go wrong?"

Naum's grandmother, Dorothea, was visiting from Albania. She said, "Oh, bo, bo. Nothing but a life of misery, being a priest, heartache and other people's problems."

"All that education and time," they said, "and in the end, what portion for the priest and his family? Well, God be his portion in the land of the living."

Naum couldn't get it out of his head. But before he could write to the bishop asking his blessing, he had to get the blessing of their parish priest, Father Marku Noni, who liked to have a drink here and there.

Les and Doreen's Happy Tap. Fishtown Tavern or the Old Philadelphia. Naum was tired of walking in and out of bars.

Saturday clouds were looking down over Philadelphia with their faces full of snow. How many bars could there be in Fishtown?

In the end it didn't matter. Because when Naum finally found Noni comfortably seated, it wasn't at any of the places he first thought to look for the old priest.

Naum walked in the door and saw Father Noni seated at the bar. He said, "Father." And thought to himself, I should've started at Shooky's in the first place.

Old man Shook, round as a wheel of Bavarian Bergkäse cheese, was known in the neighborhood as one of the few men capable of beating Father Noni at arm wrestling or keeping up with him downing shots and beers—a combination people called boilermakers—or out-slicking Noni at shuffleboard.

Old man Shook had seen a lot back home in Pirmasens, the German town not far from the French border.

He tilted his chin toward the priest on the stool and said to Naum, "So, this, you're going to study?" And kept polishing beer mugs with his thin white apron.

Father Noni picked his Panama off the stool next to him and motioned to Naum with that straw-hat grin. Titled his hat back on his head and looked at Naum the same way he did on Sunday mornings when Naum would finally find him after trolling the pre-dawn back alleys. "You found me." Always acting like a surprised kid playing hide-and-seek. Noni said, "It's not Sunday already, is it?"

Naum said, "No."

Sunday morning Naum.

Trying to get singing Father Marku to his feet and coax him into the car. Get the old man into some kind of shape decent enough to serve Liturgy for the people.

Naum on the spot. What else could he do? Coffee thermos Naum.

Helping the rumpled man get over the embarrassment of what he called his pre-existing Saturday night condition, pushing away the thermos cup and reminding Naum, "No eating or drinking before communion."

Noni sat smiling on the barstool at Shooky's and whispered to Naum, "Ya got a friend named Frank, and he's walking down the beach, and he cuts his big toe on a seashell."

Father Marku Noni took a long cold swallow from mug number three. He wiped his mustache and dabbed a napkin the length of his wide white beard. Mugs number one and two stood handle to handle on the lacquered bar top, drained except for suds running down the insides, abandoned like thick-bottomed decagonal twins.

Father Noni smiled at the empties and said, "Dead soldiers."

Naum said, "Father, please. Nativity fast is almost over."

He could see old Noni had been stuck to Shooky's stool so long that getting down and standing up unaided, even to go to the men's room in an effort to preserve the integrity of his underwear, was probably something the old man considered not worth the effort, or judging by the state of his trousers, hadn't considered at all.

Naum said, "Urata, I need your help. I gotta write a letter to the bishop if I want to start seminary at the end of January, early February, and I need your blessing. And I need some advice about a used '58 Jeep."

When Father Noni ignored Naum and said, "So he's walking down the beach, this friend of yours, Frank . . ."

Naum could see he was getting nowhere. He told the old priest, "Maybe another time, Father." Waved to old man Shook and went out the side door Ladies' Entrance.

Part II

He's Real

WEEKS WENT BY. It was the end of a beautiful post-Epiphany parish picnic at the annual blessing of the Delaware. An unseasonably warm day for early January, temperatures in the low seventies and just getting dark.

The shish-kebab grills had ashed down to low-burning embers under the canopy of bare branches at League Island Park. People sat close telling stories, having a second or third helping at the long bench tables under the pavilions. Ladies packing plates. Men gathering up so no litter would be left. Church school kids playing tag up and down the wide stone steps of the massive granite-walled Swedish American Museum.

Father Marku Noni on his lawn chair, by himself, straw Panama sideways on his head, maybe a little too much homemade raki.

Noni called Naum, pulled him close in the shadows, and confessed, "I never intended to be a priest, a real priest. I was an atheist through and through, from my university days. The priesthood was nothing more than a platform for my political views. I believed in nothing. Nothing but myself. And I did it. At least I thought I did. Promoted my ideas successfully for the past thirty years.

"But something happened to me at Nativity Liturgy, and now—" he took Naum by the hand— "now you gonna go to seminary."

He pulled his lawn chair close and put his knees touching Naum's knees. He put his face close to Naum's face, nose to nose, breathing raki in his face. "And you see this?" Noni held up the raki bottle. "Never again." And he let the bottle fall to the ground. "Never again will you have to come looking for drunken Noni on Sunday mornings. And I'm sorry you had to come to Shooky's to get my blessing to go study, to be a servant to God's people. And I'm sorry I didn't help you with your question about the Jeep."

He said to Naum, "I'm done sedating my duplicity. You're young. You're a smart man. You know, I'm sure, what it means, cognitive dissonance? Well, I can no longer hold my hypocrisy together with beer mugs of ideology and raki reasoning. Lying to the people, thinking I was fooling them, and thinking I could handle having two faces. It cut me in half, Naum."

Then he said, "Naum, *He* appeared to me at the throne in

Nativity Liturgy, and I been dealing with it since. I haven't had the courage to tell anyone, and I wish I was the priest we heard about who died in front of the altar at the moment of the consecration and remained standing. I wish it was me."

Noni had turned to the congregation Nativity night, standing in the Royal Doors, crying and sobbing, "He's real. It's real. *Krishti është i vertete.* He really is real."

No one knew what had happened or what Noni meant. The men in the parish came into the altar, thinking maybe he'd had too much Christmas raki, but he shooed them away, somehow regained his composure, and continued the prayers.

"I haven't told anyone yet, Naum. But I'm going. Going to leave Saint Alexander and go to the monastery."

When Father Noni lost his balance trying to stand from his lawn chair, Naum said, "You got a ride home, Urata?"

Naum was driving his father's lemon-cream '66 Impala. It wasn't a beater in those days. Noni rolled the window down and said, "Mind if I smoke?" But he didn't wait for an answer. He hung his cigarette hand out the window and said, "So what's the story with this Jeep? Tell me."

Naum said, "It started a few days before I came to see you at Shooky's—at my father's barbershop, Urata, a few days before Nativity."

Michael Bakalli's barber shop wasn't far from Marlborough and Girard. Three old-school chairs took center stage down haircut row. White enameled pedestals with black leather seats. Overstuffed black leather head and armrests. Ornamental ironwork scrolled around the sides and bottom. Three of the finest thrones in Fishtown.

People could hardly resist doing a checkerboard Mummer's strut across the shiny black and white floor when Naum's father, Michael Bakalli, bowed and pointed the way. "You're next. Please, take a seat," and snapped the crisp pinstriped barber cape around their neck.

Disinfected combs
Submerged in Barbicide blue
Stood upright in striated glass jars
Along dappled marble countertops
That ran above
Three-legged shampoo bowls
With neck curves so comfortably worn
Eddie Gjarper
Who went bald in high school
Fell asleep and dreamed
The same happy dream
Every time the shampooist
Massaged his dome
Eddie Gjarper
Toweled off
Sitting up and staring in the mirror
At an Eddie Gjarper
Smiling back with a head full of hair

For some reason, the whole damn neighborhood looked better in Bakalli's vintage mirrors. Regular old neighborhood folks who walked in looking Fishtown-fatigued walked out doing the two-step after a slap of aftershave and a twirl of duster-brush talc. Proud artisan barbers popping off the pinstripe cape, pushing the pedal, and letting that sweet old hydraulic chair spin and sink real slow.

A smooth cool customer stood outta that throne newborn every time. Grinning in the mirror through a Pinaud Clubman haze. Barbershop fresh and so razor-strap clean they couldn't've cared less if the whole damn neighborhood rubbernecking outside could look in and see.

And in pride of position, in the transom above the door, the art deco sign. Alabaster glass over lettering cut out of a rectangular brass face and illumined with eleven light bulbs from behind. The sign that somehow ended up in Michael Bakalli's shop when the old Broad Street Station got demolished.

BARBERSHOP: SHAVE & HAIRCUT

Classic Pennsylvania Railroad design.

The days just before Christmas were so busy you would've thought every head in Fishtown needed trimming. Men and women, nurses, boys and girls. People woulda paraded their dogs in for a haircut if they could've.

Naum's father, Michael, was handing out numbers at the door.

Ndrita, the one girl artisan, and Frank and Gucci, the two guys cutting hair, were having a quiet dispute over who got the next patron. To hell with the commission on each cut. All three claimed they could spot a good tipper by the way he walked in the door.

Young Naum was sweeping the floor. His father said learning a trade couldn't hurt. Michael insisted his son Naum the apprentice always be there, even though he was permitted to cut hair only when there was an overflow or things got backed up.

Naum hoped to sell the business after his father, a widower now, retired and moved back to Albania. Ndrita had come to Naum privately and said, "If it ever becomes available, Naum, I would love to own that railroad barbershop sign." She looked at the sign up over the door. "I was talking with my husband, Kosta, and we might even be able to get the financing to buy the whole shop—I mean, if and when your father goes back to the old country."

Naum wasn't sure what to do. He knew Frank and Gucci had agreed to partner up and buy the business if he put it on the market. But Ndrita had the biggest book, more customers than Frank and Gucci put together.

Greta, Naum's wife, had given her blessing to pack up and move with the kids to the monastery-seminary in the remote wooded mountains of the eastern region, and money from the sale of the shop would come in handy.

Toward the end of the day, a man in a suit and another in work clothes crowded in, followed by a woman in a bright red coat. There was no end in sight. Every barber chair was occupied, and in the waiting area there was standing room only.

The receptionist motioned to Naum. "Take that guy, the one in the suit," just as Frank the barber was leading his last customer to the register.

Frank told the receptionist, "No, I'll take him." Frank knew a quality suit and a good tipper when he saw one.

The receptionist shrugged and motioned toward the man in the work overalls. Naum knew the look. Take that man instead.

The woman in the red coat was a regular and said she was willing to wait for Ndrita.

What did Naum care? A few days before Nativity and with any luck, a letter from Father Noni, and the bishop's blessing, seminary was just weeks away.

He said to the man in the work overalls, "Wanna come with me, sir?" And led the way to his mini chair in the narrow hallway by the back door.

Outside, it was beginning to snow, and from the looks of the car tops and pavements, the wet heavy layer was gonna be the first of many. The streetlights had come on, and Naum could see oversized flakes parachuting in the glow.

Windshield wipers were going on a dark stretch limo just outside the shop. Every person going by seemed bundled over in packages and parkas. Traffic lights blinked in a winking synchronicity with the Christmas music Michael Bakalli loved to pipe into the shop this time of year.

"You're pretty good, son," the man in the overalls said when Naum finished. "They oughta give you one a' the big-boy chairs up in the window."

Made Naum smile.

Dusting the talc brush over his neck, Naum said to the man, "Don't get to do it too often, but I made a point at barber school to learn every time the opportunity presented itself."

"Surprised me," the man said. "You don't run into too many white barbers can do black hair, 'specially round here. Just been dropping in on one of my relations here in the neighborhood before he goes off to the Marines, young man called Getzy, maybe you know him? Works over at the junkyard with a boy they call Little Harry. Told me what you looked like. Told me you were the one to see. I was gonna ask for you at the desk, but I guess I didn't have to. Must be the man upstairs had it planned to turn out the way it did."

"No doubt," Naum said. "And I heard about Getzy leaving for Paris Island. Some of us are gonna see him off on the train down at Thirtieth Street."

The man said, "Vincent's my name." They shook hands.

Looking in the mirror, Vincent said, "Naum, I'm thinking it's worth me coming here once or twice a month . . ."

Naum said, "Mister Vincent, sir, not to interrupt, but I'm leaving myself end of next month, or I hope to. My pop's . . . my mom died a while back, and he's determined to go home to Albania. Born there, Berat, and live out his days with his family. His mom, my grandmom, Dorothea's, still alive . . ."

Vincent took a minute before he said, "I understand about your pop. But what about you? You going to the Marines too?"

"No, sir. Family and I, going to seminary."

Snow came in on the wind when the door opened. A man in a chauffeur's uniform stood in the doorway, perusing the room.

Michael Bakalli said, "Hey, ya wanna open the door a little wider so I can heat the whole a' Philadelphia?"

The chauffeur apologized and closed the door.

Tall man, regal looking, Naum thought. Looked like an officer in the carabinieri, a kinda fancy cop. He came over to Vincent and said, "Sir, you just had a call from your wife. She said it's not important, but if you forget to pick up a couple of pound cakes at Stocks, don't bother coming home."

Vincent looked up at Naum and said, "You married, right?"

All three smiled.

Vincent said to the chauffeur, "Cart, how many out there in our little entourage tonight?"

Carter the chauffeur said, "Four, sir, including me. Roz, the new secretary. Ronnie, the valet, and you know, Andres, the pilot. Had to come when he heard you were seeing Getzy, man loves rummaging through that junkyard."

Vincent reached into his overalls and handed Naum a hundred-dollar bill. He said, "This is for you. I'll pay the haircut bill up at the desk. You have time for another four heads?"

They had a walnut-cased Waterbury wind-up eight-day clock on the wall, and when Naum looked at the bill, and then at the clock, he was pretty sure he'd forgotten to wind it or time had decided right then and there to stand still.

Vincent told Naum, "My regular gal got pregnant and left the hair business. That simple." He put his hand on Naum's arm and said, "So maybe I got blessed with a new man?"

Naum said, "Mister V, I might have time for one more tonight, but I'm hoping to leave the business myself some time right after the new year, for seminary, and . . ." Naum looked at the hundred-dollar bill and said, "And this is too much, Mister Vincent. Haircut only costs four dollars."

Vincent ignored that and said, "What kind of seminary?"

"We're Orthodox," Naum said. "Saint Paul came to my grandmother's town."

Vincent asked Naum in perfect Greek if he spoke or read the language.

Naum recognized the Greek. He said, "I understand a little, sir, but I don't speak it very well."

When Gucci finished cutting his hair, Teddy the Horse walked over and joined the party at Naum's. He said "Hey" to Vincent and then told Naum, "Don't forget, seminary-man, that '58 Willy's Jeep Wagon you got on layaway, end a' January's long as I can hold it. And from what I hear about the snow on the mountains up at that seminary, you're gonna need all four wheels."

Naum said, "I'm working on it, Uncle Teddy."

Teddy said, "Maybe heaven can wait, but my boss over at Auto Heaven can't. And I'd hate to see you lose your deposit, kid. Oh, and don't forget, taxes, title, tags, you're gonna need an extra hundred, at least."

Naum had put five hundred down. Everybody in the shop knew he was having a hard time raising the remaining seven hundred.

When his father offered to help, Naum said, "Pop, self-reliance, you're always talking self-reliance. I'm grateful, but let me see if I can get an extra job or something."

When Ndrita heard, she told Naum, "I can buy that sign if your father says okay, three hundred, no problem, Naum. I'll even throw in an extra hundred for taxes and stuff."

Naum wasn't so sure of himself when Mister Vincent's secretary, Roz, came in. She said, "Mister Vincent had to go out to the limo to call his wife. He said you only have time for one more tonight, and I drew the lucky straw."

Green-eyed Roz had hair as stiff and straight as uncooked spaghetti. She told Naum, "If you just spray the ends, I'm gonna make it grow."

Making it grow, in Philly parlance, meant, don't cut it too short. Naum knew it meant, 'I intend to grow my hair into a longer style. Just edge it a little bit.'

When Naum finished, Roz handed him another hundred-dollar bill. "Mister Vincent said this is for you, like a tip. I'm to pay for the haircut separately, and he said to give you this." She handed Naum a business card and said, "He wants you to call him if there's anything he can do to help with your seminary plans."

Naum was sure the clock was going backwards.

Before she left the shop, Roz came back to Naum's station. "Oh, Naum, Mister V said we'll be back tomorrow. So I had your receptionist book two spots with you, eleven and eleven-thirty, that okay? One for Andres, that's his personal bodyguard and pilot, and one for Carter, you met him, the chauffeur. Ronnie the valet's making his grow too, so maybe next time."

The next day, the morning of Christmas Eve, Carter the chauffeur went first. Same deal. The hundred-dollar bill, haircut paid separately.

In shock, Naum.

Andres, the pilot/bodyguard said, "Mister V really wants you to be his personal barber. He'll send a jet to the seminary to pick you up and fly you and your family, if you want, to wherever he may be. Los Angeles. London. NYC. He has interests in all those places. Boca. You'll cut his hair, and we'll fly you home.

"Oh, and he couldn't help overhearing . . . Said to tell you, why not forget about that used Jeep? Pick a color. He'll send over a new one. All we need's your address. Or we could have it delivered here to the shop or to your seminary. Here's the card. Call him, Naum. Mister Vincent says he has a little shovel and he keeps trying to give it away, but God has a bigger shovel and just keeps dumping blessing after blessing on his pile."

Naum didn't have the heart to tell him there was hardly a cow path or paved road at the seminary, let alone a place to land a jet.

The pilot said, "Oh, and one more thing, if you can. Mister V would really appreciate some titles, books about you—Orthodox, is that it?"

Naum said, "Yeah."

"Couple a' books. Something you'd recommend. Be really appreciated, Naum," Andres the pilot said. "Guy never stops. Can't get enough, God and reading, or the other way around."

Christmas Eve at the shop, Naum told Ndrita, "If this happens, I will *give* you that barbershop sign."

Part III

F Cut His Toe

ON THE DAY OF THE EPIPHANY PICNIC, when Father Noni finally heard the story, he said, "So you told them you couldn't give an answer till you talked to me? And you've waited all this time. And knowing now who I really am. What I've been. Seeing me the way you saw me all those mornings, searching in those alleys, you still want my advice?"

Naum said, "And your blessing."

When Naum was with him at the picnic, Father Marku Noni on his lawn chair, straw Panama sideways on his head, maybe a little too much homemade raki, the shattered bottle under their feet, Noni still couldn't resist telling his stories.

He pulled Naum close in the shadows and said, "Ya got a

friend named Frank, and he's walking down the beach, and he cuts his big toe on a seashell."

Noni put his head down. He took a moment. Then he said, "So, Naum . . . play along with me. Say *F-cut-his-toe.* Your friend Frank, walking on the beach, who cut his big toe on a seashell, just use his first initial. Say *F-cut-his-toe.*"

Naum said, "F-cut-his-toe."

Father Noni shook his hand and said, "*Parakaló.*"

"*Parakaló,*" Noni said, "means you're welcome, and *F-cut-his-toe* is how you say thank you in Greek. The word Eucharist comes from this word for giving thanks. Efcharistó."

Naum said it again, three times.

In the car on the ride home, Father Noni said, "It's been a few days now since they offered to help you. But if you think the offer still stands, call that man, Vincent, tell him, F-cut–his-toe, but tell him you can't accept a new Jeep.

"Tell him if he will lend you the amount of money you're short for the used Jeep, you will prepare a promissory note, and you will repay him. Recommend three books—ask God to guide your choice—and you must always remember him in your prayers."

Toward the end of January, Greta, Naum's wife, called the shop the day it finally happened and asked her father-in-law, Michael, "Do you know why a man in a chauffeur's uniform came to our door and gave me a thousand-dollar check?"

Michael Bakalli looked at the sign in the transom above the door and said, "*Gezuar Krishtlindje, edhe vitin e ri*" (Happy Christmas and New Year) to Ndrita, kissed his son Naum, and told him, "Go get the ladder. I am going to Albania, and you are going to seminary in a Jeep."

Who Blesses Who

EVER HAVE THE PRIEST yell at you for not being on time when it wasn't your fault? Makes ya stand there feeling embarrassed with your robe, waiting for his blessing. And then get knocked in the nose by the back of his knuckles when he shoved his hand for you to kiss it?

Happened to me.

There were two of them that day. A real tall one and a real short one. Father Naum was gone for a couple of weeks, and these two priests were filling in.

The short one said to the tall one, "That's not the way *we* do it."

"I understand," the tall one said. "But I'm *proestos* (presiding priest)."

He didn't think I heard him when the tall one whispered to himself, "And you can hardly reach the altar, Arthur."

Well, it was partly true. The short priest had to stand on his tippy-toes to kiss the Gospel. He was wearing penny loafers, and he sorta slipped outta one reaching up there, stretching his lips. Had to shuffle-slide one shoe across the tile with his big toe to his spot on the side of the altar, where the tall priest moved his book and pointed for him to stand, like you tell a dog where to sit.

When the tall priest called the short one Arthur, the short one said, "Athanasios, please, *Bert*."

And when the short one called the tall one Bert, the tall one looked over his glasses down his nose and said, "Boniface."

The tall priest, Father Boniface, his robes were too short. His white socks didn't even cover his ankles, and one sock had a hole in the back. Guess when you're tall you're always having to bend down and yank your socks up cause your toes are so long, or maybe it was he didn't clip his toenails cause they're way down south there, and it ain't so easy to get south when your flexibility reaches a certain age and your knees and elbows'll only go so far for you. Everybody hates doing that anyway. Clipping their toes. Or maybe there're some people who like it, but I never heard nobody saying that's what they got a day-off kick doing.

The short one, Father Athanasios, his robes were so long he kept tripping, and one of the men brought him a couple of long red ribbons to tie around his waist to keep them bunched up. It made him look so much like one of those firecracker popper things, I had to close my eyes every time he pulled the ribbons to cinch himself up, cause I was pretty sure confetti was gonna come exploding out all over the altar.

It ain't easy being short. Just ask my Uncle Norbert.

I was looking at Father Boniface pretty hard with my neck bent back. I did see a coconut once over at Barenbaums'. Mister Barenbaum, the grocer, told me, "Go ahead, knock it with your knuckles." Pretty hard, coconuts. It made a sound like a bongo drum filled with water. And the knot-head coconut shape and the hairy fiber stuff around the sides wasn't all that different from what I could remember looking up at that tall priest.

Then again, those were the only two coconuts I ever met in person. Either way, I was scratchy like an itchy monkey to climb that palm tree and give that coconut a few bongo knocks on behalf of those knuckles in my nose.

Father Boniface had a voice way up near the chandelier and loud. I like to sing along. Do everything the priest does. Bow when he bows. Make the cross when he does. Kiss things. But tell you the truth, it kinda shook me a little when he started booming out like he did. It didn't sound like church singing. Not to me anyway.

It kinda reminded me of the guy in the sequin jumpsuit leading karaoke crooning last summer on the cruise, and it didn't do nothing to calm me down, any better than the seasick pills they gave me.

Only good thing was, Father Boniface didn't need no microphone hookup. I was pretty sure any people up flying airplanes heading to the airport woulda been looking at each other in the cockpit, saying, "You hear that?" —cause all the pigeons on the church roof were converting over to the rabbi's place across the street.

The big priest brushed Little Harry and all the wires away when Harry tried threading the mic through his vestments, yelling something like, "There ain't no such thing as a blessing for microphone vesting prayers." So Little Harry just laid the live mic on the altar.

The little guy, Father Athanasios, whenever Father Boniface pointed in the liturgy book for something for him to do, sounded like he had a voice full of feta, and it took him a couple a humphs and swallows to get it all out. And that made Father Boniface make faces like he was sucking on Sour Patch lemon drops and rock back and forth on his rowboat shoes and complain even more about Father Athanasios going too slow and the choir being off key.

"How long does it take to give the pitch for one *Amen?*"

I woulda tried to answer, but I think it woulda only made him madder if he knew that cause of that live mic we was all hearing, cause, boy, for some reason, the big guy was in a hurry to giddy-up and get through the Liturgy.

I never seen nobody make prostrations up and down so fast, and windmilling the sign of the cross over himself like one of those pinwheels you get down the Shore and stick to the rail on the Boardwalk in the summertime to watch the colors spin.

"The big one don't need it," I said to Little Harry, "but the little one could use a microphone."

Little Harry said, "And a step stool."

"He talks funny," I told Harry.

Harry said, "Yeah, well, he's from Boston."

Allelu-yer, allelu-yer, allelu-yer is what it sounded like to me.

Harry said, "You should hear him say the Our Father . . ."

Now the altar boy with the red hair who nobody thought was Albanian, but was, he pretended he didn't understand English and made made-up signs and signals to the tall priest, like he was wanting him to know he was hard of hearing, so the tall priest kept yelling louder and louder for the censer, and the redhead kid smiles some halfwit smile at the tall priest and goes and starts pulling on the bell, knowing the priest was wanting the censer.

And this sends the tall priest into drooling out the corners of his mouth, and when he yells for the bell, the kid walks over, making more signals, smiling, and hands him the censer loaded down with incense but no charcoal in it, and it drove the tall priest wild. Which was what the redheaded kid was aiming at all along. Standing there shrugging and smiling and making goo-goo signs like he was a baby angel innocent as butter cake.

Little Harry, who was doing rear guard in the Great Entrance, carrying the fan with the angel with the six wings, he says to me, "I saw you almost trip and look around like you wanted to slug him when the little priest poked you in the middle of your back to go faster, becausa the big priest was behind him giving him shoves in the middle of his back and whispering loud enough for anybody and everybody, 'Speed it up, Arthur.'"

We weren't used to this. Naum was always polite and patient, no matter what. He used to tell us, "So happy to see you." Even if you were late or only came once a year.

And he always thanked us for bringing him the censer and stuff. "Thank you for serving God's people." And at the end he'd say, "Good work today." He used to say Liturgy should be prayerful, peaceful, and pleasant.

All this monkey business wasn't something we were used to in church. Once, out on the playground across from Adaire School, I saw Eddie Gjarper grow a second nose right out of the spot between his eyes on his forehead, when he shoved Getzy and Getzy nailed him with one punch right between the eyes. It was like seeing Pinocchio tell a lie right there in person.

I was wondering how long it was gonna take for someone to grow that tall priest a spare nose.

But Little Harry explained not only could the short priest not reach that big guy's nozzle without a ladder or a good running jump, but there was something called propriety that Harry said prevented people punching a priest.

"Even another priest?" I asked. "Even out in the street?"

He said, "Why ya think ya never see priests out shoving people in public?"

When I gave it a little thought, I figured that was probably one of the main reasons priests were always so polite when they weren't dressed in their Sunday suit.

So back in the altar, Arthur and Bert were arguing over who was gonna give the sermon, when Arthur called Bert a *faart* . . . with his Boston accent, "Ya big fart . . ."

Which got us all trying not to laugh, and the speaker system musta been working pretty good with that microphone still lying there electric-live on the altar, cause when I peeked out the Royal Doors, the Teuta Ladies were all blinking behind their hankies and the choir suddenly went sour outta nowhere, making almost the same noise as the time all the air came outta my birthday balloon when my sister poked it with her fingernail.

I guess they made a deal on the sermon thing, cause the both of them talked to us till people were practicing yawning with their mouth closed, noticing things on the floor and the ceiling they'd never noticed before, and swearing to themselves and promising God they were gonna give more money and volunteer to come during the week and help clean if only it would be over.

The short one talked about baseball and how on October 8, 1956, in Game Five of the World Series, Don Larsen pitching a perfect game had something to do with the Liturgy. Didn't make any sense to me, but Eddie Gjarper liked it.

And the tall one was saying something about how we ought to

be like the monks, praying to be sick so we'd be more appreciative of all the stuff we got, and how it's better not to get married, and even the pope said married priests in the early Church were required to be abstinent as a sign of their being married to the Church, which got me thinking double about taking marriage advice from guys who ain't got kids or a wife.

We all knew Naum was married to Priftereshe Greta, but even our Madeline, who everybody called the theologian cause she liked to read the Bible, even she couldn't explain how a guy ends up married to a church.

I asked Little Harry what that last bit about be absent meant, and he told me it had something to do with the softball team called the Monks over at Shissler Playground, who had to take a vow not to miss a game if they wanted to be on the team.

I said, "Oh, yeah. I go to the swimo there summers. Newt's."

Harry knew none of us called it Shissler. We called it Newt's. So he said, "Then you been ta Newt's, you prob'ly seen the absented Monks sitting on the bench and the names of the churches on the backs of their uniforms, you know, like sponsored by Saint So-and-So, you know, sorta like being married to that particular parish? Unless you're sponsored by Mario's Pizza."

I said "Yeah," but I was pretty sure he was trying to make me not feel bad about my wanting to be a priest.

And then, when we came to the *Let us love one another* . . . the two of these priests started sparring over who was kissing who and how many kisses, and neither one of them greeted any of us. So we started telling each other, "Christ is in our midst," and the big one heads out the Royal Doors slap-happy, high-fiving with both hands people on both sides simultaneously down the center aisle, like when one of the Eagles scores a touchdown and goes jumping through the crowd.

Some of the people thought all that joking and handshaking and how the heck ya doing was the signal to leave, and they headed for the hall talking about doughnuts and lakror. And one of our rich guys, Kosta Koli, who Harry said had that Frank Sinatra–Pal Joey look, with the fedora tilted just right. The skinny silk tie. Even had a cigarette angled in the corner of his mouth, right there in church . . . And who was gonna say anything about it?

When Father Boniface reaches the last pew, where Kosta was balancing accounts on his smart phone, he gives the happy slap and the big hug to Kosta, and Kosta starts singing real loud: *When the moon hits your eye . . . That's amore . . .* And they put their arms around each other, swaying back and forth. Kosta and the big priest in his vestments, singing like they had too much wine, *vita bella . . .*

Father Athanasios, the short one, he's standing there in the Royal Doors watching the circus, turning the same red as his vestments, talking to himself, saying, "That's wrong. That's just so wrong." Looking like he's about to blow . . .

And I'm thinking, here comes the confetti.

By the end of the Liturgy, I wasn't sure how I was feeling about wanting to be a priest.

At communion, Father Boniface asked me three times if I was Orthodox and if I had eggs for breakfast.

"No, Father," I told him.

He said, "Then you can't commune, and you shouldn't be in the altar."

I said, "Why, Father?"

He said, "If you were Orthodox, you'd know."

I said, "I was born Orthodox, Father."

He made a face like a lemon and said, "Only Jesus was born Orthodox."

I said, "I thought I was too."

"Then why did you say no when I asked if you were Orthodox?"

I said, "That was about the eggs."

Finally he said, "What's that on your lip?"

I felt it and said, "I don't know."

He said, "Prepare better next week. And if you're not on time, better you don't come in the altar."

I wanted to tell him I was only eight years old, and about my mom working all night at the bakery and sometimes getting off late, and my father doing overtime at the putty factory, and how the car sometimes don't start right away whenever it gets below zero outside, and they gotta keep an old blanket on the engine overnight, and it still don't start on days like today, with us having to hop two trolleys and all that, and that's why I was late.

I wanted to tell Father Boniface I found out later when the redheaded kid zipped the skin off my lip that it wasn't egg. It was beeswax from my candle. From when the short priest shoved me in the back and my candle tilted in my face cause he shoved the short priest.

But he just wouldn't give me communion and I was trying to tell him . . . "Father, Father . . ."

In the church hall, I was waving the wax with the lip stuck to it, trying to get his attention. He looked down at me from the top of the palm tree and said, "It's not polite to interrupt when adults are talking."

Father Boniface and Father Athanasios were explaining to our ladies how the holy bread is properly made, how they do it at their churches. One was saying five tiny loaves. The other priest was talking about how many times he rises it . . .

When I make the meshe with my grandmother, it's never that confusing. When I asked why the ladies didn't tell them how we do it, our way, my mother said none of our Teuta Ladies Baking Society would ever argue with or correct a priest. Especially not with our Nunna Olga and old Missus Elias being there.

Magdalena Elias, old Sammy's wife, struggled to help her husband stand when the two priests came to their table, where the Teuta Ladies gathered. When they finished their lesson and left, Magdalena said, "That's not right, Samuel," when Sammy suggested maybe after seventy-five years of doing it wrong, she should give up baking the meshe and only make kurabia.

And our hundred-and-five-year-old Nunna Olga, in her pearl Sunday dress. The one she was so proud of. The one she said made her feel young. The one she wanted to be buried in. The one with the tiny red flowers. She smiled and bowed to the two priests from her seat. She made the cross to bless them, and Father Boniface said, "That's sweet, Miss, but we must remember who blesses who."

My nose was still a little sore from the blessing he gave me for being late when I came to get my robe blessed. It didn't hurt that much. Either way, I was glad he didn't bless our Nunna Olga.

Little Harry told me, "Kid, you gotta be tough to be a priest."

You ever have the priest yell at you for not being on time when it wasn't your fault and make you stand there feeling embarrassed with your robe, waiting for his blessing, and then get knuckled in the nose by the back of his hand when he shoved it at you while you were trying to kiss it?

Happened to me.

My nose was telling me the same thing.

We watched both of them taking his hand and bowing when Kosta Koli gave them their envelopes for serving.

Harry said, "And ya got lots of opportunities between now and when ya get big ta see how it's done right . . . And like the big priest said, ya gotta learn, kid, who blesses who."

What People Remember

YOU THINK ANYBODY ever remembers what you say at a funeral?" That's the question Kusheri Nastradin asked the priest Naum.

Rainy Monday morning was pressing his foggy face against the glass in a downtown Philly drizzle and spying through the oversized window at the Chock-Full-O-Nuts just off Broad and Chestnut.

The waitress brought two stainless steel spoons sticking out of ceramic coffee mugs and set them on the marble top.

Naum wanted to pay. She said, "Not now, hon . . . Up at the register when ya's're done."

The stubby mugs with the one-finger holes in the handles were white with brown-trimmed checkerboard rims. Coffee rings puddled around the bottom on the marble top where she set them. Mornings made her pour too fast.

Every day the same yakking old men took up the same high-back stools. Lined up like babies in high chairs. Shaking their rattles and crying for coffee.

Outside, the wind was knocking down the angels. The sun was doing his best, but the clouds were ganging up like they do every spring. The entire sky turned on its back and stretched out like one long rumpled gray comforter.

Nastradin told Naum, "The seasons change with rain." Seemed true to Naum.

Philadelphia City Hall was wrapped in scaffolding blacker than a widow's netting at a wake. Billy Penn was up top, looking northeast toward Fishtown and Penn Treaty Park, where he signed a sweetheart deal in 1683 with Tamanend, chief of the Lenape Turtle Clan.

Did the Quaker peace thing back then, Penn did. Paid the chief cash, right there under the old elm tree. Still standing, near what they used to call Shackamaxon village. Chief Tamanend did the Turtle Clan thing too, back then.

Leni Lenape meant *real persons*. Maybe that's how Penn and the chief made it work. Being people instead of individuals.

And it could be, that particular morning at Chock-Full-O-Nuts, Penn was up there looking out from City Hall, thinking about that treaty deal, wondering if he really was a *real person* that long-ago morning on the Delaware.

Some people in Fishtown swore Quaker dude was up there on the turret surveying the grid of his green country town with a broken stone heart, aching for his first wife, Gulielma Maria. Cause right there along the river in Fishtown, that's where him and her used to take walks, holding hands.

Somehow, the Chock-Full-O-Nuts uniform, with the apron and the checkerboard collar and the short-sleeve trim rolled up around the biceps, just made the whole homesick coffee comfort nostalgia on a rainy day thing all the more comforting when the waitress brought two nutted cheese sandwiches made with

Philadelphia cream cheese and chopped nuts on dark raisin bread from Kaplan's New Model Jewish Bakery up at Third and Poplar.

"Used to cost a nickel with a cup of coffee," Kusheri said.

Naum said, "Don't worry. My treat." And he told Nastradin, "As to your question about the funeral thing, I have no idea *what* people remember. Or if they remember anything at all of what's said by the priest, or any part of a funeral."

Kusheri was excavating excess cream cheese from between the slices of the bulky black bread.

"Just the horror of what they're dealing with," Naum said. "Somebody you love? In a coffin? Numb ya from your brain to your toes. Short-circuit all five senses. I'd be surprised if anything got through, anything at all. Maybe something on a deeper level? I doubt anybody knows. I don't."

Naum unfolded a note given to him by a father whose son had overdosed under the Tunnel. He placed it on the counter.

If you do a search for the word Sheol in Genesis and look at the context of the four times it is mentioned, you'll see if you do that all of them relate to Jacob's grief from losing his son, Joseph. Jacob claimed that if he was subjected to any additional grief, it would bring my gray hair down to Sheol in sorrow.

I used to puzzle over those verses. Not that I was incapable of sympathizing with a grieving father—it's just that Jacob's words seemed so over-the-top melodramatic and gloomy and broken.

Imagine if you were being bullied by someone you didn't know, and it briefly got physical. You managed to de-escalate back to verbal, but it raged on. From that brief physical contact, you sensed the strength and agility of your opponent. Then it occurs to you with shocking clarity and assurance that your opponent could rip your head off without breaking a sweat. And he's not ready yet to let you leave.

That's the encounter Jacob had with grief.

I understand, now that I've had the same encounter. God has granted me a lot of healing. I no longer feel like quoting Jacob.

But those verses no longer puzzle me.

Naum refolded the note, put it in his breast pocket, and tapped it in place over his heart.

Kusheri stopped evacuating the cream cheese from the bread.

A shadow of fog was seeping in through the window. It formed around the old priest and stood looking over his shoulder.

"Every time," the shadow said. "Every time each family goes through the ordeal, the priest goes through it with each family. Every time."

Kusheri wanted to say, "In the name of Krishti. The priest is there to help carry all our suffering."

Kusheri said to Naum, "What about you and your family? Who goes with you?"

Naum was thinking of the time the father had backed up over his three-year-old in the driveway. He wanted to say something then, at that house, walking by himself to the front door. He passed the mangled tricycle and prayed he hadn't come alone.

He thought of the many widows who'd told him all they remembered was wanting to jump in the coffin with their man, right then and there.

People gathering up their broken hearts out of the box,

caressing their loved one's face and kissing them, not wanting to say goodbye to the one they love.

Did anyone remember the oil and the soil poured over the face of their loved one by the priest, their face covered in a shroud? Naum hoped they didn't. He hated that.

"Who goes with me and my family? Him, I hope. But what people remember, Kusheri? Something beyond the words, maybe. I hope they remember who they really are. Where they're really from and where they're called to be."

Naum said, "If *remembered* is even the right word. And in all these years, I never saw any of the living who hadn't been believers before, suddenly become believers at a funeral."

Naum paused. "Well, maybe at Getzy's. Remember? Little Harry's friend from the junkyard, dead on the railroad tracks? Some of the people who were there, and they were mostly people of some other faith or no faith, not a lot of Orthodox that day. I mean, some of those visitors did come back."

Naum took a bite of the cream cheese sandwich. He didn't like it. He swished some coffee to get the nuts from between his teeth, returned the sandwich to the plate, and said to Kusheri Nastradin, "Now, what the dead may or may not hear? What's happening with the dead? Who knows? You wanna speculate on that, go ahead. Way over my pay grade."

Nastradin nodded.

"But, on the other hand," Naum said, "I do remember what the families *tell* me, with words and otherwise."

Naum said, "Grief and relief. Day to day. Year after year. Bobbing and weaving. I'm in the middle, praying, please, Lord, make us all accomplices in Your hope."

Naum never made notes for the eulogy. He spent time with the family. All those hours steeped in their grief.

He had seen the older priests before him stand with their hand on the open coffin and *speak the thread unwound* from the spool of our shared life.

Wound all their thoughts and memories
Around the filament of unforgetting
Twisted those thoughts and memories
Together with the thread of faith
Prayed God would weave it all in the shroud of His Son
And renew the fabric of their ruptured hope

The call of the priest, Naum thought, was to sow *that* seed deep in the good soil of the heart of a human being, where hope was hidden from the enemy. Unreachable and germinating until the planter of the vineyard returned to harvest His own.

Naum looked out the coffee shop window at a man in a raincoat and business attire fighting his umbrella, turned inside-out by the wind.

He said to Kusheri, "Truthfully, I don't remember half of what I say."

Kusheri looked at the man outside and said, "Fight it or turn it toward the wind to turn it back."

Naum said, "Maybe it's not the words we remember. Maybe it's what the words catch. Everything at an Orthodox funeral leaves an impression, somewhere, in someone."

"True," Kusheri said. "All taken all together. The prayer when the soul is departing the body. Greeting the casket at the church door. The place on the ambon where the priest stands. The position of the coffin. The timing of the censing. The reading of the scripture. Chanting the prayers. Anointing the body. The prayer of absolution. What is said when the Gospel is preached. The leading out. The hearse. All the way to the prayers at the graveside. Every action. The icon in the casket. Every image. Every word . . ."

Naum knew he shouldn't, but he wanted a little more coffee. Maybe better the waitress was on the other side of the room.

New customers were milling around behind them, waiting for a stool. Naum could see them in the wall-size mirror behind the counter.

Nastradin looked at Naum's uneaten sandwich on the plate and said, "You gonna eat that?"

When the waitress came, wiping the marble top and putting things back in place, Naum asked to pay.

She scribbled the slip and tore it off her pad. She said, "Here, hon . . . up at the register."

Naum told Nastradin, "Two things, maybe, over all these years, people've told me come back to them. One they mention is the absolution prayer."

> *May all those things which have proceeded from the weakness of his mortal nature be consigned to oblivion and be remitted unto him . . .*

The second thing that stuck with people, Naum didn't have to say.

Both men knew the chant
Knew it from their earliest memories
Had their hearts broken

Hearing their mothers
Sing it for their fathers
Sang it for their mothers
And many times
Considered it for themselves
Seeing siblings and young friends
The comfortless comfort
The ancient appeal
I përjetshëm kujtimi . . . Memory eternal.

The man they'd seen fighting his umbrella was standing behind them. He saw their cups were empty and their plates were only crumbs. He tapped his twisted umbrella on the floor.

Kusheri said Naum tipped too much.

Naum let it go
When it's over it's over
Out the door
Pulling on their hats
Hands in pockets
Both of them walking
Head down in the rain
No umbrellas
Neither saying a word
Okay with no words
Okay with getting wet
Neither wanting to sing

Not even when they had taken the final steps down into the underground and started east through the tunnels toward home.

But they did
Memory Eternal

Echoing like subterranean light
Off the tiled subway walls
The priest Naum and Kusheri Nastradin
Singing the Lord's song
In a strange land

The Box

YEARS HAD PASSED. Father Naum couldn't even remember the one-time visitor who'd brought the little golden box from Ukraine.

But I remembered.

The box sat on the altar, so perfectly wrapped in textured gold paper that Naum couldn't bear to unwrap it, to disturb its seamlessly concealed secret.

Naum didn't know what was inside. It didn't matter.

Nicholas, maybe seven or eight, wanted to know. He would come into the altar every week with his older brother, Charles, and ask Naum, "Father, what's in the box?"

When Father Naum said he didn't know, Nicky couldn't understand how that could be. Wasn't it Father's? And each time his curiosity grew.

"Tell you what, Nicky—you can have it," Naum said, "but you can't miss one Lenten service. And at Pascha, the box and whatever's in it is yours."

His parents agreed. And this was no simple thing for Vela and Ligori. A rhythm of liturgical prayer life that had been established in another world, in another time, when our faithful lived together in agrarian settings within easy proximity of the church bell, didn't always harmonize with the pace and highway distances of life in twenty-first-century American sprawl.

Ligori, Nicky's father, was a parking-meter monitor for the city. He worked long shifts, out in all weather. And though he was on his feet, walking, all day, five days a week, Vela, his wife, a nurse out at University Hospital, teased Ligori, saying he still had the shape of a sugar plum.

Ligori the meter-monitor was not popular with the working folks or visitors to Philly's downtown business and shopping areas. Time got away. Meters ran out. Ligori appeared, ticket book in hand. Many a night Ligori went home with the angry breath of frustrated parkers and their curses like film on his face.

Once, it even happened to Naum. There he was, barista coffee in hand, coming out of the University Hospital toward his car, and there *it* was, under his windshield wiper—the cream-colored dread, the thirty-five-dollar downer. And there, at the end of the block, sowing seed for the Parking Authority, was sugar plum Ligori in his summer blue uniform.

Father Naum said, "Hey, Ligor, it's me." Extending his recent issue. "I still have five minutes on the meter." Naum pleaded, "Go look."

Ligori looked at the priest and his coffee, took off his cap, and said, "We do it all the time. Most people ain't from downtown. Odds are you ain't making it back on time, and if ya do, odds are ya ain't gonna take a day off from work and come all the way back down here ta fight it. Traffic Court's a bitch. Talk about no parking. The judge himself ain't got a spot to park over on Spring Garden at his own court.

"'Sides . . ." Ligori, finger and thumb, squeegeed back the sides of his mustache. "If you can afford the coffee, a little ticket ain't gonna squash your latte."

Naum offered to buy him a coffee. "Nah, I ain't got time to stop and pee," Ligori said. "Where ya been, visiting my Uncle Llambi over at the hospital?"

Naum said, "Yes."

"You go see my Vela in there, in the hospital?"

Naum said, "No."

Ligori said, "Thanks for that."

Waddling Ligori, steady down the block. Scoping out meters. Calculating fines. Stretching over windshields. Snapping tickets under wipers. Ligori looked back and smiled, "See ya in church, Father."

For all that, Ligori was basically still a sugar plum candy kinda guy. Everybody at church liked Ligori.

Vela? More like SweetTarts, a little sour, a little sweet. Maybe it was her work and what she had to deal with day to day on the hospital oncology ward. She had the reputation of being a *real* nurse. If you were in the hospital, this was the girl you wanted. Her house was full of cards and letters from people saying, *If not for you, Vela, I wouldn't be here.*

She showed Naum something she didn't show everyone—the miniature double medals she wore, the Holy Mother and the second-century Saint Agatha of Sicily, both in silver.

A good mother too, Vela. Both her boys, Charles and Nicky, were baptized Catholic. Saturday night Mass? Her and the kids never missed.

But Charles, her older son, came to Orthodox Liturgy with

George and Jenny, his Orthodox grandparents, from before he could walk. Kid loved the Liturgy. Sat mesmerized on the front pew, swinging his legs.

After a while, Naum asked his mother, "Vela, should I bring Charles in to serve?"

Some of our people who read a lot of religious books and the Bible, too, told Naum, "No. He's not Orthodox. He can't enter the altar, and he's too young."

Naum said, "How young do you have to be not to become Orthodox?"

Vela told Naum, "Father, at home, in the basement, he has his books arranged, standing on end. Some are the choir and some are the congregation. He puts a towel over his shoulders, says he's you, stands facing his little table with a can on a string for a censer, and sings the entire Orthodox Mass. Me and Ligori watch him and get tears in our eyes. He tells us he's gonna be an Orthodox priest. It's like he's in some other place."

Some people thought to *correct* her use of the term *Mass.*

Naum said, "Sure, correcting the language of the one who taught you to speak? You'd have to be a theologian not to."

Vela told Naum, "He's not old enough to serve Mass at my church."

Naum said, "Vela, nature has to take its course. You talk to Ligor and let me know. Charles is welcome any time."

Vela said, "I believe in the Holy Spirit. I trust Him for my three boys."

By the time of the golden box, Charles was old enough to decide, and with his mother's blessing, he was chrismated and received into the Orthodox Church.

Great Lent was more than forty days. A long wait for little Nicky to get his golden box and find out what was inside.

Starting Lenten Wednesdays a little before seven PM, tired old Naum came early to light the first of the oil lampadas in the darkened church.

The people were tired too.

All day at work

Or chasing kids around the house

Shopping on the Avenue under the Tunnel

Cleaning

Washing clothes

Making beds

Scrubbing bathrooms

Caring for elderly parents

Rushing home and getting a dish ready for the Lenten potluck supper that followed Presanctified

Baking the holy bread on Saturday

Tired tired

Or just plain *retired-tired*—what Madeline called it. She told Carol she was "bored to fatigue from having nothing meaningful to do all day every day."

At all the Lenten services, Charles served in the altar. Little Nicky came out of the pews to stand with Father Naum, Getzy, Little Harry, his big brother, Charles, and the altar servers, imitating them, making the prostrations, bowing his head to touch the floor each time the prayer of Saint Ephraim the Syrian was prayed.

O Lord and Master of my life . . .

Grant me to see my own transgressions and not to judge my brother or sister . . .

After Presanctified, Little Harry and Getzy, still in their greasy overalls and work boots from all day hauling parts in the auto scrapyard, went table to table in the church hall, loading their plates with the different ethnic potluck Lenten offerings.

Vela, Nicky, Charles, and Ligori were there early, and among the few who stayed to help clean the hall after the Lenten supper. Harry, Getzy, Vela, Ligori, and the kids carted the big black trash bags down to the curb. They were always the last to leave.

There were services almost every day and evening during Lent, and even if Ligori had to work and missed a service or two, Vela and the kids were always there. Vela saw to that.

And all during Holy Week too, morning and evening, Vela and the boys were there. And even though he was worn from a day on the streets, parking-meter Ligori didn't miss one Holy Week service. No one minded if here and there during a reading the big guy in the blue uniform put his cap on his knees and his chin on his chest, and rested his eyes.

On Holy Friday evening, Naum said, "Christ Jesus descends into Hades. We gather around His tomb at sundown, and like every generation, we participate in this event made present to us in the prayers of the Holy Church, singing the Lamentations, where eternity meets time."

Little Harry was one of the four people carrying the *epitaphios*, each person holding a corner, arms extended above their heads. Harry had to walk on his toes the entire time, stretching to keep the winding sheet of our Master's burial level and to keep up with the procession around the church.

Charles, Nicky, and the altar servers carried banners, icons, candles, and crosses. The choir followed along chanting, and Deacon Dionysios, with the censer, led the way.

Naum said, "We follow Him, and our procession around the outside of the church on Friday evening is not a funeral procession, but a procession of light and gladness piercing the darkness. Following our Savior Jesus Christ as He gathers to Himself all who have gone before us in the year prior and all the faithful who, in every generation, have fallen asleep in the hope of His Holy Resurrection."

Naum walked under the winding sheet carrying the book of the Gospels. As the long rectangular winding sheet with the icon of Jesus' burial reached the front door, it was held aloft, and all God's people passed under it and returned into the church, each one making the sign of the cross and kissing the Gospel book Naum offered.

When the last person entered, Naum handed the Gospel book to the deacon, took the epitaphios on his back, and carried it to the *kouvouklion*, the canopied table covered in flowers by the Teuta Ladies. He placed the winding sheet burial icon there, in the place that represented the tomb of Christ our Lord.

Early the next morning, Holy Saturday, the Divine Liturgy was celebrated with the other prescribed services. Many families with young children who would not do well in the crush of the crowded Saturday midnight Paschal celebration, and many older people who could no longer stand for the long overnight Paschal prayers, came on Saturday morning in anticipation of the Resurrection to receive Holy Communion and join in scattering the fragrant bay leaves for the approaching King.

After Saturday morning Liturgy, Nicky and Vela helped the women of the Teuta Ladies Baking Society clean the church and get things ready for Pascha night.

At eight PM on Saturday, the evening of the Paschal celebration, Naum was again early in the church. He locked the doors and kept the lights low, hoping to be alone to prepare for the eleven PM start of the Paschal celebration, which would last till dawn on Pascha Sunday morning.

By eight thirty Saturday evening, the quiet time Naum thought he might have had come to an end. They were knocking on the door. How could he not open it? At first it was only a few, and then such a flood that by nine o'clock the church was full.

They were parleying over vantage points and positions. Staking claims over pews and seats. "I sit there every week"—the regulars negotiating, perhaps a little too aggressively, with the once-a-year Paschal interlopers.

Naum was worried but hopeful as he listened from the altar. Regulars who were generally kind contending with those who *only came for Pascha.*

Then it somehow seemed to resolve itself, and things quieted down to a friendly murmur as long-lost friends and relatives, visitors and strangers, everyone holding unlit candles, stood smiling, shaking hands, and hugging in the overcrowded aisles.

The fire marshal would have issued more citations than Ligori on a downtown Saturday night. The capacity of little Saint Alexander the Whirling Dervish parish was exceeded to a point where the walls vibrated, the roof levitated, and the bells rang with no one pulling the ropes.

Naum's wife, Greta, no more than five feet, she was the main agent, it turned out, of the sudden calm, negotiating the aisles, rearranging strollers, brokering seating arrangements, and generally serving as an ecclesial referee. Some cooperated with her. Most complied. Some who had too much pre-feast celebration actually cursed her.

Many weeks later, Naum found out the two titan Olympic wrestlers who speedily levitated the cursers on tiptoes out the door, bottles and all, were pious Greco-grappling Georgian twins.

"Negotiate?" the genial brothers told Naum. "Mamo, we don't know this English word."

Business at the *pangar*, the stand in the narthex where the candles were sold, was almost too much for Nicky Zeo and Teddy the Horse.

Teddy said, "Nicky, it keeps up like this and old Naum might even get his envelope on time for a coupla weeks."

Nicky said, "Gives it all ta Greta anyway."

Upstairs, the church hall was filled with woven baskets full of Paschal food: meat, dairy, cookies, butter, cakes, and cream, all the things people had forgone during the Lenten fast. All new again.

Downstairs too, in the church, in front of the iconostasis, specially embroidered veils covered decorative baskets dedicated to showcasing the Paschal bounty. They overflowed with red eggs and Paschal goodies from every ethnic cuisine and background represented in the parish community, all awaiting the holy water blessing of the baskets by the priest.

The police came to direct traffic and reroute city buses around the crowds that overflowed and clogged the avenue outside the church.

The walls quivered, but not with talking. There was no talking. Who knew a human hive could buzz no less vibrantly than scarlet hummingbirds or iridescent orchid bees?

Candles were not permitted to be lit. The people sat in darkness, holding their unlit candles, waiting for the Paschal Light.

When a group of men dressed in black woolen uniforms marched into the church . . .

They were decked in flaring calf-length *chokha,* high-collared coats with bandolier pockets of Masri bullets on either side of their chests, and ornate silver-sheathed *khanjali* daggers proudly displayed on thin silver-strung belts. Each broad and menacing man wore a colorfully embroidered skufia cap and jodhpur-like pants tucked into supple leather knee-high boots.

Nicky Zeo and Teddy the Horse swore they were about to dial 911. And they would have, too, if wonderment hadn't frozen them, like petrified lava on a picture panel of mosaic tile in quick-dried Pompeii.

The troop, ordered to a halt by their commander just inside the nave, formed a silent semicircular phalanx and parted the astonished crowd simply by their presence. They removed their caps, made the sign of the cross, and in unison, bowed to the altar.

Everything went still.

Getzy the Marine took cover in a pew and looked at Little Harry. "This normal?"

The tall man with the military mustache held an icon of Saint Nino of Georgia. He intoned an exotic pitch, and from the altar Naum heard a hymn ring out in a language that was neither Aramaic nor Albanian. The song of their prayer was so otherworldly compelling that the already silenced crowd, though Naum would not have thought it possible, grew even more still and attentive. Naum had no doubt God had heard the prayers of Saint Mamo Gabriel Urgebadze and sent these Georgian men to further bless the Holy Pascha night.

As the hour approached, back at the pangar, Nicky Zeo and Teddy the Horse looked out at the sky and debated about what looked like bad weather on the way.

"Should we have the procession outside around the church?" Nicky said. "And ruin all the banners and stuff if it's gonna rain?"

They sent for Little Harry and his junkyard buddy Getzy to sit at the stand where the candles were sold while they squeezed through the crowd into the small, darkened altar. When they said it might rain, Father Naum told the men, "You two stay right here."

"Nicky," Naum whispered in the little boy's ear, "Go get your mother from the pews. Tell her you need to go outside to check for rain. Ask her to take you. Come back and tell us. Thumbs down, we stay in and process inside. Thumbs up, we go outside in procession."

When Vela returned him to the altar, the little general made all the assembled servers wait. And then, without a care or a grin, gave the thumbs up.

The altar was crowded with those who served weekly—Julian, Ezra, Isaiah, Charles, little Noah—and with those who came only at Pascha, wandering sons making their yearly pilgrimage home. Fans, banners, candles, crosses, censers, and icons were assigned by Deacon Donat and readied to exit the deacon's doors.

Deacon Dionysios put Little Harry's friend, Getzy, the tall

man from the junkyard, carrying the cross at the lead. Getzy whispered to Harry, "I'm joining this church."

The servers were lined up in order and, flashlight in hand, Little Harry gave each robed server final instructions for the midnight Paschal procession around the exterior of the church.

The Paschal flame was ignited . . .

Then
As an inaudible wind
Moves branches and leaves
As a portent of rain
Silhouettes on the curtain
Over the Royal Doors
Caused by the much-anticipated
And longed-for illumination from within
Drew the mass of God's people forward
Arms extended
Unlit candles
Reaching for the Light
That came into the world
The Light that shineth in darkness
The Light the darkness comprehended not.

The curtain was drawn back, the Royal Doors were opened, and Naum came down from the ambon intoning the ancient chant.

O come and receive the Light, the unwaning gift of Life, Come and glorify Christ who is risen from the dead . . .

He was surrounded, pressed by God's people, young and old. Hope in Christ and His Resurrection shone in their faces, in the faces of many Naum knew had suffered much in the year gone by.

Candles eager for the Paschal Light
People reaching beyond themselves
Laying aside all earthly cares
Pressing toward the light
And those in the fore
With their candles now lighted
Passing the light behind
To those striving
Toward the Light of the Kingdom
Person to person
Candle to candle
Generation to generation
Even those who earlier
Had parlayed or argued over seats
Or been refereed by Priftereshe
Or admonished by the wrestlers
Or had come at the eleventh hour
All that earthbound nonsense
Laid aside and long forgotten
Happy now just to receive the light
And be
If only for a moment
Lost in the otherworldly
Ecstatic joy of His Resurrection. . . .
And outside
Far beyond the bell
Worlds above the wide front steps
The cloudless ink-black sky
Glistened with innumerable stars

Crystal, glistening, endless, and white
Like countless candle flames
Illumining a thousand
Gladdened faces
In the midnight Paschal procession
No rain in sight
Three times around the church
Everyone joining together
Raphaela
(Her name means *God has healed*)
Leading the choir
Following the servers and the clergy
The choir leading
The faithful in procession
Wound like a living spiral
Many times around the church
Those in the lead
Overtaking those in the rear
Those in the rear
Overtaking those in the middle
Those in the middle
Merging with the clergy and the servers and the choir
And everyone singing:
The angels in heaven, O Christ our Savior, sing of Thy resurrection. Make us on earth also worthy to hymn Thee with a pure heart . . .

As we reentered the temple from our Paschal procession shouting

Christ is Risen

Truly He is Risen

With the bells still ringing out above our heads, there he came, that little boy, in his cream-white robe, carrying his cross, the one he'd insisted on, the one that was too big for him. Nicky bounding into the altar to retrieve his prize.

His golden box.

But.

"No," Naum said, "Not till after."

The Orthros service *and* the Paschal Divine Liturgy were yet to be fulfilled, and the Catechetical Sermon of Saint John Chrysostom was yet to be read:

Isaiah foretold this when he said

You, O Hell, have been troubled by encountering Him below

Hell took a body and discovered God

It took earth and encountered Heaven

It took what it saw and was overcome by what it did not see

O death, where is thy sting?

O Hell, where is thy victory?

Christ is Risen, and you, O death, are annihilated!

So

When all was fulfilled

Before the baskets were blessed

Before the red eggs were handed out

With the greeting

Christ is Risen

And *Truly He is Risen* said in response

They stood together in front of the iconostasis

Nicky and Naum

And Naum told the story of the golden box

And of their deal

Of Nicky's long Lenten perseverance

And of the one-time mysterious visitor

Who gave the golden box to Naum

The visitor Naum could not for the life of him remember

Told the story to the entire happy, sleepy, smiling, hungry, Lenten-weary, Paschal-delirious, Resurrection-gathered communion.

The feast was waiting upstairs in the hall. From sundown, in preparation for Holy Communion, no one had eaten or had a thing to drink. But even so, with our little Nicky there in front, waiting for his golden box, no one was thinking of food or drink.

To Naum's surprise, the church was still overflowing, unlike what happens some years, when most people leave after receiving the Light. In fact, it seemed as if the crowd had grown.

I knew there was no way I was leaving. How could I?

Father went in and retrieved the gold box from its place on the altar. He came out through the Royal Doors and handed it to Nicky.

No one knew what was inside.

But I knew.

In front of a congregation silent with anticipation, Nicky opened the seamlessly wrapped golden box transported all the way from Ukraine by the mysterious person who had visited Saint Alexander parish in Fishtown just that one time many, many years before.

Nicky opened it in front of everyone. The box I had so carefully wrapped so long ago.

In it was an icon of Saint Nicholas.

I don't know why I purchased an icon of Saint Nicholas. I don't know why I wrapped it so. Or why I took it to that particular parish and gave it to that particular priest.

I don't know why I did what I did. I was happy just to be there. Never again was I to return to the little church.

Triumphant Nicky held the icon aloft.

Vela made the cross.

We all did the same.

She trusted her three boys to the Holy Spirit.

Our eyes were wide open.

No one said a word.

Not even me.

We sang the troparion to Saint Nicholas:

The sincerity of your deeds has revealed you to your people as a teacher of moderation, a model of faith, and an example of virtue. Therefore, you attained greatness through humility, and wealth through poverty. O Father and Archbishop Nicholas, ask Christ our God to save our souls.

Each one came forward to venerate the cross. To receive the blessed bread and a red egg, and to exchange the Paschal greeting with one another and with the priest. They sang it so many times, even I learned to sing, "*Krishti Ungjall*!"

Each one kissed the icon Nicky held for hundreds of us to kiss, my icon, the icon of Saint Nicholas. Some of the women kissed Nicky too.

Vela's boys, Charles and Nicky, helped distribute the red eggs and played epper when we went upstairs to eat, seeing who could win the other's Paschal egg by tapping the ends together, saying, "Christ is risen! Yours cracked, I win it."

Vela dabbed the lipstick from Nicky's cheeks. She warned her boys, "You better not get red dye on your new Easter clothes."

As Father Naum was exiting the altar, Ligori—it was odd to see him in a suit and tie and not his meter-monitor uniform—he and Uncle Llambi, who'd been in the hospital when Naum came to visit, they came to see Naum with a flex cooler. "Sorry 'bout the ticket, Father," Ligori said.

He took a pint of Naum's favorite ice cream from between the icepacks of his cooler, said it was Uncle Llambi's idea, and the two went padding upstairs, telling Naum, "With all these different people, from all these different countries, this sugar plum's got to sample the cuisine at every table. And those guys with the swords and bullets could *sing*."

After the cleanup, the usual crew were the last to leave.

The morning horizon over Fishtown was smearing river-gray light over the Philadelphia skyline. The heavy swollen clouds decided enough was enough, and the sky began to rain.

I was waiting at the curb for the bus. The wire trash basket chained to the wooden telephone pole was full of broken bottles.

Fatigued Naum thought it was only him and Greta when they stepped outside. He locked the door and whispered to his wife, "Gotta be back at eleven for Agape Vespers." His voice was almost gone.

Nicky and his family were under an umbrella, waiting for Naum and Greta. Little Nicky went to Naum and told the priest, "Don't worry, Father, I'll be back ta help ya."

Vela said, "You're not taking any bus," and offered me a ride.

And except for *Christ is risen*, no one said a word.

Not even me.

FATHER STEPHEN N. SINIARI is a priest of the OCA Diocese of the South. During almost forty years in ministry, Fr. Stephen served parishes in New England and the Philadelphia/South Jersey area while working full time for an international agency as a street outreach worker, serving homeless, at-risk, and trafficked teens. Born and raised in Philadelphia, Fr. Stephen currently lives on the Florida Gulf Coast with Margot, his wife of more than forty years.

We hope you have enjoyed and benefited from this book. Your financial support makes it possible to continue our nonprofit ministry both in print and online. Because the proceeds from our book sales only partially cover the costs of operating **Ancient Faith Publishing** and **Ancient Faith Radio**, we greatly appreciate the generosity of our readers and listeners. Donations are tax deductible and can be made at **www.ancientfaith.com.**

To view our other publications,
please visit our website: **store.ancientfaith.com**

Bringing you Orthodox Christian music, readings,
prayers, teaching, and podcasts 24 hours a day since 2004 at
www.ancientfaith.com

NAUM'S NEIGHBORHOOD

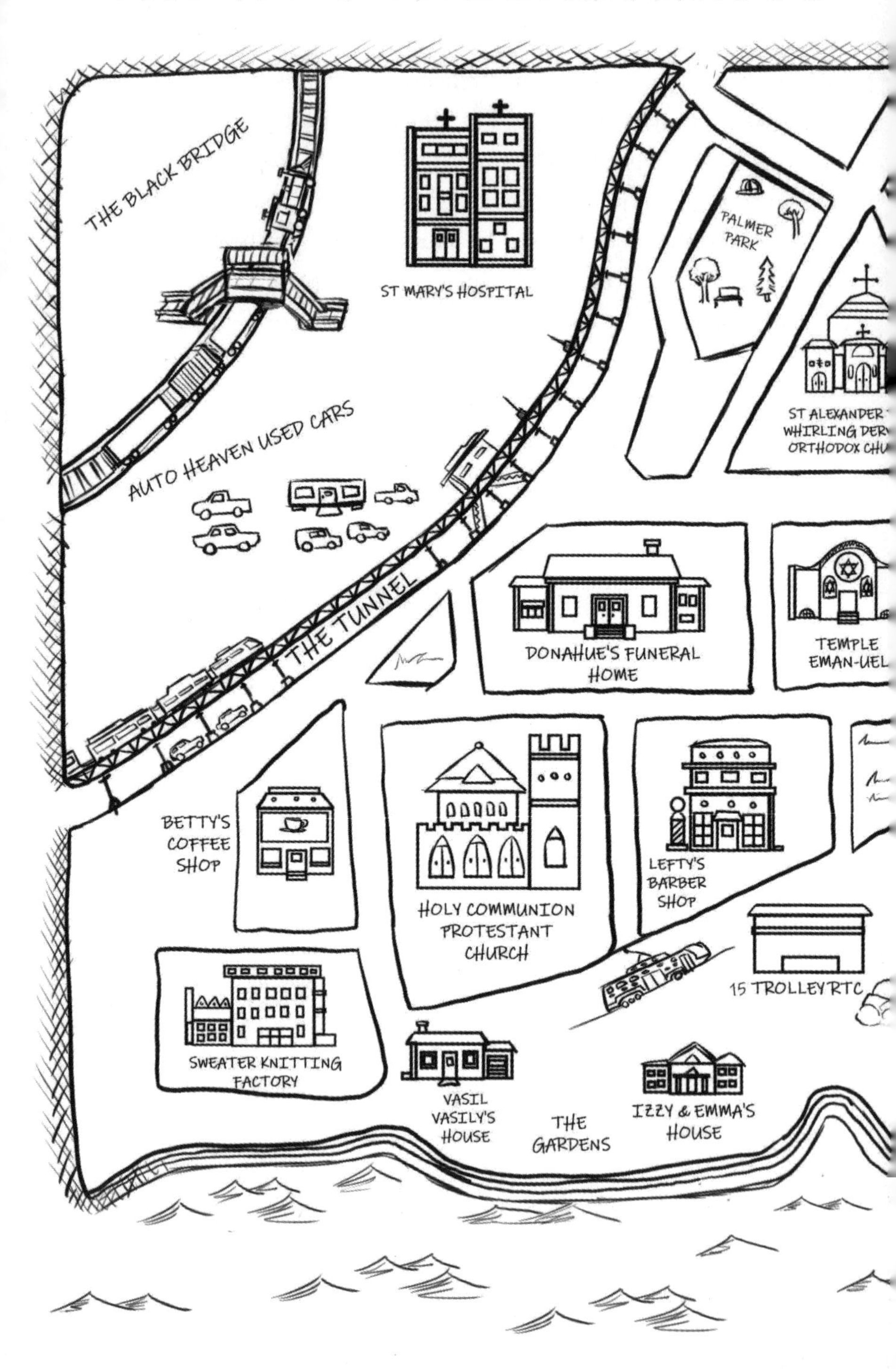

Made in the USA
Middletown, DE
25 April 2024